# SHADOW OF FEAR

## BEN NAAS

### A NOVEL

NEXT DIMENSION PUBLISHING, LLC

Published by Next Dimension Publishing, LLC

Cover designed by Xavier Comas

Interior designed by Ben Naas

Manufactured in the United States of America

ISBN 979-8-9851158-0-2

ISBN 979-8-9851158-1-9 (E-book)

To everyone who made even a slight impact on me.
From a passing smile on a sidewalk to a road-raging
middle finger. You guys are my inspiration.

# Preface

So most of those who know me (especially in high school) a lot of the characters are going to seem similar to actual people. And that's because much of the first half of this book is based off my senior year of high school. But I promise you that most of the content comes from my imagination rather than reality. With that being said, take everything read with a grain of salt. I changed a lot about the characters (including Oliver who's based off me) and their relationships with each other for both the sake of the story, as well as to just differentiate them from their real counterpart.

# Table of Contents

# Prologue

**My heart pounds** in my bare chest as I wake from a dream that's already fading.

*There was a body, but who was it? Their face was hidden by blood.*

I'm in the attic. Our attic. It's dark, the crescent moon outside giving just enough light to see the stacks of boxes around me from my position by the lone window. *I must've sleepwalked up here.*

As a kid, my parents said I would sleepwalk all the time, sometimes scaring the heck out of them as they'd open their eyes to see me standing by their bed. Often, I would wake in a weird place, but I don't remember ever waking up here. Yet now I notice a chair next to the window. A barstool. Moving past a box of books below the window, I run my fingers on the seat and find that there's no dust. Someone sat here recently. Could it have been me? If so, why can't I remember? I—or anybody else in my family that know of—have been in the attic since we first moved here nine years ago. Most of our storage we keep downstairs; this room is just for the overflow.

I find myself sitting in the chair without any conscious effort. The view through the window shows the concrete driveway, the shadow of the basketball hoop like Satan's middle fin-

-ger to the light

A warm gust of air blows on the back of my neck. It feels like someone breathing on me. I spin around, almost falling off the chair

Nobody's there. Or was that somebody standing in the corner? I search for a light switch before remembering this room didn't have any lighting installed. We never bothered to have it done. I grab the side of my leg reflexively for the comfort of my iPhone but only find the cotton of my pajama pants.

*Fear,* the faint whisper comes from the corner. A ghostly apparition cloaked by shadows is there.

*Who's there?* I try to ask, but the words get stuck in my chest. The air around me grows thin and cold. I shiver as it becomes harder to breathe.

*Fear.* The phantom was hidden by shadows; it was the Shadow.

I fall to my knees as I suffocate in the open room, sucking in the last of the available oxygen.

*I am Fear.*

Then there's only darkness.

# Fall '18

*For I know that good itself does not dwell in me, that is my sinful nature. For I cannot carry it out. For it do not do the good I want to do, but the evil I do not want to do—this I keep on doing.*

*but I see another law at work in me, waging war against the law of my mind and making me a prisoner of the law of sin at work within me.*

—Romans 7:18-19, 23

# Thursday, August 9, 8:00 a.m.

**Evil is like** a seed. It can be watered. It can be preened. But one thing's for certain: if it takes root in your soul, there's no stopping it … there is only pain and rage. Only fear.

Or at least that is what Mrs. Byers said.

"In your first section of AP English," she continues, adjusting her brown hair pulled into a loose bun, "you will come to understand the ever-potent archetype of good and evil through the Joseph Conrad classic, *Heart of Darkness*. You will see how some people try to walk the fine line between them but almost always cross over."

"Sorry I'm late," a familiar voice apologizes from the doorway, interrupting her lecture. "You won't accept the 'dog ate my homework' excuse, would you?"

It's Wes Clines, a redhead who's as skinny as he is droll. Wes isn't my best friend, but we run track together, becoming semi-close through it. Usually, he was in the normal classes, but he must have gotten a high score on the ACT over the summer. Or there was a mistake in the system.

"Ah, so you must be Mr. Clines," Mrs. Byers says with a hint of humor in her voice. "It will be a pleasure to meet you *after* you go to the office."

Wes leaves with no apparent embarrassment, while I would've been as red as a naked pastor on a Sunday morning, and returns a couple minutes later to sit next to me, flashing me some apparently arcane symbol—hands somehow creating a diamond above a heart that I could never replicate for the life of me. He calls himself a "quanite," which is like a practitioner of quantum mechanics or something.

"Please tell me we didn't have to read that over the summer," Wes whispers to me with a tinge of worry in his voice when he notices *Heart of Darkness* on my desk.

Yeah, it was definitely an error.

"Nope, but we were supposed to read and annotate 'The Hollow Men.'"

"How long is it?" Now he definitely looks panicked.

"It's a poem," I answer, only feigning irritation. I'm just glad I have somebody to talk to in this class of the high and mighty.

"Oh, good. I'll just use Sparknotes then."

I roll my eyes and shut him up so I can hear what Mrs. Byers was saying. After a few minutes of her droning on about the code of conduct, my mind drifts back to last night. I try to fight those painful memories, but they wash over me like a tidal wave.

***

"Ollie, dinner's ready," my mom calls from upstairs.

"Coming!" I yell back, a comforting scent feeding my nose as I climb the stairs. "Is that chicken pot pie I smell?" I ask, walking into the kitchen.

"Yes, I made your favorite, since it's your last first day tomorrow," Mom says cheerfully, blue eyes glowing in the lighting. "By the way, where do you want to eat tomorrow night?"

"How about Cracker Barrel?"

"Sounds great. Can you get your brothers for me? They're not answering my phone calls."

After a quick search of the house, I find them downstairs in the game room playing Fortnite. They have headphones on and appear to be talking to each other through them. Kids, I think, even though one of them is only a couple of years younger than me.

I stand in front of the TV—turning it off would have caused outright war—until my brothers take their headphones off.

"What?" the older one, Alex, asks brusquely.

Both brothers have shaggy brown hair that has never seen a comb outside of a barbershop, different from my straight blond hair I inherited from Mom. Alex at fifteen is a little heavyset, just like I was at his age, the only difference being I never had a tattoo. His is an eye with a teardrop welling up on the corner that he had gotten with some friend's tattoo gun. Apparently, it symbolizes his depression or something. It can be hard for me to be around him with his smart mouth and lazy attitude. Dylan, on the other hand, is kind of the complete opposite. He's only ten but is extremely selfless, going out of the way to help me at times.

"Dinner's ready," I answer, already heading back up.

I sit down in my spot at the dinner table, a mini-chicken pot pie in front of me. My parents are in their post-vacation-diet phase, which consists of downsizing meals rather than making them healthier.

My dad plops himself next to me, obviously tired.

"How was your day?" Dad asks me, rolling his hand through salt-and-pepper hair. He is dressed in scrubs.

"Practice was awful this morning, more running than anything else. Gotta love summer practices, am I right? But at least Coach canceled tonight's practice, so we could enjoy our last day of summer." I say this last part quietly. "It seemed yours must've been pretty eventful."

"My last patient had stage-three basal cell carcinoma, which is really hard to treat. My least favorite part of the job is diagnosing my patients with cancer. You're going to have to get used to that if you do become a dermatologist."

Dad has this idea that I want to be a dermatologist, and I haven't really helped it by acting like I wanted to as well. In truth, I want to become a screenwriter. I have even been working on a thriller, *The Stranger*. But he thinks those in the arts are a bunch of liberal hippies who will be living in their parents' basement when they're forty.

I believe—no, I know—writing is my purpose, but I'm not sure how I'll be able to tell him.

We finish our dinner with just light conversation on the day's events. After the meal, though, when the brothers are back downstairs and me and my parents are sitting in the living room, watching *90- Day Fiancé*, Mom asks me the question I had been dreading all night: "Are you excited for your senior year?"

"Yes," I answer unconvincingly.

"It doesn't sound like you are," Dad replies, pausing the TV in the middle of a fight between a middle-aged man with a pot-belly and his young Taiwanese girlfriend.

"Well, you know, I just got a lot of stuff to do this year."

"It may seem that way, but senior year is going to be one of the most fun years of your life," Mom says.

"And then it's all uphill after that," Dad jokes, and is stared down by Mom.

"It's just with football and track and scholarships and college applications, I don't know how I'll find time to do anything else," I respond. *Not to mention writing a screenplay that could change everything.*

"You'll find that you'll have more time than you'll know what to do with. Me and your dad fell in love, as you know, in our freshman year of high school. We hung out with each other most days and still did well in school. We both even had a job."

"Having high-level classes means I won't be able to do stuff with any of my friends," I say quietly, choking back a sob that came out of nowhere. I hate my damn sensitive ass. "And then

I'll have to be in group projects with people I don't like."

It's hard to explain the depth of my anxiety to somebody who hasn't dealt with that level of it. The best I could do would be to compare it to being stabbed in the stomach with a dagger and twisting. And twisting. And twisting. Until there's nothing left.

"Is that what's stressing you out?" Dad asks with concern.

"No, it's just—everything." I hide my face, ashamed of my tears. "From getting to school on time to forgetting a textbook. I just don't know if I can handle it."

"We can get you some Xanax for your stress. Your mom, me, and Dylan all take it. It helps a ton."

Anxiety runs in the family. Alex even had to transfer schools and get therapy. I have turned my back to it for years, ignoring my chemical imbalance. And I'll ignore it for many years to come. I'm not weak. I'm not.

"No, I'll be fine. I just need some sleep."

"Ollie, do you remember what I told you last year?" Dad inquires.

"Yeah, Faith over Fear."

"And don't ever forget it."

Something appears behind him. *But what about the Shadow, Daddy, what about the Shadow?*

"I won't."

# Thursday, August 9, 12:00 p.m.

**My first four** classes of the day end without many problems. In regard to anxiety, the nights are always worse than the days.

From light springs hope. Darkness, on the other hand, only brings Fear.

Now it's lunchtime. The first day of school always signifies the choice you have to make on who to sit with the entire year. A very tough choice. Do you sit with your jock, nerd, or emo friends? Or do you even have any friends in the same lunch period?

As I stand, observing the lunchroom with a tray of meatloaf in my hands, I'm saved from making this choice.

"Ollie. W-what's up?" my best friend, Gideon Slusher, calls from behind me. He has dark hair that hang down past his neck that almost seemed to complement chinstrap. "I thought I w-was going to have to sit w-with the w-weirdos for a second there."

Slushie—a middle school nickname that had just kinda stuck—has been my best friend since seventh grade, when we had first faced off on the gridiron. During a car accident that had killed his mother, he had undergone a traumatic brain injury, causing him to stutter. It was inoperable, and he will have it for the rest of his life.

We had an inseparable friendship for as long as we have known each other. Until he got a girlfriend, that is. Now I have to split time with that ginger whore. She had been with multiple guys the last couple years, trying them out like a pair of yoga pants and throwing them away once they had gotten a bit stretched out. Slushie fails to see this, believing himself to be the one. He's too good for her.

We find a spot at the end of the table and scout the lunchroom for other friends. And of course, all we see is the whore (also named Rachel Wall), who Slushie frantically waves over.

"Hey, babe," Rachel says to Slushie as she walks toward us. She's wearing an orange shirt that shows just enough cleavage to draw looks, while still being in the dress code.

I give her a big, fake smile, "Hi, Rachel."

She responds with a half-smile, eyes lingering. I hide my disgust by taking a sip of my chocolate milk.

After several minutes of Slushie and Rachel deep in conversation, completely ignoring me, a familiar voice comes from behind him. "Hey, boys. And Rachel."

Celeste Lynch sits down next to me. She's a very pretty girl with brown hair pulled into a ponytail, face dotted with freckles. She is a close friend of mine, right up there with Slushie, but nothing more. And I'm fine with that.

Yeah.

And anyway, she's hung up over someone else. I smile widely at her and mouth, "thank you." She winks at me, and we strike up a conversation about her recent trip to Destin.

Maybe I have few friends in my classes, but at least I have one thing to look forward to during the school day.

# Thursday, August 9, 2:00 p.m.

**Football to me** is usually love and hate. There are days when I want to quit and days when I am actually excited for practice. And of course, like most things in my life, there is stress involved. Most of that anxiety revolves around Coach Core. It's bad enough that he makes the receivers run more than any other position, but he also seeks perfection. One dropped ball out of a hundred meant Core would scream at you as if you had just scratched his leased Corvette and then force you to do half a million push-ups. You better believe that the receivers all wore high-quality gloves, continuously spitting on them to give them added stickiness.

It wasn't always this bad. During my first two years of high school, we had a different wideout coach who even set up a play to get me my first and only touchdown. He had to leave for family matters. If Core was coaching when I first tried receiver, I think I would have been a running back instead. But learning the lengthy running back playbook my last year is not something I want to do whatsoever.

I show up at the locker room, giving curt greetings and head nods to my teammates. Once I get my shoulder pads on, a heavy hand claps them.

"You got senioritis yet?" Coach Goetz asks in his booming voice.

At six-foot-four and 250 pounds, Coach Goetz is a large man, using his size to play D1 at Ohio State as a nose guard. After four years there, he got drafted by the Detroit Lions, only to sit the bench till he blew out his knee during garbage time. He was one of the reasons I didn't quit. He always would make practice fun, even on two-a-days during the summer, under the hot Kentucky sun. Well, almost always.

"Not yet, but it's only a matter of time," I answer.

He lets out a guffaw and announces to the team that practice starts in five minutes.

I grab my helmet and gloves and walk up to the field. Once I get there, I see Tyrese Morgan and Blake Dickman are already there. Tyrese is black and will constantly remind you of that. Blake is white and will do the same. With Slushie quitting this year—having no other reason other than he just didn't want to play—Tyrese and Blake are really the only two friends I have left on the team, not to say I'm not close with my other teammates; I just wouldn't ever hang out with them outside of practice.

"I can't believe we don't have any classes together," Tyrese says. "All I got is Dick."

"Lucky you, I have Wes," I reply back.

"Ha, have fun with that. Is he still casting spells or whatever?"

Before I could answer, a shrill whistle blows through the air. Practice has started.

Since today is Thursday, practice will be a split day: one half dedicated to offense and the other to defense. After warmups, the team splits into their respective groups. Tyrese and I jog over to Coach Core, who's wearing a *No Pain, No Gain* tee today. He loves inspirational shirts, even though he's the doesn't inspire. Immediately, he sets us on ladder drills, stutter-stepping our way through it. When we had gone through five minutes of that, Core lines us up for route running. The first route is a hitch. I, being one of three senior receivers, am toward the front of the line. And after Tyrese and the other star senior receiver, Ethan Hart, easily catch their passes without a hitch (pun fully intended), Core signals for me to go. I sprint off the line, cutting in at seven yards, perfect route. And …

*Bang!*

The ball hits me right in the facemask; not a great start to the practice.

Did I happen to mention that I start left bench?

I bashfully grab the football and toss it back to Core.

"C'mon, Behr! You're a senior now. Be a leader. Give me thirty!" Core yells at me while tilting his balding head—not a promising sign for somebody in his thirties.

I roll my eyes behind his back and crank out the pushups.

*Eat my ass.*

I stare down at my shadow and finish the reps.

Back in line, Tyrese smirks at me playfully, while Ethan just looks at me apologetically. *It's going to be a long night.* I let out a sigh.

But it isn't. Next is a go, my best route. I catch it without breaking stride, sending up a quick prayer of thanks. The other routes go just as well, only dropping on a post-corner and bobbling, but maintaining, on a comeback.

The whistle blows its glorious squeal, signaling the end of offensive drills.

After a quick water break, it's time for Team Offense. The starting offense huddles up, while I take my position at defensive end. Being five foot nine and 130 pounds, I'm a fish out of water, but I love that position. And since I really wouldn't contribute meaningfully in any other position, the coaching staff let me stay there. I'm not half bad, though, using my speed to get off the line and around the tackle quickly.

Or just getting knocked off my feet right at the start.

There's a unified clap, and the offense lines up. At left tackle, my side for this play, is Tugo, a Samoan powerhouse, who is not only huge but quick as well. He's All-State and has a full ride to Alabama. To me, he's a concrete wall. My only goal is to not fall on my butt.

"Blue forty-two," the quarterback, Brett Higgins, cadences. "Set, hike!"

Tugo may appear like the type of guy who would just knock you down and possibly t-bag you, but he's really a softy. When he blocks me, he barely puts any force into it whileI act like he's destroying me. It's a farce we started at the beginning of the year. A symbiotic relationship.

And that's how the rest of Team Offense went, with Tugo occasionally letting me get by him—only when the ball was going the other way—and me feigning getting pancaked every now and then.

The next half of practice is dedicated to defense. During defensive individuals, me and Blake line up against each other, working on defensive line techniques, such as swim and rip.

"Everybody come here," Coach Goetz commands with a wide smile, wrinkling his gray beard that only just covers his chin and not much more. "Today we're going to do something different. We're not only going to see who is the strongest physically, but also who has the strongest will. Tugo, Maclin, face-off on the ten."

Tugo and the other tackle, John Maclin, go into their defensive positions.

Goetz signals them to start, and Tugo easily pushes John five yards before Coach blows the whistle. "C'mon, Maclin," he hollers playfully. "Tugo just kicked your ass. Behr, Dickman, you're next."

We line up, and Dick smiles cockily at me, while I just keep a poker face. After Goetz says "hike," we collide and, even though Dick is larger than me, I have more resolve and hit lower, so I eventually push him back five yards. Dick always talks big but is not as talented as his mouth continuously claims.

After another ten minutes of face-offs, Coach Goetz blows his whistle to signal the end of individuals and the beginning of Team D.

I put on my gloves and join the other benchwarmers in the huddle. If it was up to Core I would be standing on the sidelines now. But the offensive coordinator, Coach Huddleston, is in charge of Scout O—the mock playstyle of the current opposing team's offense—and he has more faith in me. That being said, I don't get too many play-side pass routes and am mainly used for blocking, which I'm not half bad at.

"All right, Oliver," Huddleston says. "Run a bubble. Everybody else, you know what to do."

We break the huddle, and I nervously hurry to the far right of the field. The bubble is one of my worst routes after hitch, and a dropped pass during team would kill me. Lined up against Tyrese, I just do my best to maintain a straight face, while letting my mind clear. Thinking causes drops.

The ball is hiked, and I take a couple of steps forward, pushing Tyrese as hard as I can. I then drop back quickly as the backup wing, a large freshman named Nick White, explodes into Tyrese. The ball soars through the air, my eyes never leaving it. I snatch it out of the air with surprising ease and manage to actually break the defensive end's ankles. I'm about to make another move on a linebacker (or just get crushed) before the whistle is blown.

I bask in the hooting and hollering of my teammates on both sides of the ball, a reminder of why I kept playing, why I will never quit.

# Saturday, August 10

**Whoever on Rowling** High School's Board of Education had the phenomenal idea of starting school on a Thursday, leaving the students only two days before the weekend, is a genius. Today is Saturday, and for the Behrs, during the summer that meant boat day. Today is my turn to bring a friend, and as always, I choose Slushie. We all pile into the Nissan Armada and take off, lugging a twenty-four-foot cherry-red Yamaha dubbed *My Three Sons* behind us.

At the marina, Dad backs the jet boat, with me at the helm, into the Ohio River. Once Dad parks the tank of a minivan and boards, he takes over and lets loose across the brown waters. The Ohio River is known to many to be absolutely disgusting, and swimming in it could give you some kind of disease. That's probably not wrong, but we haven't contracted anything yet.

Once we get to a smooth area of the river, Dad stops to wakeboard. He is a fanatic for wakeboarding, thinking he's a whole lot better than he really is. He straps into the board as I take the wheel. Now in the water, he gives a thumbs-up, and I push the throttle forward, bringing him out of the water. For a man of Dad's size, it seems it would be impossible for him to wakeboard, but he crosses the wake with ease, even leaping a couple feet into the air. Our boat doesn't have enough ballast to produce the amount of wake truly needed to jump the entire wake, or at least that's his excuse. He finally draws his hand across his throat, and I cut the engine.

Now it's my turn. My love for wakeboarding isn't even close to Dad's. It's cool and all, but I could never get as good as him, and it can become frustrating and stressful. I do it mainly just to please him, to have one son who partakes in one of his favorite activities. I'm not sure if this is a weakness or virtue.

I can go straight as long as I want to, but it's crossing the wake that really gets me. And as the Yamaha takes off, I attempt to do just that but lose my balance halfway across, embarrassingly faceplanting in the water. I try a couple more times and manage to cross once but am not able to return. After that, I call it quits, knowing that any more wipeouts would ruin my mood for the rest of the afternoon.

"Hey, your mom took a video of me," Dad says with a cocky but playful smile. "Maybe you could pick up a few pointers."

"Hardy har har," I reply, glaring. Even though I know Dad was kidding, it doesn't make me any less pissed off. "Slushie, you're up. Please make me look good."

"W-what are you t-talking ab-bout. I'm about to sh-show you up." Slushie says, sporting a wide grin.

He doesn't disappoint. After three tries, he's able to stand but falls almost immediately. He eventually gives up, although not losing his good attitude. He's had so much taken away from him but can still always be happy and see the positive in everything.

Now, *My Three Sons* cruises into a cove, since Dylan, Alex, and Mom all don't wakeboard.

"How's f-football going?" Slushie asks me as we bob in lifej jackets.

"Well, Core's a douche as always. But I did catch a pass in Team and juked Tom."

"W-wait. You actually caught a pass. That's w-weird," Slush-ie jokes.

"You're hilarious," I say duly. "All I know is that I've caught more passes this year than you have."

Slushie gives me a long, hard stare, unsuccessfully holding back a grin. "So, when's your f-first game?"

"Next week. We're playing St. Clinius."

"G-good luck with that. I can still feel that hit from B-Barnes."

"Now that Barnes is playing for Purdue, their team is absolutely booty."

"That means you might actually get some p-playing time."

"I'm so glad you quit," I say sardonically, swimming toward the boat. "I'm parched. Do you want anything to drink?"

"A w-water w-would be great," Slushie replies. "W's" are always the hardest letters for him to enunciate.

As I get into the boat, I am greeted by my least favorite person ever. "Hey! Stop dripping on me!" Alex shouts at me.

"You're on a river," I disclose in a monotone voice, giving him a sideways look. We've had our fair share of scuffles in the past; there's no need to start one now. "You're going to get wet. Stop being such a wimp."

Saturday boating may be a Behr family tradition, but it doesn't mean that everybody likes it. Alex hates everything to do with the boat, which isn't surprising, since there are few things he hasn't said he didn't hate at one point or another, including everybody in his family. It's safe to say we don't get along.

After a lunch of sandwiches and chips, we board the Ya-maha, and Dad goes to work inflating the tube. Tubing is my favorite part of the lake. I always make it a mission to stay on the entire time, no matter how tired or how much pain I'm in. I'm extremly prideful, so falling off is not an option.

It's a three-person, disc-shaped tube, so me, Slushie, and Dylan all get on it, with Slushie on the left, Dylan in the middle,

and me on the right. I have, through many years of tubing, fig-
ured out the best handholds to use with each turn and how to
adjust my weight so the tube won't flip over. It's a sport of skill,
not strength (and I know I couldn't have possibly made more
of a loser statement, but it's true). That's with one person. With
three, however, there's a lot less room to maneuver, making it
harder to stay on.

Dad pushes the throttle forward, and we are off. He starts
the ride off by turning left, causing the tube to go in the opposite direction, which allows me to experience the most G's. I
lock my right elbow and easily stay on. Dad whips them to the
other side, and Slushie uses his God-given strength to barely
hang on. After a few more times of this, Dad steps it up a notch.
He turns left again but this time doesn't straighten out. A donut.
I somehow manage to stay on, but then Dad straightens out,
taking us through the wake he made. There is no hope after that,
and we all fly off in three different directions, skipping across
the water like some oddly shaped stones.

Dad gathers us back up, and we go a couple more times
before giving up, leaving for the marina.

It's days like these that remind me that sometimes I just
have to live in the now and not worry about what tomorrow
holds. To have Faith, not Fear.

# Tuesday, August 14

***Heart of Darkness*** is about a man named Marlow who takes a job to captain a boat in the Congo River to find some guy named Kurtz.

Or at least that's what I *think* it's about.

But anyways, Kurtz is a mysterious person who had apparently set himself up as a godlike figure to the Congo natives and now was deathly ill.

And man, is it boring. Some pages are just a single long paragraph describing the jungle around them. So I, of course, just do what every high schooler has done at least once: use Sparknotes.

Mrs. Byers's lecture on the good-and-evil trope during the first day of class referred to how Kurtz had first come to the Congo in search of ivory, but the life away from civilization and having power over the "brutes" turned him into a monster.

"Now that you've started reading," Mrs. Byers interrupts my thoughts, today wearing a jean dress—a jess?—with a red blouse, "you should have a grasp on the concept of conditions in the Congo that could cause one to become evil.

"Your assignment this week is to compare *Heart of Darkness* with 'The Hollow Men' you were supposed to read and analyze over summer break. As you should know, T.S. Eliot began the poem with 'Mistah Kurtz—he dead,' which obviously connects the two works. And yes, spoiler alert, Kurtz dies. Find similarities between Eliot's and Conrad's perspectives on evil."

There are still about ten minutes left in class, so I pull out my annotated copy of the poem and skim through it.

"You wanna slide that over a bit?" Wes asks as he peers over my desk very conspicuously.

"I'll send you a pic," I respond, a tad annoyed.

The poem is quite long with four parts to it, so I have to flip through a few pages to snap photos of them.

"You know, I watched *Apocalypse Now* the other night," Wes rambles. "It's apparently based off *Heart of Darkness* except during the Vietnam War. It was pretty good, but seeing Marlon Brando that fat was a bit off-putting."

Ignoring him, I flip to the last page, where something catches my eye. The last line of the second stanza in part five reads, "Falls the Shadow," which I had underlined and wrote out to the side "repetition," as it is said two more times.

However, that's not the part that draws me in. The word "Shadow" is circled frantically, almost ripped through the paper, with no annotations as to why. And the thing is, I don't remember doing it.

# Friday, August 17

**"What day is** it?" Patrick Keizer, a freshman who has the idea that we're best buds, asks as he hurries to me in the hallway between classes.

"Game day," I respond with no enthusiasm. Maybe one day I had gotten pumped up for Friday night lights, but it's been a bit. And this is also the fifth time he asked me today.

"Heck yeah it is!" he shouts into my ear as he bumps my fist, which I had laid out in anticipation, and then darts into his next class.

Yup, today is game day. That means I will have to go to the football complex right after school for the team meal—that's not the part I'm complaining about. After, we have to wait in the locker room for three hours before we take the field. Then I have to stand on the sidelines for two hours with just a twenty-minute break during halftime. And then maybe, just maybe, I might be able to play a little bit in the fourth quarter. With all said and done, I won't get home till after ten and will be too exhausted—insert joke saying that standing on the sidelines must be really tiring—to do anything but sleep.

The school day passes with its habitual slowness, and I hurry out to my blue 2015 Toyota Camry, intent on beating the post-school traffic. After flying out of my parking space and nearly clipping the car next to me, I do.

At the football complex, I take a seat by the concession stands and wait—just a bit impatiently as I'm starving from eating only school's meager lunch—for the rest of the team. It's ten minutes before the bus carrying the underclassmen shows up and another ten before the coaches allow us to eat. If you haven't seen a football team eat, it is really quite a sight. Every player storms the serving tables—seniority is of course enforced—and leaves with heaping piles of food on their plates. But don't get me started about the race for seconds.

Today the team moms fixed us chicken and waffles to celebrate our first game of the season. I grab a couple of each, drown them in maple syrup, and finish up with a side of mac and cheese and dirt pudding—the meal of champions. I sit at the seniors' table with Blake; Tyrese always likes to show up late.

"You pumped?" Blake asks, almost screeching. His long, brown head bounces with his zeal. "IT'S GAME DAY!"

Dick always gets really excited for Friday night lights—a little too much, if you ask me—and he lets everybody know. He believes that with every game he will get in and ball up. That is rarely ever the case.

"Yup, it's game day," I reply between bites of fried goodness. "I'm ready to sit the bench again."

"C'mon, Ollie, it's our senior year. Where's your game day spirit?"

"If I actually get some decent playing time, then I'll show you some 'game day spirit.'"

"It's St. Clinius. They're not that good."

*Sure, just have to convince the coaches of that.* Coach Goetz is great and all, but he always waits till we have a running clock on our opponent—achieved with a lead of thirty-six—to put the scrubs in. And at that point, we're usually in the fourth quarter and he tries to get everybody in at once, which leaves me to only get one, maybe two drives in.

I clean off my plate and go for seconds, fighting my way to

the few remaining pieces of chicken and waffles and managing to snag a piece, only having to throw a couple punches—kidding … kind of.

I later try for thirds but return with only a banana. Finished, I walk to the locker room to attempt some pre-calc homework and find Tyrese, sitting on the locker—just imagine a big seat where we throw all our stuff in—next to mine. He has a large McDonald's bag at his feet and a Big Mac between his large hands.

What Tyrese did during the team meal is a mystery. I think he just hangs out with his girlfriend—a crazy Puerto Rican. Blake proposed that he did … well, something illegal, we'll leave it at that.

"You got two?" I ask when I notice the balled-up wrapper on the ground next to him.

"Yeah, I'm black," he responds, giving me a look as if I should know better. "Team meal any good?"

"Well, they had chicken and waffles, so I'd say it was pretty darn good."

"Yeah, well, I'm trying to be healthier," he says as he takes a large bite. Looking at how fit he is, I might need to join him on the Ochocinco diet.

"Uh huh," I reply as I sit down and pull out my assignment on logarithms. But with just thirty minutes of seemingly endless log functions, I decide I need a break and take a nap.

***

I wake to rap music blasting into my ears. The pregame hype ritual has begun.

I sit for a bit, waiting for Eminem to clear my head. And after he makes me feel like a Cinderella Man, I slowly start getting dressed. Half an hour later, Goetz calls for first team, which includes me and all the other specialty players.

We head to the field and line up to run routes. There's nothing like trying to catch a ball fired at you with a good deal of people—many of them your peers—already in the stands. And I knew my papaw would've been the first one there; he never missed a game, nor tried to change who I was. With catching, I have my good days and my bad days. Today was a bad day, and now I gather with the rest of the team for warmups, head down.

After warm ups, we separate into defense then offensive individuals, coming together for a final walk-through. Through much of this, though, I just stand back and watch.

As Hunter Ryan, the kicker, knocks the rock between the uprights to end pregame warm-ups, we rush back to the locker room. There we gather around our "team chaplain," Michael Perkins, a fellow senior who is the starting fullback and middle linebacker with massive quads. Hands on each other's shoulder pads, he prays over us, not for a win, but for safety. When he says *amen*, Coach Goetz stands up and takes a deep breath, adjusting his old Rowling's cap as he always does.

"They can come to our house and throw us around," he says, looking us in each in the eye, not quite yelling but more like throwing his voice at us. "Let me tell you, they are nowhere close to the team they were last year. Now get out there and knock those little Catholic boys on their asses."

That was one of his milder speeches. At the beginning of the season, the emotion isn't quite there. Just wait.

We give a bit of a hoo-rah and line up, two by two, to walk down to the field. Some of the senior leaders rile us up, but it's not till after the captains get back when things get really hype. After giving the news that we're kicking, Ethan Hart begins the prayer.

"Dear Lord, the battles we go through life," he chants with his head down. We all repeat him.

We ask for a chance that's fair.

A chance to equal our stride, a chance to do a dare.

If we should win, let it be by a code.

Faith and honor held high.

*WE SHALL NOT LOSE!*
Day by day, we get better and better!
The team that can't be beat, *WON'T BE BEAT!*

I forgot the chills that prayer always gave me, almost as if God was giving us his blessing for each game. We charge, unified, through the paper held by the cheerleaders, toward our sideline.

After a few short words from the coaches, Hunter lines up with the kick-off unit and kicks the football to start off the game. His strong leg has attracted a few scouts from local colleges and doesn't disappoint as the rock falls into the endzone. A touchback.

The St. Clinius Cardinals' offense lines up across from Tugo's defense. The ball is hiked, and the quarterback falls back to pass.

"*Pass! Pass!*" we call out from the sideline.

The ball is rocketed to a receiver running a slant. The wideout is able to make one of our linebackers miss before being tackled by Brett Higgins at safety.

It seems the boys in red and blue will be a tougher opponent than we thought.

The next play is a run up the middle that is able to pick up five yards. The Cardinals slowly march down the field and cap off the drive with a read option, the quarterback taking it in.

With a PAT and a kickoff, the ball is in our hands. We start out with a play we had worked on during the summer. Brett throws the screen to Ethan on the outside, who then shovels it to the wing, Zane Wood. Zane has nobody in sight … and then the turf monster gets him. He still got to St. Clinius's thirty and follows it up with a long run, only barely being tackled on the three-yard line by the safety. Michael finishes the drive out with a run up the middle.

The rest of the half continued as a shootout and ends with a score of 28–28. We run up to the locker room, prepared to get a lashing. Instead, Goetz takes the starting defense outside and almost causes the walls to vibrate with his vocals. He then comes in and congratulates the offense.

"All right, fellas. The defense ain't doing nothing. They suck. No offense to those who play both sides, but it's true. We just gotta continue scoring faster than St. Clinius."

He leaves to a cacophony of "yes sirs," and we dive into our playbooks—and when I say "we," I really mean the people who actually play, while I just stare off into space—to prepare for the second half. The time comes, and we head on back out into the cool August night.

After a quick warm-up, Tyrese takes his spot on the field, ready to receive the kickoff. The kick is off, and he retrieves it at the thirty. The kick is high, and one of the gunners is already there, but Tyrese is able to send him flying with a quick shake of his hips. He takes off to the near sideline, sprinting past the kickoff team. He's almost free, before the kicker

*Lights. Him. Up.*

He pops right back up and casually walks back to the sideline, acting as if had just gotten tackled by a beefy senior, not a glorified soccer player. He will never live that down.

The offense takes the field and quickly marches down for a quick touchdown. St. Clinius then does the same. It seems both our coaches prioritized a quick scoring offense during halftime.

Through the rest of the third quarter, this trend continues, until we finally get the stop we need. It's first down right after St. Clinius had gotten the ball back, and they are looking for a big play to start off the drive. The quarterback falls back to pass, but before he can even glance over his options, Tugo is on top of him and absolutely destroys him. The ball is knocked out of the passer's hands and scooped up by Michael, who takes it in for a scoop-and-score, putting us ahead by seven after the PAT.

Into the fourth quarter, we start to control the pace of the game on both sides of the field as our defense finally begins to find some life. With two minutes left to play and the score at 49–35 in our favor, me and the other senior benchwarmers are sprinkled in. The first play is a simple sweep to my side. I block the cornerback and surprisingly am able to knock him down after driving him back a few feet. As I bend over to help him up, I recognize that he is actually a she. I had thought that she was just a hippie with her long ponytail. I help her up and go a bit easier on her for the remainder of the game, making sure to keep my hands out of her chest pads in contrast to what I had previously done and am instructed to do.

The refs blow their final whistle of the night, and we line up to shake hands. I join Blake and Tyrese at the back of the line.

"I think you committed sexual assault on the poor girl," Tyrese teases.

"No, I think that's what the kicker did to you," I retort.

After we sing our fight song, we head to the locker room celebrate to "Sandstorm." Plans are made to go to The Fifth Quarter, a party held at the local church after home games, and I decide to pass as usual. On the field, I may feel like one of the guys, but off I just … don't

# Saturday, August 18

**"*Minigolf?*" the Snapchat** reads.

"*Sure*," I reply back to Slushie. "*Who's going?*"

His Bitmoji pops onto the screen with a thought bubble. "*Just u me n Celeste. Rachel has some kind of family thing.*"

Hmm … family thing. I bet that's exactly what she's doing, I think.

"*I'll drive this time and I'll prob pick u up around 7.*"

"Aight," I text back and then open up Carrie to pass the time.

***

I make it through a quarter of King's classic by the time Slushie rolls up my driveway. He has already picked up Celeste, so I hop in the back.

"What's up, gangstas?" I ask and throw up some random gestures.

"W-why did I invite you again?" Slushie asks, giving me a look in the rearview mirror.

"Boys, boys," Celeste interrupts, wearing simply a gray T-shirt and yoga pants. "Let's go, so I can crush y'all in minigolf."

"If you mean by getting the highest score, then sure," I fire back.

We smack talk all the way to the mall like an old married couple, which I guess we kinda are. We've all been friends since middle school and always made an effort to hang out, whether it be going to the movies, bowling, or, most often, minigolf. With every round, there seemed to be a different victor, and it could get very competitive. There may or may not have been a time when Celeste pushed me into a little pond after I "accidentally" hit her ball away from mine.

We unload and go inside, hurrying past the food court to the glow-in-the-dark minigolf course, aptly named GloGolf. It's a nice place, plus there are no water hazards. We pay the teen running the register and choose our weapons.

"Hey, Celeste!" Slushie calls. "They have some k-kid clubs here."

"You know what," she replies, "I think that's a great idea. It will give me better leverage to brain you."

She jabs her club at his man parts, and Slushie jumps back, feigning shock.

"All right, morons," I interrupt. "The night's not getting any younger. I'll go first while you two are squabbling."

I place my neon-blue ball at the start of the green, getting on one knee to feign professionalism. The first hole is a relatively easy one, consisting of just a slight incline, with the hole straight ahead. I line up across the ball and give it a hard tap. It manages to somehow jump over the hole to rest alongside the wall.

"M-man, just like T-Tiger," Slushie says, giving me a slow golf clap.

"You going to go or what?"

"L-ladies first," he says, gesturing to Celeste.

"Oh, you're such a gentleman. Rachel must be very lucky." She says this last part while rolling her eyes at me.

There's a flutter in my chest as I grin back. Then my heart skips a beat when she brushes up against me as she places the ball on the turf.

*Man, I like her.* From every sway of her chestnut ponytail to every flash of a smile from her soft lips. Especially in the way her leafy-green eyes shine when she laughs.

But how can I bridge the gap that lenghty gap of a fried-zone? Well, now it may be too late.

She swings, and the bright-red ball rolls into the hole. A hole-in-one. She gives a cheer and laughs in Slushie's face. *Oh gosh, I love that laugh.*

"Ollie. Earth t-to Ollie," Slushie is suddenly snapping his fingers in my face, and I awaken from my daze. "You all right? I kn-know her, of all p-people, making a hole-in-one is s-surprising, but m-man, you look like you've seen a g-ghost."

"Yeah, I completely just zoned out."

"I know you were thinking about b-boning your m-mom. It's w-weird, but you don't need to lie about that; you're among f-friends."

"Just go." I throw the tiny pencil at him. "I don't want to be here all night."

That was a complete lie. As long as Celeste is here, I could stay here for the next week.

"You kn-know, Celeste," Slushie says as he lines up his putt, "if you show J-Jake your amazing p-putting skills, he'd have no other choice but to go out with you."

Oh, Jake Dalton. That's the guy Celeste is hardcore crushing on. There's no way I am going to be able to compete with his six-pack abs and a jawline chiseled by Michelangelo himself. I just have to hope for a rejection, but really, who could reject her? I have to ask her out, but not today. Later. I'll do it later.

"Oh, yeah. I bet he's just looking for a girl who can put a ball into a hole," she replies.

"Oh, I b-bet he is," Slushie says, giving me a look.

I manage to eke out a pretty realistic laugh as Celeste's face turns to the color of her golf ball.

Slushie putts, and it flies out of the green. He mumbles some words under his breath that would make Quentin Taranti-

-no blush as he retrieves it. We finish the round, with Celeste, of course, getting a one, me getting a two—a pretty clutch shot, if you ask me—and Slushie wrapping it up with a four.

We move on to the next green. I hardly pay attention to my putt, my mind on how I should ask Celeste out.

We finish the game with Celeste winning with a score of fifty-four, me in second at sixty, and Slushie last with a whopping seventy-six. We pile back into Slushie's beat-up Civic. The drive back is quiet, as we are all exhausted. I'm the first one to be dropped off, and as Slushie drives off with Celeste in the passenger seat, I can't help but feel a bit of jealousy. It's stupid, I know, but still.

I feel empty, which is not an unusual feeling for the post-hangout, but it's even worse now. I open *Carrie* back up to distract myself, but all I can think about is Celeste.

*Faith over Fear.*

# Sunday, September 2

**Bon Jovi screams** through the phone to wake me up. Reaching for it, only knock it off the bedside table. Finally I'm able to reach the iPhone and silence the darlin' giving love a bad name.

*Church.* I moan and crawl back into bed after I hit snooze.

Now, after an extra nine minutes that didn't do anything, I trudge upstairs in a nice polo and khakis—even though only the old people really dress up—collapsing on the living room couch. It will be another ten minutes before Mom is finished getting ready. I've lived seventeen years, and I still don't understand why married women always try to look like they're about to go on their first date.

When she's finally ready, Dad drives us to church—with just a quick stop at Micky D's.

Zion Baptist Church is a monster of a building, so big that graduation is held here every year. One would think that a building so big would attract more people from Rowling, but there are absolutely none in my grade and just a few in others.

I sit down, french vanilla latte in hand, in my small group's circle, composed of seniors and juniors.

"Ollie! You're earlier than usual," Don Freeman, one of the youth leaders, teases. His hair is spiked up as usual. "Was there no line at McDonald's?"

"You know, I just thought of your beautiful face and put the pedal to the metal," I say.

"Well, you're just in time for the icebreaker. What's your favorite Marvel movie?"

"*Thor: Ragnarok*, definitely," I answer without hesitation. "In my opinion, it was the most hilarious movie in the Marvel Universe, and Chris Hemsworth really took on the role of Thor in it."

"I think we can all agree that *Endgame* will absolutely destroy the other movies," Colton Dunner says. This may come a bit forward, but he is gay. That being said, church may seem like an odd place to spend his Sundays. There are some people at Zion Baptist that think he should be kicked out. My response to that is taken from the Gospel of John: if somebody is without sin, then they could do whatever they want with Colton. Being gay is the same, in God's eyes, as lying or porn. Colton's a really great guy who loves God. He's one of my few friends at church.

"Definitely," I respond and then give the group a look. "But mark my words, Tony Stark is going to die."

"And why is that?" Sam Calvin asks. As usual, he's wearing shorts and a T-shirt—this one has some rapper on it. Sam is the chocolate bunny of Christianity: he looks holy on the outside but is empty of God on the inside. There is a Sam Calvin in every church.

"First off, Tony started it all off with the first MCU movie. And then he stopped Thanos's invasion in *Avengers* and had arguably the best fight with Thanos in *Infinity War*."

When I first started writing, it was like something unlocked inside of me. I could predict what would happen in a book or movie. I'm of course wrong most of the time, but with fictional arts using many clichés and stereotypes, it's not rocket science.

"Speaking of predictions," Don adds to the conversation. "Remember that scene in Age of Ultron when Captain America almost lifted Mjolnir? Well, I think he might become worthy in *Endgame*. What better time for it, right?"

Our small group's Bible plan for the day ended right when Don asked the icebreaker. For the rest of the morning session, we discuss our theories of what could possibly be the last Avengers movie.

Thirty minutes later, we all stand up, laughing about a joke theory from Sam about Thor being fat, and go to the worship center. Colton and I sit in the back; that way nobody could see us if we fall asleep. I had already filled up my McDonald's coffee cup with the church's joe—which is surprisingly pretty good. Now came the battle to stay awake.

After a short, muted introduction video of the church and its doings, the band comes onto the stage, and we stand up. As the band plays—actually very well—I mouth along with the words on the screen. Everybody says that you can't hear your own voice during worship, but I can and it's awful.

After singing the upbeat "Build Your Kingdom Here," the band—aptly named The Jesus Freaks—slows it down to set the mood with "Reckless Love."

The lead singer prays us into worship, and we sit back down.

"Good morning!" our pastor, Paul Lewis, greets as he enters the stage. He's wearing the same striped button-down he wears every Sunday. "How are y'all enjoying not having your kids seven hours a day?"

"Amen," someone calls from the congregation. *Oh, no.* I wince, recognizing Mom's voice.

"Amen is right. Having four kids was the worst mistake I've ever made." Pastor Lewis says this last part while winking at his children in the front, made known to the audience by a jumbotron behind him.

"Okay. Let's settle down now that we got the silly out of us. Today we dive into a deep topic that affects all of us. I'm not saying that you guys do, but today would not be a good day to fall asleep."

I glance over at Colton to see he's still awake, but he's hanging on to every word. I too have no signs of tiredness. The black gold is doing its thing.

"Even before the Garden of Eden, sin has been wreaking havoc in lives. Eve is the one usually blamed for bringing sin into the world, which isn't wrong. But before her, there was Lucifer, an angel of God. Like Eve, he wanted to be equal with God and was thus thrown from heaven's highest heights to hell's lowest lows.

"My point here is that at birth we are marred with a seed of sin. That seed will grow as we age, but with God we can keep it trimmed, never allowing it to completely wrap us in its wicked thorns. Without God, however, it will grow out of control and overcome you with evil. That evil comes in many forms, most commonly in the form of pornography and alcohol. There are a few out there, though, that with unimaginable, horrible circumstances have been completely overwhelmed by sin and evil. Those are the psychopaths of this world, just people like you and me, who didn't have God and his hedge clippers."

I'm wide awake now, my ADD failing at distracting me with random scenarios. Pastor Lewis is in some kind of fervor. It's like he was talking directly to me. Lately my anger, which I usually keep hidden, has become more apparent. I need to learn how to control it before it gets the best of me. Learn how to fight the Shadow.

"God is the only thing that can save you. Turning to drugs or sex will just make it grow faster. Christian or not, *you* need him. Come join me in prayer."

We bow our heads, and he calls for us to come up to the front and pray for God's forgiveness and help. I glance around and see about a quarter of the congregation, including Colton, stand up. I stay in my seat. However, I do get on my knees and rest my hands on my seat, praying for guidance until tears start to appear behind my closed eyes. Praying that he will help me through my senior year and with whatever happens after that.

That he will give me a purpose and make my life meaningful.

# Monday, September 17

**BENNY: I saw** a woman today. She had some kind of pasty chalk on part of her face; probably drugged out. I ... I think she might have followed me home last night.

I take my hands off the keyboard and rest them in my lap.

"That's good. Or maybe not. Hmm," I ramble to myself. That's about my thought process for every other sentence I write for *The Stranger*. It has to be perfect, because I may never get another chance.

I started writing this screenplay around February and have eighty-one pages. I've always been aware of having a lack of talent, like not being able to sing worth crap, just being average athletically, and much, much more. And no matter how many people say I'm smart, I'm only in the top 20 percent of the class. I'll need to do better in med school if I'm ever going to be a dermatologist. Lately, I've wondered what my purpose is (if I even have one).

Writing is my purpose.

Storytelling is my talent.

I don't know what I'll do if I can't make a career out of this, but I'm not an idiot either, though, and am not going to put all my eggs in that basket. That's why I'm still going to college with all appearances of being a doctor.

Even though I'm not going to be an intern for a small movie company or something until I make it to the big leagues, doesn't mean I want to tell anybody. I guess somewhere deep inside of me I think they'd tell me I'd never become a screenwriter, or maybe even worse, they'd say my screenplay sucks. How I'm an awful writer and can't spin a story to save my life. And, also, how cool would it be to drop a published script into Dad's or Mom's lap with my name on the front?

I place my hands on my Lenovo laptop and resume to peck away at the keys.

*Faith over Fear.*

# Friday, October 5

**The coming of** October means the homecoming dance, but before that, we got some Friday night lights action.

The Brown County Panthers come to town this week, a bunch of country hicks who last year thought it would be a good idea to target one of our running backs—not even a starter—leaving him not knowing where he was. That was during garbage time, too, when we were up by forty plus. This will be a revenge game, and all of us who were there will be playing with a chip on our shoulders.

At the complex, the football moms have gifted us with a special treat: Chick-fil-A sandwiches. Chicken that is blessed by God. I only eat one, however, and follow it up with a banana. Today I know that I'm actually going to get some playing time for once, and I don't want to screw it up by puking on the field.

***

We win the coin toss and choose to defer to the second half. Hunter holds back during the kick, and the rock falls short of the endzone. Brown County's return man receives the football at their five and is only able to take it to the fifteen.

Our defense lines up against the Panthers' offense as the sidelines yells out advice and encouragement. The ball is hiked, and Brown County's quarterback hands it off to the wing.

"SWEEP!" we yell from the bench as the running back runs

to our sideline. Russell Summers, Mr. Wisconsin himself—a just-above-average end who thinks he's good enough to play for the Badgers—chases him and brings him down for a loss.

The next two downs don't go much better, and they are already punting. Ethan Hart is back to receive. The ball falls in his arms, and he runs across the sidelines, cutting so sharply that the opposing player falls on his butt. There's only one person now who can tackle him, and Ethan stiff-arms the heck out of him. Now just like that, we are up by six. Ethan is a pretty darn good player, but the boys in purple and yellow are just that bad.

Not every play is like that, but it's safe to say that we were dominating. We go in at halftime with a 28–0 lead. Another touchdown with a two-point conversion will mean playing time for us benchwarmers.

Coach Goetz doesn't even bother talking to us, and just goes into his office, probably to eat some Chick-fil-A he stashed away. I sit on my locker and try to look over the play cards, but my mind keeps drifting off to me making huge, Sportscenter: Top Ten–worthy plays.

Then Celeste Snapchats me.

I open the snap. It's a selfie of her and Jake. The caption reads: *"Guess who asked me out."*

*I don't know, Ronald freaking McDonald?*

I reply, *"Really!? How?"*

*(in the fiery pits of Mordor)*

*did that happen?"*

Before she can respond, Coach blows his whistle. Halftime is over.

We do a short warmup, and the kick-return team takes the field. I return to my usual spot on the sidelines, however, my mind is far from the game at hand. The whistle blows, and the Panthers' kicker unsurprisingly knocks it out of bounds. The ball is placed at our forty, and our offense takes the field. Brett Higgins hikes the ball and throws a screen pass to Ethan. Zane

Wood lays a hard crack block on the cornerback, while Ethan turns his shoulders, looking to pass. Brett is wide open and Ethan—a converted quarterback—hits him, and Higgins walks it in for an effortless touchdown.

The offense stays on the field to attempt a two-point conversion and start the running clock. Michael Perkins punches it in with ease as if he was going against a peewee-league team, which I guess Brown County kind of is.

Coach Goetz had already told us who would start for second defense—I'm going at defensive end—and we take the field once the ball is kicked off and recovered. I love playing defense, but all I want to do right now is to go home and eat an entire pint of cookie dough.

I line up at my position, making sure my younger teammates are doing the same. The play is a simple zone coverage, which meant nothing to me. All I have to do is get to the ball carrier. The ball is hiked, and I erupt off the line, intent to quickly jam the tackle, before getting to the passer. Instead, I'm blown up by the tackle, landing on my ass. It's a run option, the back taking the rock on my side and being almost immediately wrestled down by the freshman White. I hop up and the quarterback is instantly in my face, having done nothing else tonight.

"Stay the hell down," he says brusquely.

It's embarrassing enough to get knocked down, but another to be talked to like that by a quarterback with five interceptions in the game. I line back up, eyes straight ahead, with the ball in my peripheral, and face set. The ball is hiked, and I again dart off the line. I don't even bother this time to hit the tackle, and dash around his fat ass. The quarterback is back and looking to pass. I sprint to him, neglecting my responsibilities to contain him if he decides to scramble. I hit him low, my helmet connecting with his left knee, and hear a loud pop as he falls down. As cheap and dirty of a hit as it comes. When I come to my feet, I see a flag lying next to me, but I barely notice it and leer over the Panther.

"Stay the hell down," I say, the rage boiling inside me as I step on his injured knee—but it's not the quarterback now; it is Jake—on my way to the sideline, which is followed by a terrifying, distraught scream that sends shivers through me. Another flag is thrown, and a ref is in my face, yelling at me to get off the field. I hardly notice him. I hardly notice anything. Only the flame of ire burning from within. That and Fear. Then Goetz grabs my shoulder and spins me around, screaming in my face, asking what I just did. I wipe the spittle off angrily.

"Screw off!" I yell back at him, something I had never even thought I would, or even could, do. "Not tonight. Not *fucking* tonight."

After collecting my stuff from the locker room, pads still on, I drive home as fast as my Camry will go on backroads. I hear a movie playing from the theater room and sneak past it to my room. I do not want to explain the reason of why I'm home so early. Then I quickly undress and crawl into my bed, praying for quiet thoughts and quick sleep. It doesn't come

*"Falls the Shadow."*

The voice comes in the form of a whisper from the corner of the room. A ghostly visage arises in the shadows. No. It *is* the Shadow.

I open my mouth, but nothing comes out, and I'm stuck staring at the apparition as my body's completely paralyzed. Two dark pits I take for eyes return my gaze in silence.

This isn't the first time I've seen it. *Right?* Occasionally dancing in the corner of my eye. Or were those just specks of dust? It's been here before, hasn't it? Or were those just dreams? Nightmares?

I don't know long we stay that way, staring at each other with my mind attempting to grasp on to something—anything—tangible, before a merciful wave of sleep washes over me.

*Faith over Fear.*

## Saturday, October 6

**Homecoming. What better** word to describe it than *awkward?* With a variety of horny teenagers grinding up on each other, lonely individuals downing the free food in the corner, the frenzy waltzers and stepping-on-toes slow dancers, what was there not to love?

My friends and I are a mix of these and like to hang back mostly and chit-chat but will most definitely break it down during "Cotton-Eyed Joe."

This year will be different, as Celeste will not be going with us as a friend, but with Jake as a date. I had considered not going, but I knew that would look a bit suspicious since I've never missed homecoming. And anyway, it's my senior year; I've got to make the most of it.

With last night's encounter little more than a vivid dream, I pull on the same outfit I've worn for the past three homecomings—I am the same size as I was freshman year, and Dad is too cheap to buy me another button-down—and pose with Alex in front of the mantle as Mom takes her sweet time snapping photos. We manage to pull away and hurry to my Camry. We're running on time, but I want to get there early so I can devour some pizza before others see me eating like some kind of starving animal. Since the dawn of time, Behrs have always eaten as if the food was going to disappear before our very eyes.

When I enter the transformed cafeteria, though, I see Mitch Binford grabbing himself a Coke.

"Mitch!" I yell across the room, getting maybe a little too excited. "How's it going?"

I haven't seen Mitch since summer break. He is currently attending an academy hosted by Morehead University meant for only the extremely gifted and talented. He is a genius with a 35 on his ACT and an SAT score somewhere north of 1400. The program begins during junior year and allows the chosen students to earn the rest of their high school credits while completing two years of college. He is one of ten to be chosen from our school in the last four years.

Since he is still technically a Rowling Bearcat, he is able to attend homecoming, as well as prom and other school-sponsored events.

"Ollie!" he calls back as he approaches me. "You're looking quite spiffy."

He's sporting a sharp-looking suit with a black coat, a solid blue button-down, topped off with a pink bowtie. His jet-black hair is spiked up too. That's new.

Ah, *spiffy*, a word Wes uses whenever possible and our group eventually adopted.

"Did you not bring back some hot college chick?" I ask.

"Yeah, it's weird, right. It's like they're almost immune to my sexy charm," Mitch takes a sip of his Coke. "I thought you would have at least three girls—and maybe a guy as well—hanging all over you."

"Right. No, I'm still as single as the pope."

My last relationship was sophomore year when Stephanie asked me out. We had been pretty good friends in the year leading up to it, and I didn't want to hurt her by saying no, even though I knew it could ruin our friendship. That was my excuse, at least. I just needed a girlfriend desperately. I say this as if she was completely unattractive, but she really wasn't bad at all. She was just … tall.

Steph dumped me over text after a week. "I don't like you, but we can still be friends." She had a pretty good reason for breaking up with me, since we didn't go on one date. I think I spent that whole month debating where the best place for a first date would be. For the rest of that night, I watched *White Chicks* through my tears, hoping it would cheer me up. It didn't.

"Ah, look who's here." Mitch points at the entrance.

And speak of the devil, Stephanie walks through the double doors of the cafeteria, her arm in her date's.

"Steph, Tara," we say as they walk by us.

Yup.

As I am stewing in my self-pity, Celeste enters. Her brown hair, usually in a ponytail, is flowing down her shoulders. Her bright-blue dress, lighting up the room, draws all eyes to her.

She is perfect.

Her pure beauty completely distracts me from who was next to her: Jake, with his hand in hers. He's six-two, six-three, and like two hundred pounds of pure muscle. His jaw is like that of a Greek god, while his slicked back hair that of a movie star.

"So, Celeste can get Jake, but you can't find a single person?" Mitch asks me.

I don't respond.

"Hey, Mitch. Long time, no see." Celeste says as she approaches us.

"It's been a bit, hasn't it? Good to see you."

She turns to me and says with a wink, "Dang, Ollie, you clean up well."

"You know me," is all I say, even taking a small bow as I mentally kick myself.

"You ready for track season?" Jake asks me. He was, of course, the state champion of hurdles and high jump. And not to mention super nice. It really makes it hard to hate his guts.

"Oh, you know it." I am really batting a thousand now, ar-

-en't I?

"Well, I guess we'll see you guys later," Celeste says. "I think Jake wants to catch up with some old friends."

"Yeah, see ya," I respond, eyes burning a hole in Jake's back.

Slowly, the others start to filter in. Blake comes by himself; he has about as much experience with the ladies as I do. He just wears a T-shirt with the imprint of a tux, like he's done the last three years, refusing to buy a real suit. Tyrese arrives with his psycho girlfriend, Mia, who even when smiling, looks like she wants to saw off your penis. Slowly. His satin tie matches her low-cut dress. The color of blood, which I'm sure was the intention.

Wes then shows up with some random chick from some random school, as he is prone to do. Probably because they don't know about his uh … abnormalities. He's dressed in a red undershirt and a tie striped the same color that turned his to fire. And finally, Slushie enters with Rachel hanging all over him. Her purple dress shows most of her cleavage, while he just wears a simple button-down and tie like me, his long hair slicked back. He barely gets a "hey" out before she drags him onto the dance floor to bop to "Fergalicious." Mia, as well, takes Tyrese away to see her freshman friends.

"Guys, this is Susanah from Brown County," Wes introduces. She's a brunette with a shy smile. Too innocent for the likes of Wes.

We all nod and offer greetings. When she leaves to go to the bathroom, we jump on him.

"You brought somebody from the team we just played last night during the homecoming game," Dick asks, his face contorted in a pretense of disappointment.

I wince at the memories from yesterday. *At least they have what appears to be a case of selective memory.*

"Well, yeah. I was talking to her during the game—"

"Fraternizing with the other team not only after but *during the game?*" Mitch interrupts.

"You know, if you guys wanna be like that, we'll just go to her homecoming," he retorts before heading toward the double doors, looking legit ticked, causing me to actually feel bad for him. But not enough for me to chase after him.

For the next half hour, we small talk while I keep one eye continuously watching Celeste. Then the first slow song of the night comes on, "All of Me" by John Legend. Mitch finds a friend and takes to the dance floor. Now it's just me and Blake watching with the other losers.

"Hey, g-guys."

We turn to see Slushie standing by himself.

"R-R-Rach is d-dancing with Adam Holm." He looks extremely nervous, and his speech impediment is getting worse. "That d-doesn't m-mean anything, d-does it?"

There is only one word to describe Adam, and it rhymes with "truck toy". He doesn't date but just sleeps around. With great looks and the ability to charm everyone, no one is safe. Rachel might be Slushie's tomorrow, but tonight she is all Adam's.

"Nah, Rachel would be stupid to leave you," I try to reassure him, even though I know I'm lying through my teeth.

He nods slowly, not really believing it.

We watch together, our eyes on two different couples. Celeste is a horrible dancer—a fact I knew when we danced as friends last homecoming—so she was standing on Jake's feet as he guided her around the room. He, on the other hand, is a great dancer, 'cause why not, it's not like he has a million other talents.

The song ends, and the DJ plays "Cotton-Eyed Joe" next. The couples break apart and line up, joined by many of the onlookers, including Dick. Me and Slushie, on the other hand, sit this one out, our thoughts on something unknowingly similar.

*Faith over Fear.*

**Since Mitch will** be here for the remainder of the weekend, I had decided last night after the dance to have a little get-together, not necessarily a party. Although I think the real reason is just because I want to see Celeste without Jake hanging all over her.

The next day, I pop the inquiry into the groupchat. Within an hour, I get affirmative replies from everybody. It is on. Four o'clock my place. I can't even remember the last time I hung out at someone else's house, but I guess that's what happens when your dad makes twice as much as your friends' parents. I'm starting to think they're just friends with me because of my house.

Kidding.

I hope.

It's a half hour after four when everybody starts filtering in. They have this notion—not saying that I don't either—that they should come later to a party so more people will be there, which has grown superfluous now that everyone does it.

They know the drill by now and go around back to the basement door. There are just too many awkward conversations that can come between them and my parents, especially with Celeste, who they have been trying to hook me up with for several years now. I have yet to tell them about Jake.

"Now b-begins the hour of d-decision," Slushie says.

Our group has the hardest time deciding, well … anything, but more particularly, about what we are going to do at my house. They believe that since I'm the host, I should have plans to last the entire night. In contrast, I think that the guests should decide.

"Come on, guys," I respond. "One of y'all got to have some idea."

"You're the host, Behr," Blake says, giving almost a sarcastic shrug.

"I say we all grab a book off my shelf, sit in a circle, and read. Then we can discuss what we learned. Wouldn't that be fun?" I say, raising my eyebrows in mock excitement.

"Ooh!" Wes interjects. "I think I got my quantum energy tome in my car. There are a few group exercises in there that we can try."

"We don't want to try out any of your sex positions," Tyrese retorts. "Save that for Sarah, or whatever her name is."

Slushie just shivers at this. He had made a deal with Wes that the quanite would let him win a race during last track season when Rachel was watching if he did one technique in the book. He has never told anybody but me about that experience.

"How about we have a bonfire," Celeste offers. She's wearing short shorts today. "That sounds like a great idea," I reply, trying to keep my eyes up. "I'll grab some firewood."

"I'll come w-with," Slushie says.

"Don't forget the gas," Tyrese adds.

I've got the evidence on my right foot of why using gasoline to start a fire is a bad idea and ignore him.

I leave with Slushie right behind.

"R-Rachel d-d-dumped m-me," Slushie tells me as we walk toward the barn.

I look over at him and see he's as stiff as a brick. He is trying not to cry, but I can already see a tear welling up his eye.

"I'm p-pretty sure she scr-screwed Adam last n-night."

"I'm really sorry. Do you want to, uh, talk about it?"

"No."

*Well then.*

We walk in silence to the barn and load fresh-split wood into an ATV. When we get back, the gang's all gathered around the pit, having already helped themselves to waters and Cokes from the fridge. I run inside to grab a whole roll of paper towels, which I set in the middle of the pit and stack firewood around, lighting it up with a Zippo. It's not exactly as redneck as using gas, but it's up there.

Over the crackle of the flames, I hear a car pull up to the driveway.

"That must be Colton," I say as I walk up to meet him. "He's a friend from church."

"He's gay," Mitch adds. He had come with me to a couple of small groups back before he left.

"Yup, but probably don't want to make that the topic of discussion."

Colton is already out of his Mercury and waves when he sees me.

"Colton, how's it going?"

"It's going," he says and gives a wan smile. He was never a big fan of meeting new people, but I love bringing my friend groups together to make one ultimate squad.

"Let me introduce you to the guys and gal, and then I'll grab some stuff for s'mores."

After some greetings and me getting the goods, we just chat about how our senior years are going. It's been a few months since we've been together.

"So, Ollie t-told me that you g-got mugged," Slushie says to Tyrese with a wide smile on his face.

"Yeah, at least I didn't go out and rape some girl," he fires back.

"Wait, what?" Wes asks.

"I blocked a chick on the field and kinda knocked her over," I try to defend myself. "I thought *she* was a *he*."

"Sure, you did," Dick replies. "Your hands were all up in her boobs."

"That's what I'm supposed to do!" I respond, my voice getting louder and higher as I go, something that occurs whenever I get a bit, uh … emotional.

I glance over at Celeste to see what she thought of all this, but she is just sitting there, a humored smile on her face.

"That's what I'm sup*posed to do*," Tyrese and Dick mock in unison.

"Man, Ollie," Mitch joins the convo, "I knew you were a poon slayer, but damn."

"When did you start talking like that?" I ask.

"College is a bitch." He gives me a tired look. "It changes you."

Colton gives me an almost horrified look, probably questioning his decision to come. I just shake my head and know that I'm too strong-willed to let college change me.

"How about w-we change the subject," Slushie offers and turns to Celeste. "How's it g-going with you and J-Jake?"

I stiffen at the mention of his name.

"It's going really good, actually," she beams at the thought of him. "I think he actually really likes me. Tomorrow he's going to take me to the aquarium. What about you and Rachel?"

Slushie is saved by the bell with Tyrese's comment about the tanks not being the only thing that will smell like fish.

"Ollie, it's starting to get cold," Wes says. "We should go inside and watch a movie."

"Why don't you just surge?" Surging was something . . . well I don't really know what it is, but it has something to do with his quanite stuff. I receive an extremely dirty look in return for the question. "All right, fine." I turn to the rest of the group. "Is that good with you guys?"

"I haven't seen a good horror movie in a while," Mitch suggests.

"Ooh, yeah," Dick agrees. "Ollie, do you have *Insidious*? I just saw it on *Watchmojo* and have been wanting to see it since."

"I actually have the entire series."

"I'm feeling an all-nighter."

Everybody heads inside with Colton the only one staying behind to help me clean up.

"So, how are you liking everyone?" I ask.

He just gives me a look.

"Yeah, you have to get used to them."

One of the reasons I am always the host of these little get-togethers is because of my theater room. It really isn't that big—only the size of a common family room—but the projector screen takes up the majority of one wall with leather recliners completing the other side. I think that every time they come here they always request—demand—a movie.

Now they are taking it over, and Colton manages to slyly steal the last seat.

"Ollie, come over here," Celeste says, scooching over while simultaneously pushing Blake away.

I squeeze in between them, thrilled to be this close to her. I had already put the movie in, so I just press play. Halfway through the horror flick, I feel Celeste's head on my shoulder and look over to see she's out cold. A small smile crosses my face, and I know that I can't be with anyone else. Call me crazy, but I think she's the one.

# Monday, October 8

**There's a crunch** as I bite into the cheeseburger. I have no idea what kind of meat the school uses, but if it is indeed beef, it's poorly processed. Sometimes you might be able to find little white pieces within the meat that take little imagination to decipher what it is. It's best if one just eats the burger without looking at it, and after three years of consuming it, I've started to actually kind of like it.

I'm usually the first one to get to the cafeteria, so I just stare off into the distance, thinking about how Benny will deal with the stranger.

"What are you looking at?" Celeste asks from across him. She went with a Caesar salad, which is probably the safest choice.

"Oh, nothing," I reply, shaking myself out of my stupor and glancing at my Fitbit. "Slushie is usually here by now."

"Oh, he didn't tell you? He and Rachel broke up. Apparently, it had something to do with Adam. He talked to me about it for like all of English."

"Yeah, he told me yesterday but didn't go into much detail."

I will admit I'm a bit annoyed that all that Slushie gave me was a vulgar phrase, while he basically emptied his soul onto Celeste. We've been friends for longer, and I'd even say we are closer, but whatever. Hoes before bros, right?

"So, it's going good with Jake," I say. I probably won't like what I hear, but I need to know.

"Yeah!" she replies, putting down her fork. "I mean, he's everything I could ever hope and dream for in a man."

"Well, that's great!" I respond, putting on my best fake smile, an act I've gotten really good at lately. There's no way I'm going to be able to compete with Jake or her feelings for him. I have to try to move on.

*Faith over Fear.*

**History is in** reach today. We had won the first two rounds of playoffs and are in Regionals. This is the first time my class made it this far and only the second time in school history. If we win, we would be the first to win Regionals in the eighteen years of the football program. And with our 10–2 record, we'd have the most wins as well.

Our opponent this week is Kingsdale. The Scotties come from the mountains, which means they are massive. This is the largest team we have played this year, not to mention they have great technique and are very well disciplined. This will be the biggest test we've had my entire high school career. We will need to play *perfectly* to be able to even have a chance. There will be no room for mistakes. We are thirteen-point underdogs, and we'll use that to strike a fire under us. We're not going home tonight.

"Seniors, this could be the last night you wear the R on your chest," Coach Mazuk emphasizes.

Coach Mazuk was our coach back in middle school. Young and ripped, he's very different than Goetz. When I first started playing football, I was just a chubby kid who didn't even know how to get into a three-point stance. The first practice consisted almost entirely of conditioning, something I was entirely unused to, and I was *this* close to quitting. But at the end of practice, he said something that changed my life forever.

"Some of you are probably going to quit no matter what I say, but there is one thing I want to leave you with," he had said, looking every one of us in the eye. "Football will give you another family you'll have forever. The memories you make here will be with you till the day you die.

"Life is always going to knock you down. It will be even worse as you get older. But if you can endure these workouts, then you're one step closer to getting back up each time life gives you a right hook. Don't let life win."

And some did still quit, but I stayed and really did start to make friends that felt more like brothers. Brothers that I still have today. I owe who I am today to Mazuk.

"I would give an arm and a leg just to play one game," Mazuk continues. "Go out there firing on all cylinders. Play like you'll never play again."

He gives us a look as he did so many years ago to thirty worn-out kids. "I've known most of you since middle school. I've been with y'all for the good, the bad, and the ugly. You guys are the best, most talented class I've ever coached. Now go out and prove me right."

For the next hour, alumni and coaches going all the way back, talk to us seniors. And when it's all over, I don't see one dry eye. Even Tugo is sniffling. Afterward, we hug each other and then begin preparations for the night.

***

Following warm-ups and the team prayer, Coach Goetz gives his speech.

"Now, I'm not going to get all emotional like all your former coaches; I don't expect to lose. If you play like you've been playing all season, though, we're going to lose. You have to take it to the next level. Give everything you have and then more. And if you don't, you'll regret it for the rest of your life.

"You've got the tools you need to win. Now do it! Play for the person next to you. Play for the ones who came before you.

after you. And give those son of whores the biggest ass-whooping they have ever had!"

We all jump up and holler in agreement. I'd be surprised if any professional coach can give a speech that motivating.

"*Unleash the violence!*" Tugo howls, and we echo him back.

It's game time.

***

A 21-to-7-point game in favor of Kingsdale at halftime is not how we imagined the game to go. Zane is the only reason we are in the game, giving us our only score on a powerful thirty-yard run. Higgins can barely hit a receiver and even got replaced by Ethan until the reason he was switched to receiver is revealed. Even Tugo hasn't been a force, allowing two sacks while not even getting one on the other side of the ball. We will need a full, 180-degree turnaround to be able to win this game.

Coach Goetz comes in surprisingly calm and takes the starting offense outside while Core grabs the defensive starters who don't play both sides. After ten minutes, we leave the locker room without a speech. The starters know what to do, and I guess that's all that matters.

A lot can happen in twenty-four minutes.

***

By the end of the third quarter, we had tied the score because of Higgins's amazing turnaround. I swear, he had just one incomplete pass, and that was only because it was deflected at the line. He is on fire. Tugo is leading the defense now with six tackles and a sack. I don't know what the coaches told them during halftime, but it sure is working. Kingsdale only had a couple first downs this half.

But I think I spoke too soon, as the Scotties just complete an end-around and get over twenty yards out of it. The defense must be shocked by this because the beefy fullback is able to take it another seven yards. Kingsdale is already lining up for another play, while our defense is scrambling around like chickens with their heads cut off. Coach Goetz runs halfway out onto the field to call time out. And when he comes back to the sideline, his face is beet red—whether from anger at his defense, exertion by his sprint, or being berated by the ref for his misdemeanor, I don't know.

Kingsdale does get a first down, but our defense then holds them to a few yards, leading them to punt. But something isn't right; the upback is usually right in front of the punter, except now he is playing to the right of the ball, on the heels of the end. It's a fake. Goetz recognizes it, but as he yells to tell the return team, the ball is hiked. The back darts off the line, not even bothering to fake a block, to run a corner fade. He is untouched at the line, and nobody guards him. The punter is the backup quarterback and throws a beauty. The ball is caught, and the upback takes it up the field. Zane is the only one back to receive and is juked out of his shoes as he goes for the tackle. Touchdown Kingsdale.

There is 8:24 on the clock, and we're down by seven.

For the next bit, it's back and forth, neither of our defenses giving up an inch. It's punt after punt—our return is much more alert now—until, with two minutes remaining, we get our first first down of the quarter. And then another. The offense is steadily marching down the field, not wanting to score too fast and allow Kingsdale a chance to score. But then we hit fourth down on the twenty-three-yard line with 1:12 left. A field goal won't win this game; we need a touchdown.

Higgins is in shotgun, with Michael next to him and Zane at the wing. Ethan is out left with Tyrese on the other side. Brett claps his hands, and the ball is hiked. Ethan makes a move and then bubbles out, with Zane sprinting to make the block on the corner. But instead, he stops and creates a wall with his arms for Ethan to run behind. The back flinches, expecting to be rocked, which gives Ethan enough time to get a couple steps of separation from him. The safety is an All-American, however, and recognizes this almost before it happens. He pursues, angling to meet Ethan at the goal line. Higgins notices the safety and launches the ball high, nothing more really than a jump ball. The two players pinpoint the football and attempt to outleap each other. Both hands are on the ball as they fall in the endzone together, but it is Ethan who stands up with the rock raised high over his head.

We go wild on the sidelines, everybody chest bumping and headbutting. When Ethan trots over, Coach Goetz picks him up and wraps him in a choking bearhug, laughing like a child. Everybody wants a piece of him.

But the game is not over yet. After the extra point, it is a tie game with fifty-four seconds remaining.

Hunter squibs the ball, which is fallen on by the thirty-six. The Scotties' offense lines up with, presumably, a series of plays in hand. Our defense will have to be ready and quick on their feet to be able to get a stop.

The quarterback hikes the ball and runs to his left and hits his receiver for a twelve-yard comeback but is tackled before he can get out of bounds. The offense runs up to the line with the QB yelling "Elvis," while strumming an air guitar. This time he runs to his right and throws to a wideout running a post-corner. But Tyrese comes from his safety position to cut off the pass and intercept it. With the home crowd cheering him on, Tyrese jukes out defenders before he is eventually run out of bounds at their thirty-five. He makes one mistake, however: not falling down immediately after he caught it, and now there are only three seconds left. Hunter has never had a career kick over fifty, and this would be for fifty-two. He has drilled a few of them this far in practice and already has a full ride to Thomas Moore, but this a whole different atmosphere.

We don't want to go into overtime. We may have the momentum, but we're tired, and mistakes are bound to happen. I'm not sure we can survive another quarter.

Hunter takes his steps. His face is poised, but he is noticeably sweating on this cold November night, where all he has done is kick. He measures it up, nods to the holder (Higgins), who motions for the ball. The snap is good. The hold is good. And the kick is … GOOD!

With the clock striking zero, we storm the field and carry Hunter off the field. Coach Goetz somehow manages to get us to line up and shake hands with Kingsdale, before running up to the front of the stands to sing our fight song with our student section:

Onward Dragons, onward Dragons,
Win this game tonight.
We are here for, we will cheer for,
Rowling's orange and black.
Rah! Rah! Rah!
Onward Dragons, onward Dragons,
We will do our best.
We are proud to say that we're from RHS!

Finishing with a large cheer, we run over to where the coaches are standing for the postgame huddle.

"You boys don't know how proud I am of you," Coach Goetz says, choking up, something he was prone to do at the end of the season but never with a win. "To go out and play the way y'all did in the second half, coming back from a fourteen-point deficit, is the Mamba Mentality. You guys know I'm a big Kobe fan, not just because of his athleticism, but because of his attitude and work ethic: the Mamba Mentality. Today all of you had the Mamba Mentality."

Goetz dries his eyes. "Tonight is for you to celebrate—there will be no film and weights tomorrow—but if I hear any of you have been drinking or smoking grass, you will be sitting next week."

Before we go and live it up tonight, we spread out around the logo in the middle of the field for prayer and invite Kings-

-dale to join us. This is a tradition Michael Perkins started a couple years ago and is one of the most important aspects of the game. Without God, there is no football. No family. A few of the Scotties don't join us, but most do. With a Scotty between each Bearcat, hand-in-hand we pray as Michael leads it. After the prayer, we give a few courteous condolences to the losing team and hurry up to the locker room.

No win is the same without "Sandstorm," except on this occasion we do it twice. Plans are made to go to The Fifth Quarter and this time I decide to join them.

# Monday, November 19

**Home is where** our story begins.

They should throw that on a t-shirt. Perhaps on a bumper sticker? Or maybe on some piece of decoration at Bed Bath & Beyond, targeted toward sentimental mothers who live in rural areas.

Oh, wait. They do have that, and sure enough, Mom bought it when we first moved here nine years ago, and to this day, it lies above the fridge. I think it was the rooster, randomly placed on the sign, that really drew her in. For some reason, ever since we moved out to the country, she has had a thing for chicken decor.

"Ooh, that glass hen will look great on our mantel."

"That painting of chicks would be perfect for our bedroom."

And on and on.

*Mi familia y yo* have lived in rural Verona, Kentucky, for the better part of the last decade, moving here in the summer before my fourth-grade year. Our family was about to grow, with Dylan soon to be born. And it sure did grow; one kid, four dogs, and a cat, oh my. Having that many animals becomes a real pain, and really the only one I actually like is Benny—I sure did name the main character in *The Stranger* after that good boy.

And certainly enough, as I open the door, I hear him greet me with his shrill bark that almost sounds like someone is tor-

-turing him. Since I have a dual-credit anthropology class that's only on Tuesdays and Thursdays, I'm the only one home, meaning the dogs are my responsibility. Yay. Benny is a Frenchie, a pretty solid one at that, and as I let the dogs out, I pick him up and kiss him on his squished shnoz.

With the dogs outside to do their business and the cat fed, I settle down on the couch with a bowl of Flamin' Hot Cheetos and watch reruns of *Friends*. Coach gave us the day off with instructions to watch film—as in, for the *starters* to watch film, not little ol' me—so I got nothing going on. I'm also not taking the hardest of classes this year, and the little homework I do have, I'm able to get done during school. Plus, I've been able to keep a 4.0 GPA without really doing too much studying—no biggie or anything—so I don't have to worry about that either. I can just take the day to relax.

I get up to let the dogs back in and grab an Ale-8 on my way back. With Benny and the terrier, Dalton (named after the Bengals' quarterback, lying on top of me, I feel as snug as a bug in a rug on drugs, and it's not long before I drift off to sleep.

***

"Ollie, dinner," Mom says as she wakes me up. "I made spaghetti."

Ah, spaghetti, one of the few meals she makes, or anywhere for that matter, I do not like.

"Awesome," I lie through a yawn and get up, unburdened by the dogs, who are probably choking down some Blue Buffalo right now.

After dinner, I head downstairs to watch some Netflix, having decided to pass on seconds but am stopped by Dylan, who's already in his PJs.

"Ollie, do you want to play poker?"

This might seem like an odd request coming from a ten-year-old, but we were raised to play poker. It was something we used to do as a family every Friday night. Now it's just on occasion.

"Yeah, let's do it."

I go over to the game closet and pull out the poker set, which is basically a briefcase, complete with locks.

"Who's all playing?" I ask as I shuffle the cards.

There are affirmations from everyone except Alex, who claims he has homework to do. Yeah, whatever.

"All right, are we playing Texas Hold 'Em, Omaha, 7-Card—"

"Let's just do Texas Hold 'Em," Dad calls from the dinner table, working on thirds.

I set out five piles of about $500 worth of chips (one $100, eight $25, ten $10, and a handful of $5s) and wait for the others.

We planned on playing for only an hour so Mom and Dad can watch their *90-Day Fiancé*, but it isn't until three when Dylan takes all our chips with his first-ever royal flush to the sound of Dad complaining about his crap hands.

My top choice of colleges is Eastern Kentucky, which of course would require me to dorm up with Slushie. But tonight, however, has made me start to consider staying home and commuting to Northern Kentucky. For one, staying away from home for great periods of time could be devastating for my mental health. And to be honest, I don't think I could be away from them that long.

# Thursday, November 22

**Thanksgiving is a** time for gratitude. This past year has had its ups and downs. From the difficult decision of becoming a screenwriter to making history by winning Region. From discovering I have a crush on one of my best friends to seeing her dance with someone else.

But now, standing on the snowy field of what could possibly be our last practice, I am extremely thankful.

Practicing—or playing, for that matter—in the snow is another mark we made in the record books. Although it does make it difficult to stay focused, especially knowing that our opponent, Patterson, had beaten the former state champs 40–21 Friday. Even Tugo is enjoying the weather, laying on his back between plays to make abnormally large snow angels.

Nobody wants to practice the morning of Thanksgiving, but us seniors all linger around afterward, all the same, trying to take it all in. Alas, we all have plans with our family for the afternoon and need to get back. I, myself, have a long haul down to Elizabethtown, two hours south of here.

There is one Thanksgiving tradition that is held almost religiously—and it's not the homemade yeast rolls—The Turkey Bowl, an event of the world's greatest athletes (in the Behr family at least) hashing it out for pure blood and glory. And that's for two-handed touch. We did tackle once, but it resulted in multiple visits to the hospital.

The Turkey Bowl is one of the things I look forward to the most during the holidays, and I'm giddy with excitement as I warm up in the front yard. The teams consist of me and my brothers versus the cousins. My team is the reigning champs for the last two years, probably due to the fact I'm the only person here to play more than a couple years of football. But my cousin, Jacob, is the top striker of his high school soccer team. He has the speed to cut and get upfield, which could be a major problem.

Jacob flips the ball in the air. I call stitches, and that is exactly what it is. Our ball.

I'm back to receive, with Alex and Dylan in front of me to block. Jacob chucks the rock rather than kicking it and risk shattering a window. It's just to the left of me, and I receive it deftly. I run behind Dylan while pushing him toward the pursuing Jacob. Once he gets close, I push Dylan at Jacob, allowing me to get behind him. After that, all I have to do is juke out some younger and less-athletic cousins, before high-stepping it to the endzone. To celebrate, I fall onto the ground and row an imaginary boat with the football. I hop up to chest bump Dylan.

Now it's their time to receive, and I throw a pop-up to the cousins. Jacob reels it in, but with the additional time the ball is in the air, I reach him before he can go anywhere. Harry, the older of the two other cousins, quarterbacks. Jacob runs a quick slant, which I cover well, but with a pump fake from Harry, he cuts into a go. There's a very good reason I don't play defensive back, as Jacob takes it in for seven—there are, of course, no field goals, so the extra point is already tacked on. We might need to double cover him instead of having Alex blitzing after five Mississippi.

We play a few more series, with us scoring once on a flea-flicker to Dylan from me and holding Jacob's team to just the one touchdown, the double coverage working very well. But now it's time for a little Thanksgiving meal halftime.

We have a pretty large family, but our grandmother—who took the name of Granjerry—cooks for an army, although you don't hear anybody complaining. There is a turkey, ham, stuffing, yeast rolls—which are indeed homemade—corn pudding, green beans, mashed potatoes with gravy, cranberry salad, and a hodgepodge of pies: pumpkin, pecan, derby, you name it, all laid out over a sturdy oak table, specifically made for this occasion.

Papaw is a large man who used his size to play football for the University of Kentucky. He says grace as his bald head gleams with sweat, and blesses the food as we hold hands around the smorgasbord, heads bowed. With the conclusion of the prayer, it's every man for himself.

Like every Thanksgiving, the men leave for the living room to watch the games on the fifty-five-inch curved smart TV, while the women take their meal to the dining room. The Lions and Bears are on, with Detroit having a four-point lead in the third. I don't really care much about who wins; all I want is for Le-Garrette Blount to get me some fantasy points. After seconds and finishing with a variety of pies covered in whip cream, we start the second half of the Turkey Bowl before we all fall into a food coma.

The second half has always incorporated much more sluggish play, as we are weighed down by a week's worth of food eaten in an hour. We halfheartedly play and leave large gaps in coverage. This type of play leads to a high-scoring afternoon.

The first team to seven touchdowns wins the game, and the score is 42-42, our ball. I take my turn at quarterback to rest my aching stomach and make a few random and superfluous gestures before hiking the ball. Alex and Dylan both jog skinny posts, cutting in at the same time. Jacob is playing safety and favors Dylan, while Harry gets lost in the sauce, trying to cover Alex. He is wide open. I lob it up to him, and he ... drops it. Harry grabs the tipped ball and takes it in for a touchdown as my weighted stomach prevents me from stopping him. Instead of ruining the day by yelling at Alex, I just return to the living room. At least Blount had gotten me 26.3 points.

# Friday, November 23

**There's nothing that** can get you as hyped as watching an underdog movie. The morning before Semis, we get together as a team to watch *Creed II*, and what a start to the day. Ivan Drago's son Viktor beating the snot out of Adonis Creed and Creed going to Russia—after a lengthy training montage, of course—to do the same to him. Man, I'm ready to take the field. I can see some of my teammates fidgeting in their seats, others with their eyes closed, visualizing tonight. You could feel the energy we are giving off like the smell of ozone on an overcast day. The calm before the storm.

We're major underdogs in this one, with the Patterson Indians being -27.5 favorites. And there is no "you'll get 'em next year." It's now or never. Win or go home. It's time for an Outstanding Orange Upset.

***

It was close in the first quarter, with a 7–7 score halfway through. And then Patterson started to heat up. By the end of the half, they had another three touchdowns to our one. We had tried to pull together for the last twenty-four minutes and did score once in the third and twice in the fourth, but it wasn't enough, as the boys in green and black scored almost twice for every one of our touchdowns. It was a game of offense, and ours couldn't keep up with Patterson's gunslinger of a quarterback and future

future collegiate wings.

Final score, 28–70. Pathetic.

This is not an underdog story.

Now we stand around Coach Goetz with heads down, not allowing ourselves the leisure to sit. The tears had started well into the fourth quarter, and there is no sign of them stopping anytime soon. For everybody except me, at least; my face is still dry as the Sahara.

"Boys, there are n—" Coach can barely get out the words as he chokes up. "There are no words to describe how proud I am of you forty-eight. You have gone where no team has gone before, leaving no doubt that you are the best to ever wear that uniform. It was a tough, tough loss, especially for you seniors. Patterson will probably win State by a wide margin, but you gave it your all: putting twenty-eight on them is nothing to snoot at. I know you all will do great things in the future."

With that, he walks to the center of the field, and we follow him to pray, even though none of us feels like doing so.

Afterward, I allow myself to fall to the turf in a daze. My brain is finally processing what is happening. This will be my last time wearing pads on this field—or any, for that matter—under the lights. There will be no more games, no more practice, no more two-a-days, no more team meals. No more of something I've spent six years of my life doing. The tears that had been locked up finally begin to flow.

I feel a firm, calloused hand grasp mine and pull me to my feet.

"In all my years of coaching," Coach Goetz says, "I've never seen somebody with so much heart. You've never complained about your lack of playing time but battled hard in practice. And when you got in, you would never let someone twice your size bully you around. And, hell, I don't think I've even heard you swear.

"I just wish I had more like you, and then maybe we would

be on our way to Kroger Field."

I just stand there, not knowing what to say.

"I love you, Ollie. And my door is always open if you need anything."

He nods almost to himself and leaves to console others.

In the locker room, there is a lot of crying and hugging going on as expected. I take a seat at my locker and stare off into a corner, not really thinking about anything.

"Ollie, I love you, man," Tyrese says above me. He pulls me in for a hug.

"I love you too," I say quietly.

After several more hugs, I gather my things and walk to the parking lot. I look back one last time onto the lit-up field. Six years of hard work, sweat, and occasional tears, and it's all over.

I force my eyes away from the gridiron and continue on toward the next chapter of my life.

# Monday, December 24

**My favorite occasion** of the year has to be Christmastime. I mean, what's not to love, with presents and cookies, reruns of *The Polar Express*, and building gingerbread houses.

Tomorrow is the big day, and the excitement I've been trying to contain for the past week finally floods out. I know that at this stage of life, I'm not going to be getting much more than clothes and money, but nothing can beat the thrill of waking up Christmas morning and seeing the stockings filled up, with brightly wrapped presents lying below them.

A sudden vibration jars me out of my thoughts. I pull out my phone and answer.

"Can you come up here?" It's Mom, and it sounds like she had been crying.

"Yeah, what is it?" Mom may not be as stoic as Ronda Rousey, and will shed tears for just about anything, but crying is crying.

"Just come up here."

I hurry up, horrible thoughts flooding my head. Everybody is already upstairs and, scanning the room, I freeze on Dad. His eyes are filled with tears. The last time I've seen him cry was six years ago, when his parents both passed in a freak incident. If the tone in Mom's voice wasn't enough, *that* surely was. Someone has died.

"This morning, your Papaw—" Mom can't finish, as she bursts into tears.

Dad goes to console her. "Your Papaw had a heart attack, during surgery," he says. "They couldn't bring him back."

Papaw, a cardiovascular surgeon, having a heart attack while probably doing open-heart surgery. What the hell?

"I kept telling him he needed to retire!" Mom exclaims. "A surgery room is no place for an eighty-year-old."

I can't believe what I'm hearing. A month ago, he was a-okay and his usual self. How could this happen in such a short time?

"Ollie, are you okay?" Mom asks.

I see that I'm the only one not crying.

"Yeah, I'm … going downstairs."

In my room, I recognize my bed has yet to be made. As I go to do so, flashes of memories with Papaw come to mind. Taking me fishing on his brother's farm. Convincing me to follow in his footsteps and play football, then not missing a single game. He was the one person who truly believed I could achieve greatness outside of the classroom. I collapse onto my mattress, tears finally springing loose now that no one is looking.

***

Christmas is canceled. Granjerry decided that burying Papaw the day Christ was born would be fitting. So, Christmas morning, while everyone else is opening presents with glee, we're piling into the Armada, a dark cloud over our heads.

Mom's sisters' families had stayed the night in Elizabethtown in anticipation of Christmas, so they and Granjerry are already at the funeral home when we get there.

I walk around the parlor in a borrowed suit, straying away from my grandfather's face, abnormally stretched with cotton. Toward the back of the room, there is a collage of pictures Granjerry must have strewn together last night. Most were taken recently, but there are few here and there that are from back when Papaw and Granjerry had first started dating. I had never seen pictures when they were this age. They looked so happy together.

"Sixty-four years." Mom sneaks up on me. She's wearing a black dress and no makeup for good reason, as she's crying. "That's how long they were married. And they were dating for a few years before that. High school sweethearts."

"Wow," is all I say. Sixty-four years. An eternity in my eyes. I want to be with someone that long. Have that love that sparkled in their eyes. I want … I *need* Celeste. And then my imagination, my imagination that has been such a gift lately, takes over, and then it's Celeste in the coffin. I feel almost guilty my eyes water for her, not the man who lies there and had meant so much to me.

For the next half hour, we have to shake hands with a bunch of old people I don't know, trying to keep at least a small smile on our faces. The actual wake itself is fairly short, just as Papaw always liked it. The pastor gives a quick sermon over Psalm 46 and concludes with his "deep" condolences to the family. I stay dry-eyed through the whole thing.

The funeral is right after, to follow Granjerry's wishes. It's a gloomy day, as if God sanctioned the sun to never shine over the burying of the dead.

My brothers, cousins, one of Papaw's friends, and I were asked to be pallbearers just this morning, and all I could think about was tripping and spilling Papaw's body out of the casket, but it's not exactly something I can say no to. Fortunately, though, proceeding went as planned, and the casket made it safely into the lowering device.

After a short prayer from the pastor, he hands the stage over to Granjerry for her eulogy.

"'There are only two things in life that I've ever wanted,' Joel would always say," Granjerry begins, standing in front of the pulpit in her black shawl. "'To marry you, have kids, and for them to have kids that I could spoil.

"'And what is the other?' I would answer.

"'Well, for the Bengals to win the Super Bowl, of course.'"

She smiles over us. "We had three beautiful daughters, who had six handsome sons. He got what he always wanted.

"Now, it was 1966 when I first met Joel in my sophomore English class in college, and from that moment, I knew he was the one for me. It was love at first sight, and I know it was the same for him." She stood tall, putting on a brave smile. "Neither of us could gain the confidence to even talk to the other, and it was not until we were paired together to write a paper, on love of all things, that we actually started talking to each other. But it was not until a year later, as I was studying outside my dorm, that he finally found the courage and asked me. He could lead a platoon into the jungles of Vietnam, but he could not ask me out.

"Speaking of Vietnam, he spent over three years fighting there after he earned his bachelor's. And even when he was given permission to leave with an honorable discharge, he stayed, stating his reasoning as he had another family to protect. He cared for others so much that when he returned home for the final time, he applied for medical school and earned his MD to help the sick and injured. He worked so hard, even at an age where most surgeons retire. I kept telling him he was going to give himself ..." She stops for a minute, trying to maintain her composure as wind whistles through her orange, curly hair.

"He loved you all, he loved me, but most of all he loved God," she continues, wiping a tear that escaped from her eye. "I cannot talk about him without talking about our Lord. Constantly, I would find him with his nose buried deep in scripture, and I thought I was the English teacher. His favorite verse was, *'Now faith is confidence in what we hope for and assurance about what we do not see,'* from Hebrews 11:1. I do not know what the future holds, but if he was here, he would say to have faith and that all will work out."

She again pauses, perhaps thinking on her words as if she didn't truly believe them.

"He was the embodiment of how a husband and father should be," she resumes. "I still can't believe that's him in that casket. I keep thinking he will get up and say something snarky.

"Now I better quit before I start to waterfall; Joel always hated funerals and really just sorrow in general. I want to leave with you all this: that he loved you very much, all of you. Do not ever forget that."

Mom and her two other sisters go next; these are much more tearful.

Afterward, we leave to go to Granjerry's house and try our best to celebrate Christmas. But there is no joy. None whatsoever.

# Spring

*The only thing to fear is fear itself*
—Franklin D. Roosevelt

# Wednesday, January 16

**Today is the** first day of the rest of my life.

Or at least I hope so.

I have just wrapped up my final draft of *The Stranger*, and now I need to write a query to send to an agent that meets my needs. Having done my research, I know that the query is going to be a major factor in selling my script. I've also heard some agents—if not all—will even reject a screenplay just because of a poorly written query.

There are plenty of screenwriting managers out there who will help bring your script to the silver screen, but I feel extremely confident in *The Stranger* and really believe this is God's plan for me.

Now with Google Docs pulled up and my personal information written in the heading, I ponder what to say. I need to separate myself from the competition, and I think that will be my age. I mean, a seventeen-year-old writing an eighty-plus-page script? That has to mean something, right?

I begin to type.

*Hi. My name is Oliver Behr. I am seventeen and attending Rowling's High School as a senior. I will be pursuing higher education at Northern Kentucky University in the fall as a biology major.*

I contemplate this and decide to delete the second sentence as I had already written my name on the top margin. In addition,

I remove my major. I don't want to lie to them, but I also want them to believe I'm all in with this screenplay.

After a few more changes, I'm finally finished with the first three sentences. Only like a hundred more to go.

Next, I write a couple of sentences containing the genre and word count, then give a brief abstract.

Now comes the part where I have to convince them that *The Stranger* will be a success. Knowing my age will be my greatest asset outside of the script itself, I lean heavily on it. Maybe a little too heavily. I know I will bring a new perspective to a Hollywood full of balding men. I just have to show them that.

Finally, I thank them for their time and type my name at the bottom.

With that done, I can now look for an agent. I start to scroll through some names I pulled up on Google and barely make it past the first page before I come across Janna Bromwell. Something just called out to me about her, like some kind of divine intervention. There really isn't much in her bio, just that she only accepts young-adult scripts and especially enjoys thrillers. But I know that she's the one. I had originally planned on sending *The Stranger* to as many agents as possible, but I now realize that's not necessary. I edit my query in compliance with her suggestions and email it, as well as the screenplay manuscript, to her.

Now all I have to do is wait for my dream to become a reality.

# Tuesday, January 22

**I've never been** worried about a class. Not for pre-calculus, or the sex-ed chapter in health, or even fifth-grade art taught by a chick with a shaved head, a thousand tattoos, and at least one criminal offense.

But a class where basically my only grade is from speaking in front of thirty people for ten minutes? Yeah, that would be rough. And that's exactly what Public Speaking is. It's a dual-credit class out of NKU, so I don't *have* to take it till college, but what's better, giving a speech in front of thirty people you've known most of your life or to a hundred randos? Yeah, neither of them sounds good, but the former is way cheaper.

"You ready, Ollie?" Ethan asks as I take my seat next to his. His longs legs are man spreading in my area, but I don't say anything. He's one of the nicest guys I know and probably didn't think anything of it.

The first speech is an introduction of a classmate. So, not only do I have to present a speech, but I also have to listen to one about me. It just gets better and better.

Ethan had chosen me to be his partner over his popular friends, because, well, I'm just that awesome, definitely not because we had just been randomly paired.

"Oh, yeah, you know it." Cause I sure don't.

Due to my last name, I'm one of the first ones to go. I stand up behind the podium, start the timer on my Fitbit, and begin.

"Now Ethan, here, is the GOAT." And that's about how it goes. I do manage, however, to not say any "ums" or "likes"—a point deduction each—and maintain decent eye contact, so at least I didn't fail.

I return to my seat, red-faced, and try to avoid looking at Ethan, who's grinning madly, holding two thumbs up. After several more people go and outshine me, Ethan is up. We had prepared what we are going to say last week, so it shouldn't be anything unexpected, but that doesn't make me any less nervous.

"Ollie is cut from a different cloth than us. I've never seen someone get a sack and, before celebrating, help the quarterback up. I think I even remember him saying 'nice hit,' or something like that after being lit up at the line."

*He must've forgotten about the homecoming game.*

"He is the nicest guy I know. I mean, he looks at the positive in everything, and I don't think I even heard him cuss once. He is just a class act. And did I *mention* he's a lady killer? I mean, watch out, girls, he's coming for you. And y'all men better keep ya girl close, because Ollie's always on the prowl."

When we discussed this, we had agreed maybe to just mention my good-*ish* nature and definitely not talking about me killing any chicks. As his speech wore on, I recognize that he's not going to say *any* of the things we talked about. All I can do is duck my head in my arms to hide my reddening cheeks. Ethan is a great guy, but sometimes he can be a little over the top. I hate having everybody's attention on me when I'm giving a speech, but I think it's even worse when that attention is still on me as someone else is delivering the speech.

"How was it?" Ethan asks as he sits down, his brown, mussed-up hair bobbing slightly.

"Did you practice?" I ask, trying to keep it light by throwing on my self-defense smile.

"Oh yeah. A ton. But my mind went completely blank up

there, so I rambled on a bit. I didn't embarrass you, did I?"

"Oh no," I lie, smiling. "It was great."

**"How d-does it** feel now not being able to k-kill anybody and g-getting away with it?" Slushie asks.

Today is my birthday, and I'm officially an adult. I've been really struggling with the concept that I won't be able to commit assault without any large consequences.

Kidding.

Kinda.

I'm just glad Slushie, who had only turned eighteen in November, will stop calling me "child."

"I don't think that's how it works, bud," Celeste chimes in.

We're enjoying our break from school, by eating some rock-hard chicken sandwiches at our usual spot.

"I mean, I can still get away with it," I respond as I turn my head, eyebrows raised. "I may know a guy who knows a guy."

"Anyways," Celeste interrupts while giving us both a look as scary as a playful puppy, and then turning to me. "So, what are you doing tonight?"

*Well, I was hoping it'd be you,* a James Bond–like voice comes in my head. I just barely hold back a smile.

"I don't know. I got track workouts today, and the fam ordered Graeter's cake. We're not doing anything crazy."

"Hey! We should go mini-golfing Saturday. Our treat."

"That sounds great, but you know my pride won't allow a

girl to pay for me."

"Your pride will kill you one day, Behr. Slushie can pay then."

"Uh …" Slushie starts.

"On that note," I say, winking at Slushie, "let's play two games, get some dinner beforehand, and maybe some ice cream afterward."

I'll probably end up sneaking some cash into his pocket somehow. They both have to pay car insurance and stuff, while Dad handles all that for me, so with the odd jobs I take up, I tend to have more money than they do.

I also do have a deadly amount of pride, which may very well indeed kill me.

***

"HappybirtdaytoyouhappybirthdaytoyouhappybirthdaydearOlliehappybirthdaytoyou," Dad raps frantically, leering over the Graeter's ice-cream cake with a large knife. "Now let's eat."

After a hearty dinner at Cracker Barrel, it's time for the main event.

"Doug!" Mom yells, halfheartedly slapping him.

"All right. All right!" He brings his hands up in defense and backs up. "But let's hurry. I think she's starting to melt."

"She?"

"He. She. They. Princess Consuela Bananahammock. I don't care." I interrupt the domestic dispute. "Let's forgo the foreplay and dig in."

"*Forgo*," Alex says.

"Foreplay?" Mom repeats.

I gesture at Dad, and he quickly sinks the knife into the cake.

We take our plates to the living room, where President Barth is discussing events ongoing in China. Apparently, they're building an army and accumulating nuclear bombs. But I feel like the Chinese are always doing that, anyway. It's just a façade to flex on the world.

"What have you done today to celebrate your adulthood?" Mom asks.

"Well, I bought a lottery ticket after school and then registered to vote," I answer. "Oh, and tonight the boys are taking me to the strip club. You know Bootylicious in downtown Cinci?"

"Stop that," she replies and then, on second thought, glances at Dad, who shakes his head.

When she looks away, he gives me a wink and a thumbs-up.

I give him a small, confused smile and make my escape.

I have some writing to do. I'm thinking a sequel.

# Monday, February 4

**When I had** first started track and field back in the eighth grade, I was a chubby, unathletic kid who had just tried out for the team because Slushie was on it. It wasn't super easy to get on, but I was mentally tough due to football and earned a spot. It's definitely not because I was the only one there who wanted to be a thrower.

Now it has grown into a strong passion, right behind writing and football. And this year, I'm gonna try sprinting. Coach Core may be a bit of a douche, but all the conditioning he made us do noticeably boosted my speed, and I've nearly dropped ten pounds since last season. Also, I've grown tired of not really being part of the team, since we throwers kinda do our own thing.

For all of January, we had just been doing workouts and maybe doing some sprinting drills every now and then. Today is our first real practice of the season and, to be honest, I'm a little nervous. I just hope I don't get dusted by some freshman.

"Ollie!" Celeste yells behind me as I walk toward the track. "What's up?"

I turn around and grin up at her in her Mercury.

Saturday, she had crushed us in minigolf. Both rounds. But the way she smiled …

(*Why is she here?*)

That question is answered as Jake gets out of the passenger

seat.

"Jake's car broke down, and he asked me to take him," she continues.

"Well, that's nice of you," I respond dryly.

She rolls out, and I follow Jake down.

"You pumped for your first day as a sprinter?" he asks as he slows down to walk beside me. He's wearing a tank top, exposing his toned muscles.

"Oh, you know it." I wonder how I can spike him while making it look like an accident.

I see Slushie—his hair tied back into a man bun—and Tyrese stretching on the track and hurry past Jake to them.

Slushie sees me first and calls, "Hey, Ollie. You ready to eat my d-dust?"

"You mean," Tyrese contends, "are you ready to eat my ass?"

"How about you eat this," I jab my spikes toward him, and he doesn't even flinch. He knows I'm the last person to do harm to anyone.

*The Shadow laughs in my ear.*

We warm up on the track for a couple laps and then stretch on the field.

"All right, boys," Coach Register says to us after we divide into our "factions," if you will. He's shorter than me, and that's saying a lot, but during the yearly coaches' relay he's always carrying the team on his back. "Since you've been working your butts off for the last month, I'll make today light. I want to get a glimpse at who's the fastest, so I can start setting relay teams. You all will just do a 100, 200, and 400. Untimed, only against each other. Three heats, boys first, then girls. Divide yourself as you think is best."

I know my strengths and forgo my pride for today as I join the third heat, made mostly of underclassmen. The girls go first, so I try to stay warm bouncing around in my brand-new spikes.

I was feeling good before practice, even a little excited, but now I feel nothing but fear. I keep thinking I will fall on my face or get embarrassingly crushed. It's an apprehension I've had before the few races I ran and one I'll have for the rest of the season.

Nerves suck.

But as I settle into my blocks after the first two boys' heats go, it's as if they were never there. It's time to prove myself. Show my worth.

Coach gives the cadence and claps in lieu of a gun. I'm first off the blocks—probably due to the necessity of having a quick reaction time to survive as an underweight defensive lineman— but come out too high. I push myself as hard I can, and then somehow harder, finding something deep inside me that I didn't know I had. And then it's just me and the track. No one else. Nothing else. Vin Diesel had said there is nothing like the ten seconds of a quarter mile. Put that in running terms and I agree. There is *nothing* like a race.

I cross the finish line with no one around me. It may have just been a bunch of freshmen, but I'm feeling good about this season. Real good.

# Friday, February 22

**Now begins the** first of many "last time evers."

Since fifth grade, I've been going to a weekend church retreat called the Push. The Push makes for a fantastic time, where you get to hang out with people you normally just see once a week, while also making an impact on the community. The weekend is filled with enjoyable events like paintball and Call of Duty tournaments, while still setting time aside to dive into God's Word.

This year will be extra special, not only because it's my last Push, but also because I managed to convince Slushie to come. And by convincing, I mean I bet him that he would have to come if I beat Tyrese in a forty-yard dash. Tyrese is pretty fast, but there is a lot twenty dollars can do.

Part of the arrangement is that I have to pick him up, which I do after grabbing us some never-frozen beef from Wendy's. The Push begins at the church, where we find our groups and wait for worship to begin.

Colton and the rest of the seniors are chilling in the back.

"Colton, you remember Slushie?" I ask as we approach them.

"How could I forget?" he replies, smiling at him.

An Indian man separates himself from his conversation with Don and approaches us. "I'm Tyriel," he says. "I'm from the Cru organization at UK."

Every year a Cru—short for Campus Crusade for Christ—member helps out alongside our small group leader.

"Yo, Ollie. You see that we're at my house this year?" Sam stands up from where he was crouching against the wall. "What you feeling we do first? I got the latest *COD* and *Halo*. My dad also just bought a pool table. Top of the line."

*It's a Christian event. It's a Christian event. It's a Christian event.*

"They all sound great, Sam," I answer, throwing on my biggest fake smile. "We'll just have to see when we get there."

The way our small groups work is that each incoming freshman class is given a leader who sticks with them till graduation. Every year, the senior class's leader has to come up with a sermon and lead each sermon for the weekend.

So, Don leaves to prepare, and fifteen minutes later we enter the worship center.

After a few songs by the Jesus Freaks, Don takes the stage, looking confident.

"As many of y'all know," he begins, "this is my first time preaching in front of a large crowd, so try not to be too harsh," saying this last part with a nervous laugh, which we half-heartedly join.

"With my kids all graduating here in a few months, I thought I'd preach on God's plan and will for us. I don't know about y'all, but when I graduated high school, I had no idea of what I was going to do with my life. I was scared of something I called the Next, what lies beyond. I went to college, majoring in business, not knowing what I was going to do with it. It stressed me out and put me in a really bad place. I prayed and prayed for God to put me in the right direction. And for three years, nothing happened. Senior year, I was taking macro and was big struggling; I was in my professor's office *all the time*. Well one of those days, while we're reviewing for the midterm, he offered me an internship at Fidelity. Said his brother was pretty high up there and could get me one instantly. Now, several years later, I'm slowly climbing my way up the corporate ladder, loving every bit of it.

"I know the fear of the unknown. Fear of not being rich. Fear of getting a job you'll hate. Fear of not being successful. Even fear of loneliness. If there is one thing I want you to get out of this weekend, it is that God's got a plan for you. One He created before you were a twinkle in your mother's eye. Put your trust in Him, and He will deliver. Embrace the Next."

Don looks up from his notes and flashes a smile. "Well, guys, I ran through my sermon a lot faster than I thought I would. But if any of you, not just my seniors, have questions, come find me anytime this weekend. Let's pray."

Closing my eyes, I know *The Stranger* is God's plan for me. Don's sermon has confirmed my faith in that. I mean, my whole life has been leading up to this. Being an average athlete and academic, but with an underlying skill of writing, creativity, and imagination that I finally have combined just in time for graduation. It's like a screenplay itself, except this one is real and written by God.

As Don concludes the prayer and we rise for the Jesus Freaks, I know now that I am ready for the Next.

***

The services are amazing, but, man, it's the nights at the host home that I'll remember the most. The good, the bad, and most certainly the ugly. Like, for better or for worse, I'll never forget the time when Mitch dumped water on Sam as he was sleeping, causing him to jump out of his sleeping bag buck naked. A scarring sight indeed but very memorable regardless, although, I'm not hoping for any repeats this year.

When we get to Sam's house, we have a short discussion on Don's sermon, about which I keep my feelings to myself as I always do, still listening nevertheless. Afterward, we begin a pool tournament of nine-ball, and the table, I'll admit, is pretty nice. Sam easily sweeps the room, as he most likely practices every

-day, whereas my only experience is from GamePigeon.

Now it wouldn't be Push without a little *Call of Duty*, and the tourney wages again as Sam pulls out *Black Ops 4*. As he starts working on the bracket, Don pulls me away for a second.

"You were pretty quiet today," he says. "Which isn't entirely unusual, but how are you feeling about post-graduation?"

"I'm feeling good," I answer, actually meaning it. "As you know, I'm going to NKU to pursue a biology degree and be a dermatologist."

"Well, that's good. Not nervous about college, then?"

"Nah, I'm ready to get outta high school."

"Now, I remember at church camp that you had expressed fears of finding love. How's that going?"

Church camp has a way of loosening lips. And wetting eyes, for that matter.

"Great!" Now I lie. "I'm actually talking to this chick in chemistry." I'm not even taking chemistry.

"That's really good." He looks over at Slushie, taking his turn at the controls. "Slush, right? How's he doing?"

"Slushie. Yeah, I think he's doing good. He looked really in tune to your sermon."

That's a complete lie. I kinda forgot about him during the service, but it seems like the right thing to say.

"Does he go to church?"

"No, but I'm working on him. I'm hoping the Push can really make an impact on him."

"Well, coming here is a big step in the right direction."

I nod and return to my spot. It's my turn, and I'm up against Sam. I'm not too shabby at first-person shooters, and I constantly kill him, a wide grin on my face each time I do.

# Thursday, March 7

## From: Janna Bromwell
Re: Query; The Stranger

I inhale sharply, my heart beating out of my chest. All the Faith I've had in this script since I first started writing it dissipates. Now, as I open the email, all I feel is Fear.

"Thank you so much for giving me the opportunity to read your screenplay. But unfortunately, after further consideration, I have decided to turn down your script. There are many agencies out there with varying interests, so keep submitting.
I wish you the best of luck with your writing career.
Sincerely,
Janna"

Short but like a stake to the heart.
"What am I going to do?" I ask the A. J. Green Fathead above my desk.
I try to visualize myself as a dermatologist. Going in to work every day, looking at disgusting skin diseases in places I never want to see, not to mention touch. Hell, I'm not even able to watch *Dr. Pimple Popper* without gagging. I can't do that. I can't see myself as doing anything else other than writing, no matter

how hard I try.

*Probably shows how good of an imagination I have.*

I won't let her keep me from obtaining my dream. There are hundreds of agents out there. One of them has to see what I see. That The Stranger can be something great. That *I* can be something great.

I push away from my desk to look out my window at the rustling trees and swirling dark clouds. A storm is coming.

*Faith over Fear.*

# Friday, March 8

**"You can't just** wait until you get in your car," I mumble to myself through gritted teeth as I throw my bag on the ground.

Celeste and Jake are full-on mouth-sucking in the parking lot.

"That bastard better be keeping it in his pants," I rant to Benny as he whines from his cage.

I let out a hot sigh and let him out along with the others.

Once they're outside, I fall down heavily in front of the TV and turn on *Friends*. A minute in, I shut it off. This is Celeste's favorite show; I can't watch it without thinking about her. I stand back up and go to the fridge. My eyes linger for a second on the opaque blue bottle of Skyy, before reaching down for a water.

I have track practice in an hour, and the last person I want to see is Jake. It's times like these when I miss football. At least there I can hit somebody without getting in trouble for it, even get congratulated for it. Oh, I wish Jake had played football.

I let the dogs back in, wiping their asses with a discolored towel by the door. I sling my backpack over my shoulder, grab a banana, and head downstairs. And then I step into something warm and soft that sends up a familiar, rancid odor. Recoiling in disgust, I look around the room, searching madly for the culprit as my rage boils from within.

"Who the hell' shit?" I scream, my nails biting into the skin of my closed fists.

Dalton is the first one I see.

"Was it you?."

He cowers down, expectant of what's to come. I run at him, kicking his fat ass into the wall. He cries out in a mixture of terror and agony as the mutt tries to run away.

"You think you can escape me?" I let out an unfamiliar laugh. A laugh filled with anger and pain. It was a laugh of someone who's out of their mind. A symbol of insanity and evil. Of Fear. "You think your fat ass will be able to escape *me?*"

I reach for him, and he bites me then runs under the couch.

"Ah, you bitch!" I yell, I reach under the couch, and this time when he bites me, I don't let go, only squeezing tighter. Once I pull him out, I backhand the hell out of him.

"Don't you *fuckin'* do that again!"

He whimpers into submission. I hold him by the scruff and bring him to his cage, throwing him in. I pick up the entire kennel and carry it to the back porch, setting it up on the railing of the two-story balcony in a way that if Dalton shifted his weight any way he would teeter the crate off the deck and himself along with it.

"Let's see if this teaches you."

Dalton makes a sorrowful, heartbreaking sound full of fear that pulls at my heartstrings for a second.

*No, he deserves this.*

I storm out to my Camry, intent on getting to practice early, so I can burn off this steam.

I viciously jab the key into the ignition and rip the gearshift into reverse, veering out into the garage. I smash the gas to speed off down the road. Flying around a sharp bend, I slam the brakes in response to a truck turning out of a badly placed subdivision. My heart thuds in my chest, as I get closer and closer, with Fear and anger. I quickly swerve into the opposite lane, which is thankfully empty, smashing my horn. I return to the correct lane and roll down my window just to flip him off.

"There are too many idiots on the road," I grumble, knowing full well that it was my fault.

As I continue to drive, my speedometer closer to the speed limit now, my mind begins to wander as it tends to do. I think back to Dalton's cries of fear and pain. Of the expression on his face. What could happen if the cage falls off the railing.

*Or if somebody saw what I did.*

But most importantly, how could I do such a thing?

*What have I done?*

I turn into a Marathon parking lot, so I can go back home.

When I get to where my story begins, I rush to the back deck and cry out in surprise when I see Alex, petting Dalton through the cage.

"Alex ..." I fight for an answer.

"*Falls the Shadow.*"

I just stare back him, not comprehending what was happening.

"*Between the idea and the reality. Between the motion and the act,*" Alex recites in a trance. "*Falls the Shadow.*"

"Who is the fuckin' Shadow!" I scream back at him.

A sharp pain attacks my brain that feels like feedback, so bad that it knocks me to my knees. It only lasts a minute, and when I look up, Alex is gone.

*Where did he go?* He was right here. *And what the hell just happened?*

I slowly remove Dalton from the kennel as the smell of urine attacks my nose. Letting him inside, I move in a trance to the fridge. I think I'm going to need that vodka.

*Faith over Fear.*

# Tuesday, March 12

**Track meets have** a completely different air to them than football games. There isn't any hype. No goosebumps or cold chills as you take the field. Nada. It's a five-hour venue, where your first event could be hours before your next. Or maybe it could be the very last race. That doesn't make it any less fun, though. The extra time allows you to basically hang out with friends for a while. I've enjoyed track for the last four years I've run—or thrown, I guess—and I'm positive I will this season, even more so now I'm a sprinter.

The meet is at Lincoln P. Douglas High School, just about fifteen minutes from Rowling. Since it's our first meet of the season and my first as a sprinter, I'm a bit nervous, but no surprise there. I try to visualize success, yet all I see is failure.

Once we find a place to set up camp, we just do a quick warmup and stretch, knowing a lot of us won't be running for at least another hour. The first event of the meet is the 4x8 relay, and with Slushie currently doing long jump and Tyrese preparing for the 110 hurdles, there's only Wes. So, I leave him and try to find Colton, who is running distance for the Douglas Vikings. I spot him along the fence surrounding the track and go to him.

"What's up, Colton?"

"Oh, hey, Ollie." He pushes off against the fence. "Not much, you?"

"Just a little nervous, I guess."

"Yeah, you'll do fine. What events are you running?"

"The 100, 400, discus, and the B team of the 4x2."

"Man, your coach really must want to test you; the 4x2 is immediately after the hundred. All I got is the 1,600, 3,200, and high jump."

"Yeah, I guess he's trying to see how fast I really am." I nod over at the track. "You guys got anybody good in the 4x8?"

"I mean, we were runner-ups last year—"

"To whom were you runner-ups, may I ask?" I give him a side look with a half-smile.

"It's not like you were part of it," he replies, staring me down before breaking into a smile. "But what I was going to say is that we got a new girl as our anchor, and she's really good."

"Well, I guess we'll see."

The gun fires five minutes later, and the runners are off.

It is close for the first six laps, with Rowling slightly in the lead, and then Douglas's anchor makes them look silly, beating us by at least six seconds. As she crosses the finish line, she looks around, eyes falling on us—on me, actually—and smiles. And she is hot. I mean H-A-W-T hot. A goddess even as sweat glistens off her mocha skin and her dark hair is in disarray. I smile back shyly before breaking eye contact. All thoughts of Celeste fall out of my head for the time being.

I turn to Colton. "What'd you say her name was?"

"Well, one thing, I never said her name. Two, she goes to our church."

*Well in my defense, guys and girls are separated for the most part.*

"And three, she's way out of your league." He sees my face fall and adds, "Her name is Jensen."

***

After about forty-five minutes, the hundred is about to start. Me, Slushie, Wes, and Tyrese all warm up down the length of the field. It's not a half-bad day for the middle of March, but there is still a nip in the air, and I really don't want to tear a muscle during my first race.

The girls are just finishing up, and we are assigned our lanes and heats and instructed to line up in the order given to us. And before I know it, Tyrese and Wes are already setting up their blocks. Again, the nerves hit me, but this time much harder. I take slow, deep breaths and try to clear my head of all the negativity swirling in it. If I think I'm going to trip, I'm going to trip. If I think I'm going to lose, I'm going to lose. If I think I'm going to win, I, yeah, I will probably still lose.

The gun jars me from my thoughts, and the runners are off. I can't tell who won, but it had to be between Dick, Wes, and some redhead from Douglas.

"All right, p-partner," Slushie says to me as he sets his blocks. "S-see you on the other s-side."

I just nod, my jaw locked up with fear. The gun fires again, and this time I think Slushie is the clear winner.

As I kneel to my blocks, I look over to my right and see a buff guy in the green-and-black uni of Patterson, sporting a Popeye tattoo. Dang, I think he was one of their starting linebackers when they whooped us in the Semifinals. If I can only beat one person, I hope it's him.

I take a couple good run-outs, and the nerves start to fade as my mind empties. This is not a sport for thinking.

"On your mark!"

I take a final deep breath and exhale as I curl into my blocks.

"Get set!"

Every muscle fiber in my body tenses up, anticipating the gun.

*Bang!*

I explode out the blocks, but not quicker than my opponents. But soon enough, I pull ahead to where it's only me and Popeye. The crowd fades from existence as I run just behind him. About halfway, I really start to accelerate. I slowly gain on him, but he's heating up too.

*30 … 20 … 10—*

With a last, impossible burst of speed, I pass him only by the hair of my peach fuzz.

"Yes! Ollie!" Coach Register yells by the timekeeping bench at the finish line.

"Did I do good?" I ask as I bend over with my hands on my knees.

"Heck yeah, you did! You got first in your heat and a 12.69. I really wish we had run you earlier. You are a beast!"

I think what makes me happier than getting first, running a pretty darn good time, and even beating Popeye is his compliment. All my athletic career, I've never had somebody say something like this to me, that I could actually help the team in some way. And I'll be damned if I let him down.

# Wednesday, March 20

**"Have you guys** made a bracket yet?"

We're enjoying another meal at the lovely Rowling's cafeteria when I bring up the Big Dance as the First Four wraps up tonight.

"Yeah, I filled out a couple," Slushie answers.

"Is that for March Madness?" Celeste asks.

"Just the one for the track team," Jake replies from his spot next to Celeste. "You're in it, aren't you?"

"No, they must've missed me."

*Yet again.*

"Here, I'll go add you right now. What's your email?"

*Damn his niceness.*

Jake had started sitting with us at the start of the calendar year, since his previous class was only for the semester, and now he's just a library aide, meaning he has nothing to do but flirt with Celeste for thirty minutes a day. Even though I've started to develop a small crush on Jensen, it doesn't mean I still don't dislike him.

*"The following students are asked to please come to Meeting Room A by Mr. Lu's office,"* the intercom blares. *"Philomena Ball, Oliver Behr, Madison Bender, Kassidy Chasen, Wesley Clines, and Jacob Dalton. Thank you."*

Around this time of year, Mr. Lu pulls students from their classes—or lunch period—for a meeting on their plans after high school. And not just one-on-one either (that just wouldn't be awkward enough); no, they need to have six people to add to the fun. And now I get to be in a group with Jake. Yay.

We get up together and walk to the meeting room, me pacing myself a couple steps ahead of him, so we're not walking side by side. Once there, I park it next to Wes, who's already seated. And Jake, of course, finds the need to sit next to me, causing the room to be of middle school standards: boys on one side, girls on the other.

"We will try to make this meeting as short as possible," Mr. Lu begins as he's joined by Vice Principal Durbin. "All I want to know is a general idea of postgraduate plans. Like what college are you going to, if you are going. What are you going to major in and what you are going to do with it? And if you're not planning on attending college, what are you going to do? We'll start alphabetically with Miss Ball."

"I'm going to the University of Kentucky and majoring in accounting."

"Very good. I might need you to prepare my tax returns. Ha. Mr. Behr?"

"I'm planning on going to NKU and majoring in biology." I've said this so many times, it's like I've rehearsed it. "I know I want to do something in the medical field, but I'm not quite sure, although I'm leaning toward dermatology."

"That's a very good field to be in, and NKU is opening up their medical school in a partnership with UK and St. Elizabeth this year, if you didn't know. Miss. Bender?"

Madison and Kassidy are both going to culinary school, while Wes is going into chemistry at Western Kentucky, although not sure about the exact occupation. Now it's Jake's turn.

"All right," Lu says as he pushes up his ever-slipping glasses. "Let's wrap this discussion up with Mr. Dalton. Go ahead."

"Well, I'm going to Michigan State for track, but I haven't decided on what I'm going to do after."

I look over at him. Jake always seemed like a guy who had his stuff together. Me and him—to my chagrin—may be more alike than I thought.

"I have no interests, outside of track, that I can make a career out of, and I'm nowhere good enough to go to the Olympics or even go pro. Not gonna lie, I'm a little worried, especially with all these guys knowing exactly what they're going to do."

*If you only knew.*

"We can hook you up with our Career Services lady, Mrs. Meece," Mr. Lu says, looking a bit shocked, as we all do, at the most likely president of the Class of 2019's lack of direction. "She'll help guide you in the right direction. Stay after, and I'll get you the information."

As I leave with one last look at Jake, I recognize there's much more to him than what meets the surface. That we are more alike than I had previously thought. What I will do with that information, to help or to harm, I do not know.

# Tuesday, April 2

**There really isn't** a better way to spend spring break than on a cruise. Eight days of having nothing to do. Food at your every request, an all-you-can-eat buffet, lobster and steak dinners, soft-serve ice cream, and other things that don't have to do with food. And with the stress I've been under lately, I need a week of peace.

Our first day was just a sea day, where most of it was just spent eating—if you can believe that—and lounging around the pool deck. Today will be our first stop of the trip at Grand Cayman.

Spring break is a dangerous week for athletes. We spend months and months training our butts off and could lose it all in seven days. It's happened to me, and I know it's happened to many others. The only way to prevent it is through constant conditioning. My situation, however, is a bit different than others; I don't exactly have a place to sprint—unless you can count a tiny track full of powerwalking moms—so I have to make do with the small gym on the boat. Since my family and I plan to leave the boat around ten, I have to wake up at eight to get a decent run in. Oof.

On the way to the workout room, I grab myself a banana from the buffet—straying away from the pastry section to avoid the temptation—so I'm not running on an empty stomach. The fitness facility itself only consists of about a dozen treadmills and ellipticals, plus a couple of benches and a rack of dumbbells. Although, in the cruise liner's defense, most people don't come aboard for the workout equipment.

To accommodate for the lack of running room, me and Coach Register had planned a workout that would only involve a treadmill and thirty minutes of my time. I start at a steady pace, and with each quarter mile, I bring up the speed a couple of notches. For the last tenth of the mile, it's a full sprint. Then I restart after a mile, for a total of three. So, nothing killer, but hopefully it will maintain my conditioning.

The workout goes well enough, and by the time I'm done, I am soaked in sweat.

In our stateroom, everybody is up and bumping into each other as they try to get ready in the cramped space. Half an hour later, we're upstairs eating breakfast, and twenty minutes after that we're making our way down the ramp into Grand Cayman.

It is a beautiful place, containing reefs filled with a colorful variety of fish like huge tarpon that will scare the heck out of you when they appear in the corner of your eye, resembling a more deadly sea creature. And when you're not in the water, it would be hard for you not to notice the iguanas, as common as a deer in Kentucky, crawling around the bright hibiscus and towering palm trees. It's no wonder money launderers like to hide their money here.

This is not our first time in the Caymans, and we find ourselves a nice snorkeling area with a decent beach for Mom and Alex to relax on while me, Dad, and Dylan swim with the fishies. We suit up and jump, having to go through a school of large, ugly tarpon—a kind of wall to keep humans from exploring the magnificent world beyond. After keeping our arms tucked to our sides to prevent contact with their slimy, scaly bodies and using our legs to propel ourselves through the clear water, we reach the reef. Hordes of sergeant major greet us, as we enter and slowly move along the top of the sea. Everywhere we look, there is a brightly colored parrotfish or flounder, staring up at us with one eye before skittering off. In crevices, blue lobsters peek out, while needlefish float among the coral. A pufferfish blows up in fright as we float by to inspect it. Fifteen minutes later, we reach the end of the reef and return to the beach, taking our time.

All that snorkeling worked up our appetites, so we climb the steps to the cabana just five minutes down the beach. We are greeted by a pretty, tan woman, wearing nothing but a bikini, who points us to an open table on the deck.

"What to drink?" she asks, sticking out her hip and placing her hand there.

"Two Caribs, please," Dad orders. "Do you want one, Ollie? The drinking age here is eighteen."

"Do you even have to ask?" I respond, having never drunk more than a sip of any alcoholic beverage.

The hot mama comes out with the beverages and lays down a beer in front of me. She pulls out a bottle opener from nowhere and cracks it open. I take a sip, aware of everyone's eyes on me. You know when you wash your hands with sanitizer and then eat a bag of Doritos, licking your fingers afterward? It tastes like that but much worse. I try to hide my immediate soured expression, but it's too late.

"I'm glad you don't like it," Mom says as she takes a long gulp from her Carib. "I won't have to worry about you drinking in college."

I take another sip, this time keeping my face neutral. "You know, if I start drinking now, I'll get used to the taste by the time I turn twenty-one."

Dad lifts his drink to me and is stared down by Mom.

"What?" he asks, acting confused. "He makes a good point. And it's not like you didn't do your fair share of drinking at Kentucky."

She lightly slaps him on the arm. "Don't encourage him."

He motions the waitress over. "Can we get three shots of tequila?"

"Doug!" Mom screams at him.

"What, he won't like it. Might as well turn him away from it now than be introduced to it at a frat party."

She glares at him and turns away, comically looking like a little girl being declined ice cream before dinner. Dad's going to be sleeping in the hall tonight.

"Do you all want to order any food or just drinks?" the sexy waitress asks as she brings the shots.

"In a little bit, darling," Dad replies and, as she walks away, her hips swaying, he looks at us and points at his wedding ring, mouthing "married."

We roll our eyes at this old act.

I pick up the shot of the light-golden liquor and take a whiff, my nose wrinkling at its acidic scent. With my heart accelerating with anticipation, I throw it back. It has a taste not that much different from pure hand sanitizer, followed by a sharp burning sensation in the back of my throat as it goes down. I noticeably grimace, to the pleasure of my family. But then there's a large, warm feeling in my chest, almost like a hug from a loved one you haven't seen in a while. My head then begins to clear, the total opposite of what I thought it would do. Dad thought this would turn me away from alcohol, but never have I felt anything like it. Nothing so freeing. Nothing so *therapeutic*.

# Wednesday, April 10

**Since the first** track meet, I've been eyeing Jensen every Sunday at church and every Wednesday at youth group. It's amazing how someone so invisible to me a couple months ago has become almost an obsession. Now prom is coming up in a couple weeks. There's a problem, however—she is so out of my league I don't know if I'll have the nerve to ask her out.

"Are you going to do it?" Colton asks.

"Do what?" I inquire, confused.

We're sitting on a couch in the commons, waiting for the Wednesday night youth group service to start.

"Ask Jensen out. I'm not stupid; I've seen the way you look at her."

"I'm not going to ask her out," I respond, my voice squeaking like a cartoon lie-detector.

"I mean not ask her out-out—she's way out of your league," he says and elbows me playfully. "But to prom."

I sit quietly for a minute, picking at a loose strand on the cushion, before replying, "Even if, hypothetically, I did ask her to prom, she'd say no."

"Well, if it's any consolation, she's been throwing some looks your way."

"Really?" I quickly look up.

"Yeah, I mean not as much as you and much more discreet,

but yeah. And word on the street is she has yet to find a date."

"Well, if I did like Jensen and had plans to ask her out, then I will definitely take that into account."

Colton laughs and slaps my back. "Whatever, Ollie. Let's go inside; the service is starting.

***

Wednesday night services are usually kept fairly short, to allow more time for the evening's true purpose of social gathering. And when the sermon is concluded with an amen, I pull Colton back down as he was standing.

"Can you get me in a conversation with her?" I ask, looking around as if the Mafia is after me. "Like introduce me to her."

He smiles widely and answers, "Of course." He nudges Sam sitting next to us, on his phone and oblivious to what is going on around him. "Can you call Jensen over?"

He shrugs. "I thought you were gay, but whatever." Standing up, he spots her and hollers, "Jensen!"

I wince and hiss through gritted teeth to Colton, "You couldn't have made it a bit more discreet?"

"Like you?"

"What is it?" Jensen asks, walking toward us as Sam moves away on his phone.

At the sight of her, I freeze, half of me wanting to escape, the other just wanting to shut down. Not a part of me wanted to ask her out at that moment. And to be honest, I don't think I've ever been as frightened as I am now. But it's too late as she has already reached us. I throw on a smile that couldn't have been much more real than the Joker's. Her smile, on the other hand, brightens the entire room.

"Hey, Jensen," Colton interrupts my near mental breakdown. "I'd like for you to meet Ollie. You've probably seen him around, but I just found out you've got similar interests."

We both give him a questioning look as she asks the question we're both thinking.

"Each other," he throws a large grin and turns to leave. "I gotta go to the bathroom. Have fun."

I swear at him under my breath before seeing Jensen staring at me amusingly.

"Uh … he, uh … I, uh … hmm."

*Is it possible to die from pure awkwardness?*

"I saw you running the other meet," she breaks through my stuttering. "You're pretty good."

"Yeah, I saw, yeah, you're good too. Fast," I glance at my watch. "Oh, look at the time. Uh, I got a test tomorrow that I, uh, should probably study for. Hm."

I start to pull away.

"Sure, it was nice meeting you." She again smiles brightly, her teeth sparkling. Braces. She doesn't seem at all fazed by my awkwardness.

"Yeah, yeah, uh, bye." I move to the door and nearly eat it tripping over my own feet. I finally make it out only to come face to face with Colton.

"How'd it go?"

"Awful," I reply as I knock past him to the parking lot.

As I lie on my bed an hour later, wallowing in self-pity, my phone rings. It's a facetime from an unknown number. Normally I would have declined it immediately, thinking it's some kind of pedo or something, but this feels different somehow and I answer.

"Hey, Ollie." It's Jensen, her pretty face filling the screen.

"Oh, uh, hi, Jensen." In the corner, I can see myself blushing.

"I was wondering if you would like to go to prom with me?"

"I, uh, um." I take a deep breath before continuing, allowing the words to settle on my tongue before spitting them out. "Yes, of course, I would love to. I'm really sorry about earlier, Jensen. I don't know what happened."

She smiles and waves her hand. "You're fine, it was cute."

*She said I was cute.*

It was anything but. However, I still beam at the compliment.

For the remainder of the night, we just talk, getting to know each other more. And when we finally hang up, I would've sworn we were only on the phone for half an hour at the most, but according to my alarm clock, it had been close to two.

Man, I like her.

**I hate scrolling** through Instagram and seeing nonstop pictures of people dressed to the nines and posing with friends and their dates. It seemed like after an hour I'd still be rapidly swiping up on my phone, while still acting like I care and double-tap the screen. Well, it looks like now I'm going to be doing the exact same thing.

We're released several hours early from school, so girls can get all dressed up and look like they're about to walk across the red carpet while giving guys the time to trash talk each other on Fortnite. Once everyone is ready, then begins the lengthy photography session, only comparable to the one on your wedding day. But before that, I have something much more important to do.

When I arrive at Jensen's house in a rented tux, I take a slow, deep breath. Ever since she asked me out, we've been talking a lot, and I've been falling hard for her. But there are still fears of her laughing at me as she opens the door, asking why a girl like her would ever go out with a guy like me, before slamming it back in my face.

I exhale and get out of my Camry. I climb the steps leading to her door, pausing with my hand poised to knock, feeling as if I am being lassoed by two cowboys in opposite directions. But before I can act, the door is pulled open, exposing Jensen to the world.

She's wearing a sparkly, red dress, while showing off her light-brown skin. Her dark hair flows down her shoulders in waves that you could get lost in and never want to come back. And I do, in fact, find myself standing with my mouth slightly agape, unable to do anything.

"How do I look?" she asks, blushing slightly at my expression.

"You look," I say, gazing deep into her hazel eyes, a slight smile coming to my face, "like an angel, so beautiful that God had to throw you out of heaven because the other angels lusted over you."

Her blush deepens. "That's really sweet, Ollie."

"Let's go before the others start dinner without us. You know I'd hate to pass up a good meal."

In Cincinnati, we meet the others outside an Italian restaurant called Philomena's that overlooks the Ohio River.

"Ollie, I respect you doing a little pre-prom hanky-panky," Tyrese says completely straight-faced, wearing a slick white coat, black button-down, and a satin tie, "but a man has gotta eat, and there will be plenty of time for that after."

I start to get flustered and glance over to see Jensen's face is even redder than mine.

"Tyrese!" His mom comes around and slaps him straight across the face, not holding back at all.

Rose Morgan had raised twelve kids and did not take crap from anyone, so when she "offered" to take the pre-prom pics—having had taken a couple photography classes in undergrad, fancying herself a pro—there was no way to refuse her.

"Sorry, ma'am!" he cries. She may be the one person who can shut him up.

"Before y'all go messing up yo nice clothes, I'mma get just a few photos before dinner," Rose announces, meaning it would be more like fifty. "And I don't want to hear no complaining either."

Following a chorus of "yes, ma'am," she leads us past the restaurant to the Ohio River behind it.

"This is perfect," Rose expresses almost to herself as she regards the muddied waters. She then turns around, giving us her thoughts—demands, "We'll do girls' individuals first, followed by boys'. After that it'll be couples, ending with a few group photos."

As the girls pose, I finally get the opportunity to find out who everyone brought, as no one is going alone.

"So, Slushie," I ask, "who's that chick you brought?"

"Well, you kn-know I've been w-working at Chick-fil-A. She's the one who trained me." He is cleanshaven for the first time since like sophomore year—must be some girl for him to do that. His hair, however, is still long. And he's wearing simply a gray coat, white undershirt, and charcoal tie. "W-we started t-talking, and she invited me to her church, Pentecostal T-temple—you kn-know the one five minutes from the complex. I liked her, so I d-decided to give it a shot. I got saved last w-week and am going to get b-baptized this Sunday."

"That really great, Slushie, truly."

Although, I do feel a bit ashamed that it was some girl he just met who brought him to Christ, rather than his best friend.

Tyrese brought his *lovely* girlfriend. Blake was asked out by a bit of a socially awkward girl and is going with her as friends. He is actually not wearing a tuxedo T-shirt but the real thing instead. Mitch is back again and brought a pretty girl from Morehead. He sports a black coat and a green striped tie to match his girl's dress. And Wes brought, uh—

"Hey, Wes, is that the same girl you brought to homecoming?"

"No, remember we broke up a couple of months ago. This is Kylie from Kingsdale."

"Where do you even meet these chicks?"

"I met her at one of our track meets." He's got on a bold baby-blue coat with a matching tie. "Isn't that where you met Jensen? Oh, and how's it going with you two, anyway?"

I look over at Jensen as she's posing, resembling some of the best models.

"It's been great," I reply, turning to him and grinning like an idiot. "Really, really great."

"Well, I'm glad for you. Are you going to ask her out on a date after this is all over?"

"I want to, but I don't know." I return my gaze to Jensen. "I just don't know."

***

Dinner at Philomena's was amazing, and with our stomachs full of chicken parmigiana and spinach ravioli, we leave for the dance. Prom takes place every year in a barn, although it's not quite your baby-Jesus-in-a-manger type of barn, instead one built entirely for quaint weddings set in the countryside. It's a massive facility, consisting of two seating areas with a large dance floor in between, all complete with a bar, serving, of course, only water and soda.

We arrive a few minutes late and park in the grass in front of the building. Inside, we move among a throng of people, admiring our surroundings. We find a corner in the back, and I leave to grab Jensen and me something to drink.

"Man, Ollie, you're looking good."

I turn around to see Ethan and his girlfriend, Kaitlyn.

"Thank ya. You're not looking too bad yourself," I return.

"Is that who you brought?" He gestures with his cup over to Jensen.

"Yeah, she goes to Douglas. Met her during a track meet."

"I told you he's a lady killer," he says as he looks over at Kaitlyn, who smiles politely. "A lady killer. But I'm proud of you, man. She looks like a keeper."

I gaze over at her. "Yes. Yes, she is."

It's just fifteen minutes into the dance when we get our first slow song. And, without my even having to ask, Jensen pulls me onto the dance floor.

"Do you know how to dance?" she asks over the melancholy tunes of "Ruby Tuesday."

"We had to waltz once during school, but that didn't go too well."

"This is much easier. First, put your hands on my hips."

I do so a bit awkwardly, and she laughs—no, giggles, a symbol of her purity.

"Relax," she instructs as she places her hands on my tense shoulders. "Now, just sway to the right, sliding your feet along just slightly and the same way to the left."

I do so; it isn't nearly as difficult as I thought it would be, and before we know it, we're oscillating in tune to the music.

"Jensen, this has been an amazing night," I say. I open my mouth to continue, but then see, over her shoulder, Celeste dancing with Jake. And, man, is she beautiful in her violet dress with an evergreen trimming that really brings out her eyes. Jealousy begins to pour into me until I fix my gaze back onto Jensen. In her eyes, I find true happiness, something I've been short on for a long time.

"I, uh ... um. Sorry," I take a deep breath and ready myself. "I like you, Jensen, and was wondering if you would like to go out with me. Like out-out."

She smiles, and her eyes seem to sparkle twice as much as her braces. "I would love to."

Not only do I find the joy I've been searching for from her response, but also hope. Hope for a future that is seeming to clear up with each passing minute.

# Thursday, May 2

**After another short** track season, Regionals has arrived, and this will be my first time suiting up in May, as I had managed to earn a spot on the 4x2 team along with Wes and two juniors, Gary and Mike.

Since Register is one of the best coaches in Northern Kentucky at running meets, we almost always host Regionals. There will be ten teams competing this evening, including some familiar names like Patterson, Kingsdale, and, of course, Lincoln P. Douglas.

Me and Jensen have been Snapchatting like crazy but have yet to go on a date, and this will be our first time seeing each other since prom as she has been a bit sick lately. I know it's just a coincidence, her falling ill right after I ask her, but with my history of girlfriends—or more like, lack thereof—it doesn't seem like a good omen. Not a good one at all.

With my lone event of the 4x2 scheduled two hours away, I sneak out of warmups to find Jensen. She's stretching with her 4x8 team when I pull her away.

"Ollie, I'm sorry we haven't been able to hang out," she says. I don't know if it's my blindness caused by my feelings for her, but she seems sincere. "I've been a bit under the weather lately."

"Yeah, you look great now, though. I mean, not as if you never looked great."

I wonder when this awkwardness will go away, but at least she has a humored smile on her face.

"I know you've got a race to prepare for—and good luck with that, by the way—but I was wondering if you would like to grab some dinner with me this weekend? Maybe catch a movie afterward?" I ask as I mentally pat myself on my back for not messing up.

"Of course. Do you want to try that new place that just opened up? Oh, what's it called, Aunt Juju's?"

*See, there's nothing to worry about,* I conclude as I smile at her. *It's just a coincidence.*

The meet begins forty-five minutes later, kicking it off with Jensen's 4x8. I go to find Colton in the throng of athletes gathered along the infield, so I won't be stuck cheering against Rowling with other Dragons.

"So, Jensen said you two are dating now," he says, raising his eyebrows at me as I approach. "How's that going?"

"Well, we haven't been on a date yet, but we are going out this weekend. I really think I'm falling for her."

"Aw, that's good. But you better sink your claws into her, because you won't find another like her."

"Man, it almost seems as if you like her."

"Ha, good one." He looks over at Tyrese standing with Slushie and Wes. "But your friend there. *He* is hot.

"Ha!" I laugh. "Sorry. I don't that's the direction he swings."

He doesn't seem hurt. Or at least on the surface.

"Have you got a guy you're crushing on?" I ask after a minute.

"No," he says with just a little sorrow in his voice. "There just aren't many gay men in the area, and the few that are are the more flamboyant types, which I'm not into."

I just nod, not sure what else to say.

I'm saved from an extended silence by the beginning of the race.

Jensen is again the anchor, so it's six laps of Douglas chasing Rowling before she takes off. It's not even a full lap until she takes the lead, her long, dark legs propelling her there. And by the end of her second, she's got a large lead and coasts down the homestretch. It looks like she and the rest of her team will have a chance to be back-to-back state champions.

I go up to congratulate her, moving my way through the mob of track stars. When I reach her, she smiles and separates herself from her team.

*Hug her*, my inner wingman says—or more like demands.

No, we haven't even been on a date yet. It's too soon.

*She just won a huge race, and all she wants is a hug from someone she cares about. I mean, just look at her.*

I don't even know if she car—

*Hug her.*

I will later.

*Hug her, you pathetic idiot.*

"Great job, Jensen," I finally say.

"Thanks" is all she says as she is again smothered by her fellow Vikings, with a look that may have been disappointment. Or maybe nothing, just my imagination.

*You're going to need to grow up if you're going to be able to keep her.*

I know.

***

With the 4x2 about to start, me and the others get some last-second handoffs in as we attempt to keep the nerves at bay.

Like Jensen, I'm the anchor, although I presume it to be for different reasons. No one has said anything about it, but the other three sprinters all have at least a second on my time, meaning any one of them would have a more likely chance to catch up with a sprung lead. Register's running this team to get a large head start, so I won't be able to mess it up. I want to compete, not be carried.

We split to our positions, me and Wes to the 200 start line, and the two juniors to the finish line.

"You nervous?" Wes asks me.

"Nah, it will be a walk in the park."

"You'll be fine. We'll get you in a good position to finish on top."

*That's what I'm worried about.*

"Here," he says, putting his hand on my shoulder and closing his eyes. "I'll surge you. I've already used most of my energy on myself, but it'll give you an extra boost."

I remain still and allow him to do his thing. I mean, it couldn't hurt, right?

Five minutes later, the flags are raised to signal the runners are ready, and the gun fires a moment later.

Gary is the first leg, and as he takes off, it almost seems as if he was running at half speed through the first hundred. Once he gets closer, I see the reason why: he's limping and grabbing onto the back of his leg with his free hand, meaning he probably pulled his hamstring. When he hands the baton off to Wes, we're in last place. But not all is lost as Wes has the fastest 200 on the team and shows it by passing three guys before handing it off to Mike.

I had already taken my steps during Wes's leg and now wait for Mike. I'm surprisingly calm. Actually, I'm excited. I finally have a chance to bring something to this team.

Mike passes another, bringing us to second, and then I'm taking off at 80 percent to allow him to reach me in his winded state. The word "stick" is screeched, and I stretch out my left arm behind me in the perfect form I'd been practicing all week. With baton in hand, I accelerate, giving everything to beat— wouldn't you know it—Patterson's Popeye just ahead of me. After fifty meters, I recognize I can win as I've narrowed the distance between us to ten. At a hundred, with the extra burst of speed buried within all track athletes, I pass him, running faster than I ever have. Now there's nothing between me and victory beside straight rubber. But hitting the last fifty, I realize that there's another competitor: myself. My right leg falls slightly left, tangling up my feet while spiking its twin for good measure. I tumble onto the track for one as I see Popeye pass me from the corner of my eye.

It's over. Done.

I feel rare tears fall down my cheeks. Not for me or the pain from the fall or being spiked—which had caused my leg to bleed pretty profusely—but for failing my team. For failing Coach Register, who had given me the opportunity.

Through the tears, I see Jensen followed by the trainer and some of the guys. She wraps me up and holds me, telling me everything's going to be all right. I cry harder in her embrace.

A bittersweet end to a bittersweet season.

<h1 style="text-align:center">Saturday, May 4</h1>

**May the fourth** be with me—sorry, I just had to—as I go on my first date. It hasn't exactly been a great first week for us as boyfriend and girlfriend, so I'm going to have to bring everything tonight or risk losing her forever.

After taking suggestions from the boys—never a great idea, but I'm desperate—I show up at Jensen's door wearing a button-down shirt with gray slacks (both just ironed, of course), topped off with some cologne I found in the back of Dad's closet. Man, I hope I didn't overdress, and woo ... I think I may have put too much Versace on. When Jensen opens the door, I see that's exactly the case: she's just wearing jeans and a red blouse.

"Uh, I may have overdressed," I say, my face burning as if she had just ripped off her top.

*I wouldn't be that lucky.* My cheeks redden further at the thought.

"But you look good," she says. "Now let's eat. I'm starving."

Aunt Juju's is a restaurant based on homestyle cooking that had just opened up. I've heard it's really good, but I was thinking something more along the lines of a fancy Italian place like Philomena's, but considering the thickness of my wallet, it's probably for the best.

We grab a table up front—no "wait to be seated" sign

here—and pick up the semi-greasy menus.

"Welcome to Aunt Juju's!" a waiter exclaims energetically as he pops around the corner. "Now make yourselves at home while I grab your beverages. What we having tonight?"

We both order water and return to our menus without speaking to each other. Being a major overthinker, I had prepared some conversation topics to get the ball rolling but now can't remember a single one.

The jubilant waiter returns with our drinks and takes our order—meatloaf for me and chicken tetrazzini for the lady.

"So, just a couple weeks left of high school, huh," I finally say once the waiter leaves. "What are your plans after?"

"I wish I could say I'm a hundred percent sure, but I'm not even close," she replies, taking a sip of her water. "I love cooking and am really considering going to culinary school. My parents don't exactly agree with it. They want me to use my 31 ACT and be an engineer or some other high-paying job."

"A 31 ACT? Dang, I can see why they think that. But I do understand. I, uh … have a dream too that my parents would disagree with as well."

"What is it?"

I pause before answering. "I want to tell you, but not yet." I can't let my feelings uncover a secret I've kept for so long. "It's not illegal or weird or anything. But it's something I haven't told *anyone*."

"Why have you kept it a secret?" she asks, not fully able to hide her disappointment.

Huh, I've never really thought of that. I mean, there's the fear of disapproval from Mom and Dad, but I can deal with that. I think it might be because of the fear of them reading my script and saying it's awful. That could break me, maybe even cause me to quit on my dream.

"It's complicated," is all I say.

"Meatloaf for my good sir," Mr. Smileys announces with the

steaming plates in his hands. "And chicken tetrazzini for m'lady."

That ends our conversation as we quietly eat our dinner—which is surprisingly really good.

I handle the check, and we leave for the theater. Since Jensen chose the restaurant, she allowed me to pick which movie we watch, and, after much consideration, I went with *Pet Sematary*. It's not only a flick I've wanted to see since it first came out, being a big fan of Stephen King, but it's a horror movie. So, in theory, she'll get scared, and that's when I come in to comfort her. Her knight in a mommy's boy armor.

At the movies, we settle into the recently added leather recliners just as the previews begin. And after suffering through several raunchy trailers, where I sit stiff in my seat, staring at the bottom corner of the screen away from the uncomfortable scenes, the film begins.

A quarter of the way through, Jensen takes my hand, which I may or may not have held out, palm up, on the armrest since we sat down. I look over, and a small smile dances its way up her cheek as she keeps her head forward. I lean back, completely ignoring the movie. I can't say for sure what love is, but what I feel for Jensen I've never felt before. Maybe I do love her. It may be jumping the gun a bit since I've only known her for a couple of months. But I've never cared for anybody as much as I do her. Not even Celeste.

The climax is now underway as Ellie comes back to life—in different circumstances, I would be ticked at how different the movie is from the book, but I'm in too good of a mood right now. And just as I hoped, Jensen reacts, but only by squeezing my hand tighter. These new seats are great for comfort but were not created with cuddling in mind.

The movie ends, leaving me with the idea that maybe there shouldn't have been a remake. I drive her home, talking all the way back with her hand in mine. I then walk Jensen to her front door, as I've seen in dozens of movies.

"Well, good night," I say, standing just a bit awkwardly on her doorstep.

"Thank you for tonight," she replies, lingering in her doorway—or is that just my imagination? "It was amazing."

I turn to leave and stop. "I think I forgot to mention that you look great," I say as I return to her. "Beautiful, actually."

"Actually, I think that was the fourth time you said it," she alleges. Yup, she's definitely waiting for me to do something.

Again, the two sides of me rage within: the awkwardness of the old me and the boldness of the new.

I throw out the past and chase a future, now bright as I go to kiss her. I lean in to her soft, expectant lips and connect our two lives as one. The kiss itself is rather sloppy, not at all like the movies, but it's amazing all the same. When we separate, however, the smile she wears doesn't reach her eyes. It's one given to a freshman asking for directions, not to a lover. It's a polite smile, not a happy one.

We part without another word, and I now know I love her, but the question is: does she love me? Maybe the future is not quite as bright as I thought it was.

*Faith over Fear.*

# Thursday, May 23

**Well, it's finally** here—the last day of school. To be honest, it had felt like a pretty long year, but looking back now, it's like it's only been a couple of months. I've made a lot of memories at Rowling, many bad, but most good. And as I walk in, after being in this building since fifth grade, eight years—almost half my life, which is crazy, come to think of it—it's hard to contemplate that I will never tote my backpack through these doors again.

Class, in essence, is already over—final exams had been taken yesterday—now all that's left are goodbyes.

Mrs. Byers has a sensitive soul. It's not a bad thing but can make holocaust documentaries rather unbearable. Most of us in our AP English class have had her since freshman year, so she's gotten to know each of us fairly well. It doesn't help that her daughter is graduating as well. There will be tears.

And even before I take my seat in the back, I can see that her eyes are already moist. I really hope she doesn't start crying; it will make staying dry-eyed much harder.

"I don't want to say much just yet," Mrs. Byers says, her voice shaking as the bell rings, "or else I'll start crying. Here's the senior video."

The same Hunter who had kicked the winning field goal against Kingsdale created the video. Usually, we have a pro-

-fessional come to film it, but Hunter is an avid videographer with already a hundred thousand plus subscribers on YouTube, who may one day be directing movies in Hollywood. And, who knows, he could very well direct *The Stranger* or another one of my future scripts. On that note, however, I've gotten many rejections since the first query and have stopped sending them out. Although I do have another idea for a movie set in a dystopian world that I feel really good about. I still have faith that is God's plan for me. This is just a mountain I have to climb, and I will not falter.

The video begins with the principal, Mrs. Bartowski, congratulating us for our accomplishments. She's followed by other teachers, including Mrs. Byers, saying, in a sense, the same thing. The video then moves to us holding up a sign with a word or two from "The Climb" as the song is played over it. It ends with a montage of pictures of us.

It's very well made, and plastering the lyrics from the Miley Cyrus song onto posters was a nice touch no other videographer had done in the past. It also manages to produce tears from many of my peers, including Mrs. Byers, to no one's surprise, but my eyes are still dry as a desert. I'm still sad, however, and do have to hold back the waterworks a bit, but I'm ready to move on to the next part of my life. I've spent a long time at Rowling and want to spread my wings a bit, even if it's only to a commuter college.

Mrs. Byers had written us each a letter, saying that she would break down if she tried to talk to us individually. I open mine once she has handed it to me, readying myself to battle tears.

*Dear Ollie,*

*It has been a blessing to have you in class, and even as you try to go unnoticed in the back, I have seen your humility. You may not be the best writer in this class, but you have improved so much more than the others. It is your ability to tell a story, however, that stands out, whether it be a creative free-write or a research project regarding society's impact on mental illness in teens. The latter of which brought items to my attention I never even thought about. With all your skill, you never once boasted about it, and that is an attribute that will take you places many in this class will never be able to reach.*

*What I am getting at is, you have so much potential with whatever you decide to do. I do not think I need to tell you not to throw it away, but college is a tricky business these days. Its pressures have changed many of my past students. Do not let it take away what makes you, you. I know you will succeed in all you do.*

*With love and best wishes,*

*Erica Byers*

I sit back in my seat a bit surprised. I really had thought I'd gone unnoticed in the back and never knew I made even a slight impact on her. But what affects me the most is that she believes in me, in my ability to spin a story and write. I've never had someone say that to me. Ever. A tear finally breaks through the façade that I had spent so much time building up.

***

The moment has finally come for us to leave Rowling for the final time. Mrs. Bartowski sends us off with a farewell address of sorts.

"Every year, around this time, we are forced to say goodbye to a group of bright young men and women. It's not something I or the other members of the faculty can ever get used to, but this year's seniors mean more to me than the past others, because they welcomed me to Rowling freshman year and are the first class I've seen go from start to finish. I know you all will do great things. Now everyone please stand outside your rooms and send off the Class of 2019."

We walk through halls that had felt so long as freshmen, now as small as a rat's maze, and leave through the glass double doors one last time.

****

Four years ago in eighth grade, we had to make a time capsule. There was a broad outline to follow—more as a suggestion, rather than the rule—that said to add items such as photos of family and current prices of everyday items. Family and friends were also encouraged to add letters not to be opened till the last day of senior year. Today.

The Class of 2019 meets at the nearby park, where some of the teachers have set up a lunch catered by none other than Chick-fil-A. After snagging a sandwich and water, I find the boys and Celeste at one of the picnic tables.

"D-do you remember w-what you p-put in your capsule?" Slushie asks me as I sit down.

"Uh, some pictures of the fam, gas prices, and the letters my parents and grandparents put in," I answer. There's something else too that I can't recall for the life of me. "I think."

"I'm a bit nervous for the letter we wrote our future self," Mitch says, having already graduated from whatever academy he was at—Murray, Morehead?—last week.

So, that's what I was forgetting.

"Remember when I had a crush on you back then?" Mitch asks Celeste. After a quick nod and a glance at Jake beside her, he continues. "Well, I think I babbled on and on about you. I might have even written a poem."

"Oh, I gotta read that," Blake interjects and is stared down by Mitch, although Celeste sure seems interested.

As we are finishing our lunch, the teachers start passing out the capsules in their fancy shoeboxes. I'm given mine and crack it open, going for the pictures first. The first one is just of me, and man, I was ugly—not that I'm Prince Charming now. I was pretty chubby back then, but that's not the worst part. The buzz

150

cut I had didn't in any way give me the badass look I was going for then, probably due to the thin-rimmed glasses I wore and braces—which only Jensen can rock.

Next, I open the letter I wrote myself and realize that I didn't forget it, I blocked it out of my memory. Right from the start, I had asked future me how it was going with Rachel. Now it all comes back to me, fantasizing being with Slushie's ex. Well, at least I didn't write a poem about her. The letter then takes a sharp turn into a more serious tone I didn't remember possessing.

*Never forget that money is great and all, but it's not everything. As everyone says, it will never buy you happiness. Get out of your comfort zone and ask someone out, even if it's not Rachel. In my little life experience, I've found that love is the path to true happiness.*

Eighth grade was the first time I ever considered killing myself. Rachel had just started dating another guy, and my young, stupid self had thought I would never find love. I remember, plain as day now, walking to my bedroom window—I was living upstairs then—and wondering if I jumped out, would I die. Suicidal thoughts have come and gone since then as I battle them in secret. The suicide of a teammate sophomore year showed me that there is more than one victim. Killing myself would be selfish.

I wipe a couple of tears that had escaped quickly from my face before anyone notices and dig through the box, coming across a letter from Papaw. The first paragraph was just him humorously babbling on about what to write. Then he moves on to talk about how proud he is of all I've already done. But the next paragraph is what gets me.

*I'm guessing that you have read about 3,500,000 books by now and if you can remember everything you have read, you should be a walking encyclopedia, full of facts, history, myths ,and stories. These are the backbones you can use to create a successful career. You would make a great screen writer, Ollie. All the most famous authors like King and Grisham will tell you that being a voracious writer can lead to being a great author. Reading is one of the greatest assets that come with writing.*

*I know that a lot of people, like your dad, will be telling you to find a job that will make you a lot of money. But all that matters is that you're happy doing what you're doing. Whether it is writing, playing football, or being a dentist. Do what you're meant to do. Don't let anyone ever tell you differently.*

I finish the letter, mostly reiterating the same thing, and no longer are my eyes dry. He was the first one ever to believe that I will succeed, not by doing something that will make me rich, but something that I will actually love. Even though he didn't know I would ever write something of significance, he still believed I would be great. If only I could thank him.

My doubt and Fear evaporate from me, leaving solely hope and Faith. I can do this.

# Friday, May 24

## "Oliver Joel Behr."

I walk to center stage under the bright lights.

"Don't forget to smile," Mrs. Bartowski says as I approach her in casual attire.

It's ten in the morning on our second walk run-through, and I'm ready to go home and take a nap. With the most insincere of smiles, I go to her with an open hand.

"Shake with the right, grab diploma with the left," she recites. She's a bigger woman, and her hand envelops my own. "Tilt head down to the right and smile for the photographer."

I do as she says and exit the stage. I gotta say, I'm looking forward to graduation, but not at all for the walk. I can see myself all too well tripping over my cursed feet and eating vinyl. Also, the idea of being the center of attention for hundreds of people doesn't exactly pique my interest. I'm ready to get this over with, even though I know I'll regret that line of thinking soon enough.

***

"Oh, look at my little graduate," Mom exclaims as I walk upstairs a few hours before the ceremony. "Don't you just look so *cute!*"

"I don't even have my cap and gown on," I reply, wearing the same button-down I wore on my first date with Jensen, with the addition of a tie.

"I just can't believe my little boy's about to graduate."

I shrug and change the subject. "When are we going to dinner?"

"In about thirty minutes. Still want to go with BJ's?"

"Well, since Uncle Jeff's paying, most definitely."

"Before we leave, though," Dad intrudes, "why don't you open your presents."

He runs—okay, maybe not the best way to put; he walks kinda quickly—to their bedroom, returning with a large gift bag, seemingly heavy by the way he is lugging it. I'm fully conscious of the smile taking over my face; opening presents will never get old. I dig in, and the first object I pull out is a nonstick skillet. Confused, I reach back in and grab a pack of various cutlery. With a quick look inside the bag, I see that the contents are all types of home goods, appliances, and tools. I turn to my parents to see what's going on and find Dad holding out a key.

I slowly reach for it, finally starting to realize what's going on. "What?" is all I ask as I slowly take it from him.

"It's your new apartment," he answers.

"There's two bedrooms," Mom adds, "so you can room with Gideon or somebody if you want to. We'll be paying for everything."

"You're kicking me out?" I ask in complete shock at their ambush.

"My dad did the same thing when I graduated, and I can't thank him enough for it," Dad explains. "Sometimes we just need a little push."

I begin to finally come out of my daze. "I'm going to Northern instead of Eastern, because I wanted to stay here for a couple of years. I could've gotten a much better scholarship there, but decided I wanted to be with you guys for a little longer. And now you're kicking my ass out."

"Ollie—" Mom starts.

My blood begins to boil. "No! Don't give me that shit. I hope you enjoy my room. Turn it into a dog playroom like I know you've always wanted to." I move to the door. "I'll meet you at BJ's, but only for the sake of Jeff and Granjerry."

I turn around. "Thanks for ruining this night for me. Happy *fuckin'* graduation to me!"

Mom lets out a sob and dashes to the room. Dad stands there for a moment, perhaps deciding whether he should reprimand or apologize. He opens his mouth, then closes then opens it again. "We were just trying to help," he says with sorrow in his voice before going after his wife.

I return to my bedroom feeling like the bottom of a litter box.

***

Dinner went as expected, and now I wait in the choir room of Zion Baptist, fully adorned in my orange cap and gown along with a fair share of neckwear. A yellow cord for my acceptance into NKU, a black sash with the Senior Beta crest, and a medal to acknowledge my academic achievement of a 4.0 GPA across four years.

"I'm surprised you're able to hold your head up with all that ice," Celeste says, leaving Jake to approach me, stunning in her black gown. "Especially since you already have a big head."

"Yeah." I give a weak laugh. "I just can't believe this is it."

She notices my abnormal pessimism. "Is everything okay?"

"I just got kicked out of my house." I could never lie to her.

"Really, just for no reason?"

"They gave me the whole 'sometimes a bird just needs a little push out of the nest.' But they left out the part where the chick occasionally falls to its death."

"Ollie, I'm so sorry." She grabs my hand, eyes full of apology, but what I only take for pity. "And tonight of all nights."

"Yeah." I turn away from her, taking my hand out of hers as I start to feel my eyes water. "I just want to get this night over with."

"Everybody get in your places," Mr. Lu directs, pushing up

his ever-sliding bifocals

Celeste hugs me quickly before I can resist and goes to her position. I stay where I am for a second, a little stunned, before moving to mine.

We're marched inside the worship center like an oddly dressed herd of cattle and led to our seats. Five minutes later, the choir fills the terrace, all dressed in white with the occasional orange or black gown dotting the group. As tradition goes, they must first sing "I Will Remember You," by Sarah McLachlan before choosing their own; this year going with Juice Wrld's "Graduation." After bringing tears to many eyes, Mrs. Bartowski takes the stage, her eyes themselves wet. She manages to hold it together as she praises us for our many accomplishments and everything. Basically, the same crap everyone else has been feeding us as if they'll even remember us five years from now. Just blah blah blah.

This goes on for about ten minutes, and just when I thought it was over, Mr. Lu does the same thing, followed up by some teachers. Finally, in the time I could've spent watching an episode of *Breaking Bad*, we're given the cue to line back up in the choir room. Now, the walk.

One by one, seniors cross the stage, not a single person even stumbling.

I've barely spoken a word to either of my alphabet neighbors ever—and certainly am in no mood to start—so all I can do is nervously tap my finger on my thigh. Philly Ball is called upon the stage, and now I stand right behind the curtain leading out to the worship center. Man, I hate having a name so high up in the alphabet.

"Oliver Joseph Behr."

*It's Joel, bitch.*

I cross the stage slowly, aware of the hem of my gown brushing the top of my loafers. During the graduation run-through this morning, we were instructed to tell our families to hold their applause till the end, which they were reminded of at the beginning of the ceremony. But I had at least expected something like a little clap, nothing like the hooting and hollering given to Philly and the couple others before her. Though, as I approach Mrs. Bartowski, it's dead silence.

*Oh, I hate this damn school so much.* I shake with the right, grab diploma with the right, "forgetting" to smile, and then give the photographer just a glance with my sour complexion—better than the middle finger I wanted to give this total stranger.

Well, at least I didn't trip.

*Fear.*

# Summer

I must not fear. Fear is the mind-killer. Fear is the little death that brings total obliteration. I will face my fear. I will permit it to pass over me and through me. And when it has gone past, I will turn the inner eye to see its path. Where the fear has gone there will be nothing. Only I will remain.

—Frank Herbert
*Dune*

# Monday, May 27

**"When I was** around your age," Dad says, "my father told me something I'll never forget."

We're sitting on the couch after I just had a mental breakdown over a paper I had to write overnight.

"Something I even remembered the night he and my mom were killed."

Four years ago, a burglar had come to my grandparents' house just to find some quick cash and go. But Pops heard the commotion and thought it was my dementia-riddled grandma. He wore a crucifix that had been in his family for years. The thief saw the metallic object and shot and killed him, thinking it was a gun. Mamaw, hearing the gunfire, wobbled down the stairs, and the freaked criminal shot her dead before she reached the bottom. He was never caught.

"Faith over Fear. Make that your mantra. Live by it, and you will be fine. Let that Fear win, and it's all over."

"What is Fear exactly?" I ask, inquiring about his definition for it, of course.

"Well, Ollie—" He pauses to think, obviously having never pondered it before. "Fear … Fear is all things bad."

***

Today's move-in day, and I will need every bit of my Faith to be able to conquer my Fear of the unknown. The apartment they rented for me is in Alexandria, not too far from NKU. *Guess that means I'll be able to sleep in a little more.*

"Just because you're moving out doesn't mean we're not going to be a part of your life," Mom says, carrying a box up the stairs. "You can call anytime, day or night."

"Maybe not at night," Dad contradicts as he lugs up one of three boxes of books.

"Whatever," I retort. I have calmed down a bit since graduation, but I have yet to fully forgive them, and it's going to be a while before I can.

When I unlock the door, I see they spared no expense. I set down the bags I was holding on the couch, placed to the side of the room in front of a plasma TV. On the other end is a kitchen, with all the works. Ahead, there are three doors, and after further inspection, discover they are bedrooms with a bathroom connecting the two between them. They certainly didn't kick me out onto the street.

"You can use our laundry whenever," Mom continues. "You can drop off the clothes, I'll start a cycle, and we can all go out to eat."

"Not too often, though," Dad adds.

"Don't listen to him. You can come home whenever you want."

*Home is where our story begins.*

So, what does that mean for me? Is this the beginning of a new chapter? Or the start of a sequel? Is this The Next? Or maybe … this is The End.

"Thank you, Mr. and Mrs. Behr. This is amazing." Slushie trots on through the open door with his own entourage.

"Really," Mr. Slusher starts, holding his young daughter's hand. Slushie's mom didn't die immediately in the car crash that gave him his stutter. She was over eight months pregnant and passed in the hospital after going through preterm labor due to the extreme stress of the situation, miraculously giving birth to Riley. "Let me pay for Gideon's rent."

"No, no, no," Mom declines. "If Gideon didn't come here

willingly, I'd be paying him to stay. I'd feel better off if Ollie is living with such a good kid as him."

This time, Dad agrees and nods his head.

"If you need *anything*—"

Mr. Slusher is cut off by both parents' adamant reassurances.

"Let's leave and let them settle in," Dad suggests.

And after a few more trips to deliver our stuff, they do.

Sitting on the couch, feet propped, while flipping through channels on TV and talking to Slushie, I realize this won't be as bad I thought.

It's not The End, only The Beginning.

# Wednesday, May 29

**My parents may** be paying the rent for my apartment, but I'm on my own for everything else. And for that reason, I've been searching for job opportunities the last couple of days. After thorough searches through Indeed and Glassdoor, though, I haven't found anything of interest. Work is not supposed to be fun, anyway, and I need the money, so I applied for a few.

I'm sitting on the couch, casually scrolling through LinkedIn with *Friends* reruns on TV, when Slushie enters the room.

"D-don't you w-watch anything else?" Slushie asks, sipping a coffee.

"C'mon, it's a classic. You need some culture," I return. "What are you drinking?"

"It's a Sw-swolboi from Swolbois. It's a really good ... restaurant? I guess that's w-what you w-would call it. They m-make protein coffee and stuff. It's like a healthy Starbucks, I think"

He takes a loud slurp and looks at my open laptop. "Hey, you're st-still looking for a job, right?"

I nod and he continues. "W-well, unless you ch-changed your mind on Ch-chick-fil-A ..."

"Nope," I quickly interject. He had just started working there and has been trying to get me to join him. Having to spend all day around the holy chicken may deter my love for it, and we can't have that happening.

"Then, Sw-wolbois is n-new and n-needs employees. I think they're having open interviews, actually."

This seems like an opportunity I can't pass up, and before leaving, I quickly print out a resume from my brand-new HP OfficeJet my parents bought me.

***

"Oliver Behr, like the paint." I give the hulking man with blond curly hair my name.

"Huh, I didn't know Oliver was a paint." He scrawls my name onto some type of documentation, spelling my last name-like the animal.

I open my mouth to object but then quickly close it. No need to undermine a potential boss. I'll be Ollever Bear for now.

"Do you work out at all?" Tanner, the owner of Swolbois, asks.

"Yeah, me and my roommate lift at Planet Fitness," I lie. It was the first gym that came to mind.

When I first arrived, an attractive employee watching the counter made me a French Toast Swolboi—the house favorite—for free while I was waiting for Tanner, who really couldn't have been much older than twenty-five.

"Dope," Tanner replies. "That's where I worked before I started this place. Do you know McKaela who works there?"

"Uh, I don't know," I answer, my eyebrows furrowed in fake thought. *Should've gone with Crunch.*

"She's the short one with blonde hair in a bun."

"Oh yeah, her." I'm really digging myself a hole.

"That bitch is my ex." His complexion turns stormy.

I take a long sip from my coffee, not knowing what to say, as if anyone could.

"Anyways—" He's back. "When can you start?"

"As soon as possible," I immediately say, sitting up on my stool.

166

"All right, see you tomorrow. Twelve p.m. sharp."

I return to the apartment to find Slushie watching *South Park.*

*Hates on* Friends *but watches cartoons as an eighteen-year-old, smh.*

"We're going to Planet Fitness," I tell him, standing in front of the TV. "Let's go."

**I've been putting** off getting a job ever since I was fifteen and could legally work at most places, fearing that it will take every minute of every day. I also have a bad case of FOMO, and it pains me to see my friends hanging out without me—however rare it is.

Standing outside of Swolbois with my company T-shirt on—a smiling coffee pot with jacked arms coming out each side and "Swolbois" written under it—Fear takes over, and I consider just turning around. No call, no show. But Tanner sees me through the glass doors and motions me in.

"Here, let me introduce you to the crew," Tanner says once I reach the counter. "This is Brie," Tanner says, leading me to a curvy ginger, making a Swolboi.

"Like the actress," she discloses, looking up at me and smiling politely.

"Or the cheese," Tanner adds, winking at me, with eyes lingering on her voluminous backside.

"And over here," he continues to a muscular brunette, slicing up bananas, "is Chloë." He leans toward me to whisper in my ear. "Doesn't really look like a Chloë, does she? But I'm telling you, she's a tiger in bed."

*Oh no, I'm employed by a pimp.*

"Finally, we have Emma, who I believe you've already met," he says, pushing through the set of swinging doors to the back.

The pretty worker who had made me a free coffee is sitting

at a table eating a sandwich.

"She's on break now, but she'll begin training you once she's done. For now, why don't you get to know each other." He gives me another wink, unseen by Emma, before going back up front.

"Hi," I greet her, sitting across from her a bit awkwardly. "I don't know if he mentioned it at all, but my name is Ollie."

"Yeah, he told us this morning," she says, eyeing me behind the Reuben. "Are you a gay?"

"Uh," I stutter. *Is it too soon to quit?* "No."

"Hmm. It's just that you're the first guy he's hired. Not trans?"

"Nope."

She goes back to her lunch as I gaze at the back of my hand as if it's the most interesting thing in the world.

"Sooo," I say, fighting for something to fill the void. "Tanner is an interesting guy."

"Yeah," she replies, finally finishing her meal. "As long as he's romping Chloë, he's cool."

"Oh." I mentally tap my index fingers together. "Awesome."

"What am I doing?" she asks herself, smiling warmly for the first time. "I'm scaring you off."

I try to deny it, but she waves me off.

"He's really not that bad of a boss. Excluding some of his extracurricular activities, he's really not that bad of a guy either. You've just got to give him a chance.

"It's not a hard job, either. It's never too busy, being fairly unknown right now and a bit pricey. There's also a TV in the dining area, and we get free coffee. Tanner doesn't really care what we do, as long as we get closed on time. The day can go by pretty quickly.

"So, you gonna give it a chance?" she asks, her face pleasant but also pleading.

"Yeah." I nod, smiling. "I'll give it a chance."

"Sweet." She stands up. "Now let's make a Swolboi."

# Saturday, June 1

**"Why did you** have to choose those pics of me?" I ask Mom.

Today is my grad party, so my family and I have been setting up for it all morning. On the table, next to the gift box, are a multitude of photos of me. Moms always seem to present the worst pictures of their kids, and Mom's no exception.

"You look soo cute all naked in the bathtub," Mom explains.

"Yeah, and what about this one?" I ask, pointing. "Do I look *cute* here?"

It's me shirtless on the beach back in middle school, my man boobs sagging unapologetically.

"You always look cute to me."

It has been over a week since they kicked me out, but I'm still salty and just want people to get here so I can get away from them. Thirty minutes till the party starts.

And it's fifteen minutes later when Jensen comes. She's wearing a tank top and short shorts, her hair tied up in a ponytail. What throws me off the most is her smile, one of apology, not happiness.

"Hey, Jensen." I stiffly hug her. "What's up?"

"Oh, not much," she answers, returning the hug the same way. "This setup looks great."

"Thanks, it was mostly my mom's idea. I was just the laborer."

"Here, I got you something," she says, pulling out a card

tucked into the back of her shorts.

It's a picture of a French bulldog, similar to Benny, with the words "Happy Graduation!" on the front. On the inside is the same dog, this time with its tongue out, saying "Now let me lick you."

She then reaches up and kisses me. It's less sloppy than the first but no warmer.

I look behind me and see both parents smiling widely at me with two thumbs up. I return my gaze back to Jensen, my face burning.

"I also got you this," She unveils a twenty seemingly out of nowhere.

"You didn't have to get me anything," I reply and glance over my shoulder, smiling coyly. "Or at least any money."

"Well, I felt like I should get you something, since I won't be able to stick around."

I almost ask her why, when I realize the reason for her dress. "Track."

"We have State next Thursday. Coach is working us to the bone. Wants us to get another ring. I'm sorry."

"No, I understand," I say, a bit hurt.

"I'm really sorry again."

In her defense, it looks like she means it.

We talk for a little while longer before she leaves, just as other cars are pulling in.

Mom had invited about every person she ever came in contact with. You sliced my lunch meat? Invited! Gave me an oil change? Invited! Bullied my son in middle school? Hmm, maybe not. But your dad is the CEO of Graeters'? Invited! And make sure to bring some ice cream.

I walk around, thanking everybody for coming and their gifts, while mentally keeping count of how much I was getting. After a while of doing this, I make my escape, popping a squat at my friend's table.

"How much have you made so far, Ollie?" Mitch asks.

"I don't know. I wasn't really counting."

*It's $635 and a lottery ticket from some guy I've never seen before.*

"Where's Jensen?" Celeste asks me. "I haven't seen her yet."

"Yeah, she swung by earlier," I answer, my face dropping a little. "She has track practice."

"Oh, that's rough."

"Yeah, but it's fine." I glance back at her and see she's not buying it. "Anyways," I try to change the subject, "did you guys have track practice today?" aiming my inquiry at Slushie, Tyrese, and Wes. Colton is talking to Don over by the pool.

"W-we have it n-now, actually. We t-talked to C-coach about it, and he said it's fine. State's only Thursday." Slushie winces as he recognizes his insensitivity. "B-but I'm s-sure J-Jensen's relay is m-more imp-important than ours."

"And I'm not going to State," Wes says in a neutral tone, but unable to meet my eyes.

Now I'm the one wincing. I unconsciously scratch at the spike wound, not completely healed after having to get stitches.

"Hey, Ollie!" a loud, bellowing voice acknowledges from behind me.

It's Coach Goetz.

"Hey, Coach! Thanks for coming."

"Yeah, you got a hell of a mom there. Tracked me down at my son's baseball game."

"Well, she's a really talented stalker."

He guffaws. I just half-smile.

"Slush!" he hollers his way. "Missed you this year."

"It looked like you d-did pretty w-well w-without me," he replies, taking a bite of his pulled pork sandwich.

"Who knows, maybe you could've helped us get to State."

Slushie just nods, knowing full well that anything short of Patrick Mahomes would still get us an L.

"Well, it was good seeing you boys again, and congrats on

graduating."

He makes his way to the food tables.

***

Two hours have gone by, and most people have left. Only Slushie, Celeste, Dick, and Tyrese are still here. They're getting close to calling it a day, when a car rolls up. A latecomer. I don't recognize it, so I just assume it's some fast-food employee who served Mom in the past week. Actually, I think I have seen it, but I don't remember where. The high school parking lot, possibly?

Right as the door opens, though, I recognize who it is.

"Wow, who's that?" Blake asks as the cute blonde walks up to us.

"Emma," I say, not bothering to hide the surprise from my face. "We work together."

"She's part of the sex ring, isn't she?" Tyrese conjectures.

"Shh," I hush them quickly. I stand up to greet her. "Hey, I didn't think you were coming."

"Well, you had mentioned it at work, so you practically invited me," she replies in a pompous manner, with undertones of something else. "You had also said your dad smoked some pork, and I never turn down some home-smoked pig ass."

"Oh, and happy graduation or whatever." She reaches into her pocket and pulls out a crumpled twenty-dollar bill.

"You didn't—"

"Shut up, just take it." Emma stuffs the money into my hand she had pulled from my side. The action causes a familiar tingle to go through my body. "I'm going to go eat now."

Once she leaves, my friends start giving me The Look.

"She's either a self-entitled bitch," Tyrese begins.

"Or she likes you," Celeste finishes.

I don't respond and just turn to watch Emma. Why can't anything be straightforward?

# Thursday, June 6

**Every year, State** for track and field is held at the University of Kentucky. We had already run on it this year during another event, and man, it's an experience. There's something just aesthetically pleasing about running on a bright-blue track.

Coach Register let me hop onto the bus with the State team, so I sit with Slushie while Tyrese is by himself. Wes decided not to go.

Once we get there, I separate from the Rowling crew to find Jensen. With a suggestion from Register, I elected to wear my track uni under a T-shirt and shorts, so no official will try to kick me out. So, now I walk across the recently mowed field, shirt off in the ninety-degree weather. I find her talking to Colton and some others. She sees me and walks over.

"Thanks for coming," she says, hugging me. "I'm sure watching a five-hour track meet on summer break isn't super fun."

"I wouldn't want to be anywhere else or with anyone else," I reply, returning the embrace. My body relaxes against hers. I'm starting to get comfortable with this. "So, is the order of events different than usual?"

"Just a little, but the 4x8 is still first."

I try to think of something else to say.

"How's Swolbois?" she asks, filling the conversation gap.

"Uh, it's good. The owner's a little weird, but the coworkers are cool. I also get free protein smoothies, so that's always nice."

I see the Vikings getting ready to warm up.

"Well, it looks like they're needing you. Good luck."

She leaves as I kick myself for my terrible social skills. Why is it so hard for me to talk to her?

*'Cause she's not—*

I try to cut that thought off.

*—the one.*

I need to have Faith that she is the one. Without Faith, there is only Fear. With Fear, there is nothing but darkness.

***

I'm forced to the stands along with the rest of my team as the meet begins.

It's Rowling, Douglas, Kingsdale, Patterson, and four other teams competing for the state title in the 4x800 relay. The first runners for each team line up, while the crowd goes deathly silent. After an eternity, where you could hear a pin drop from a mile away, the gun fires. Emerging from the mob is Rowling, followed closely by Kingsdale. Douglas's starter hangs back with the others. After the first lap, Rowling remains first, with Kingsdale second, Schusterville third, and Douglas close behind in fourth. Patterson and the rest are trailing by ten meters. Fifty meters after handing off to the second legger. Once Douglas's third legger gets the baton, they've passed Schusterville. With another lap and a half, they're in second, fifteen meters behind Rowlings.

Now it's the final leg, two laps left, and Jensen has the baton. She starts to gain on Rowling's anchor, Sadie. With one lap left, Jensen's right on her heels. She reserves her strength till the home stretch. Sadie realizes this and finds a little gas in the tank and keeps the lead, at least for the moment. But with twenty-five meters left, Sadie starts to falter, and Jensen goes to pass her. Then their feet get tangled, and Jensen goes down while Sadie stays up.

176

I'm already standing and run down the stairs. That was no accident. Sadie finishes, barely fazed, without a look back in Jensen's direction. She tripped her. I leapfrog the fence against the official's protests. I first go to Jensen, but then I see Sadie sneering at her. Fucking *sneering*.

"Hey," I move her way. "You bitch! You did that on purpose."

"Oliver!" Register approaches me, his face turning an unnatural shade of red. "You better get back to the stands, or you're going to have to find your own way back home."

"She tripped her!"

"Their feet just got tangled." He starts to grab my arm. "An unfortunate turn of events."

I rip away from him and stare at him in a mixture of shock and anger. "You *told* her to trip Jensen." I get up in his grill. He's the polar opposite of Coach Goetz and actually smaller than me, but he doesn't back off. "You little bastard"

"Ollie," pleads Jensen, her words tinged in pain, "please stop."

With one last glare, I turn away from Register and move to my girlfriend, where she lies in my shadow.

*Faith over Fear. For from Fear emerges rage.*

# Tuesday, June 18

**Today a labor** rep from the Fair Labor Association swung around Swolbois to check on how Tanner is treating us. Dressed in a black pantsuit with her equally dark hair pulled in a bun so tight that it must hurt, made for a quite intimidating sight. Tanner brought her to the back, saying he didn't want to disturb all the nonexistent customers.

"I think I know why Tanner hired you," Emma says as we try to act busy in the empty parlor.

She's here to make sure we're working in a clean environment, being paid fairly. and that there's no sexual harassment.

"Yeah," I agree, cleaning a blender—for the frappuccinos—for the fourth time. "Maybe I should ask for a raise."

She giggles youthfully at that.

"May I have a moment with both of you?" the agent asks. She must've sneaked up on us as we were talking.

We nod, and she quickly references her notepad.

"What is your hourly wage?"

"Sixteen," Emma answers.

I nod in agreement. Business may have not been booming just yet, but having a light crew, and with Tanner possibly trying to keep us quiet, gave us nice pay.

"And is there any gender inequality in the workplace?" She gives me a hard look.

I raise my eyebrows, but before I can defend myself, Emma

bursts, "No, there is not. Everybody is paid the same and has equal responsibilities. Thank you, but this isn't some third-world sweatshop."

I find some newfound respect in Emma, while the rep glowers and leaves.

Five minutes later, the doors swing open once more as Chloë enters, sporting a bandage across a portion of her forearm.

"You got a tattoo while clocked in?" Emma interrogates.

"Yeah," she replies. "The tattoo place is right across the street. Also, we're dead as can be. I know Tanner won't mind."

*I wonder why.*

"What'd you get, anyways?"

"It's a symbol I found on a card some traveling Gospel-spreader or whatever gave to me. If you read it from the outside of my arm, it will read 'Death.' On the inside 'life.' Kinda symbolizes how people think I'm all big and bad when really I'm just a perfect sweetheart. Or something like that."

"Did someone say tattoo?" Tanner asks, emerging from his hidey hole in the back.

Chloë shows him a picture of the tat both ways on her phone before showing us.

"That is pretty cool, although I don't know if it's as good as mine," he says.

"What's yours?" I inquire before Emma lightly elbows me in the side.

"I'm glad you asked," he says, pulling down his shirt and smiling proudly.

It's a naked mermaid, the tail wrapping around his nipple, with what may be—

"Is that—"

"A vagina? Yes. Inspired by a shark's labia."

I don't bother to respond and turn to Emma. "Do you have any tattoos?"

She nods and pulls up her luscious blonde hair. Right behind her ear is a sword surrounded by orange flames.

"After I graduated, me and some friends went to a tattoo place," she explains. "I didn't want to get anything big, and this one kinda called to me. The lady called it 'A Trial by Fire'"

"That looks like it would be a painful spot."

"To be honest, we weren't exactly sober when we went," she says and looks at me. "What about you? Got anything?"

"No, although I've been thinking about getting one of a phrase my dad had told me. Faith over Fear."

"Yeah, I've seen that before."

"Well, the way he described it is much more unique than something you'd find at a Christian clothing store. He said it's like a scale. As long as Faith is heavier than Fear, life is great. If it's balanced, you have to do everything to bring Faith down. But if Fear ever crashes down and sends Faith sailing, it's game over. It will take the power of God Himself to right the scale."

"Well," Emma says after a minute, nodding to herself, "I think I'll never look at those two words the same ever again."

A customer walks in to interrupt our worthwhile discussion, and we return to our duties.

I hadn't really been thinking about getting a tattoo; with my parents' strict discipline, I could never. But I'm out of the house, out of their jurisdiction. If I were to get a tattoo, that would be the way to go. No two words have ever meant so much. A wider reach than heaven and hell. Greater than life and death. More powerful than good and evil.

It's the balance that ties all things.

# Friday, June 21

**I've recently come** to the decision that the reason I never got an agent for *The Stranger* is simply because it's not an original idea. And I'm sure, like everything, my writing will improve more with practice. Now that I've actually written a screenplay, I now know what I did wrong and right. I have experience now, and I'm still only eighteen.

I've got an idea for an apocalyptic story, where global warming causes the permafrost to melt, which unleashes a dozen diseases. Most are known and have vaccines. But some have never been heard of. I've been trying to come up with names for them, and during a grocery run at Kroger, a pyramid of Coronas drew my eye. Coronavirus. It just rolls off the tongue.

I still believe that my age and original idea will give me an edge over other amateur screenwriters. And as I begin typing, I realize the words come easier than they ever had.

*The Stranger*'s failure was just a test, I now know; this script, *2020*, will be my big break.

# Sunday, June 23

**When I moved** out, Mom and Dad offered to take me to lunch every Sunday after church with the rest of the family. Unable to to turn down a free meal, I agreed. Also, I'd like to see Dylan more. And I'll admit, I even miss Alex a little bit.

I had met them at church, and we took one car to Chuy's, Mom's favorite restaurant, not mine. Now we sit around a basket of chips and creamy jalapeño, chatting between bites.

"You got next week off, right?" Mom asks, rubbing my shoulder with presumably greasy fingers.

"Yeah," I answer. "But—"

She cuts me off. "Good. I'm so excited to spend time with you all week."

"Actually—" I shift in my seat, unable to meet her eyes, or anyone's for that matter. "I've already rented out a cabin in Gatlinburg with some friends."

"Without my permission?" she challenges, beginning to turn red now, angrier than I've seen her in a while.

"Your permission?" I repeat, my voice rising at its usual emotional pitch. "Your permission? I'm eighteen and out of the house. I don't need your fu—frickin' permission."

"We can stop paying for your apartment. If you don't go."

"No," Dad finally mediates. "We're not going to do that. He's an adult now. He can make his own decisions."

I turn to him, happy to finally have an ally, only to find disappointment.

"Hey, Ollie," Dylan speaks up. "Did you get a tattoo." He winces as he realized he just snitched.

My sleeve had rolled up during the argument, exposing the "r" of Fear on the inside of my right bicep. I'd gotten a tat of *Faith over Fear* not long after our discussion at work. Maybe it was an act of rebellion against my parents or maybe just a whim, but it happened, and there's nothing I or anybody else can do about it.

"Yes, I did," I reply, rolling up my sleeve. "Again, I'm an adult, and I can do what I want. Anyways, Alex got one, and he's only fifteen."

His friend's older brother had given him it with his tattoo gun.

I can hear the whining in my voice, and Alex gives me a dark look across the room, but my parents just look at each other sadly. It probably had to do with the reason Alex got his tattoo; an eye with a tear welling up in the corner on his wrist to symbolize his depression or some other emo shit.

"Oliver Jo—"

I stand up and storm out of the restaurant, not even bothering to let her finish, with no plans to continue this weekly tradition.

*Faith over Fear. For Fear gives birth to loneliness.*

# Thursday, July 4

**For the past** couple of years, we've—me and my friends, that is—been trying to go on a road trip, and it just never happened. We could never find a time when everybody was available. There was also the issue of money and helicopter parents. But now we're all adults, have jobs, and don't have summer practices or whatever. But even with all that, some of us still couldn't go. Mitch has an internship at a cancer-research facility, Colton is counseling at Zion's church camp—although I doubt he'd survive living with Dick and Tyrese for a week—and Wes never responded. I think he's still pissed I lost the race.

Gatlinburg is about the closest vacation spot that is still far away enough that we feel like we're adulting, while not having to drive cross-country to the nearest beach. I'd been looking forward to this since graduation, and it has yet to disappoint, with each day full of activities, from mini-golfing—where you know I showed up and took the dub—hiking, and even a junior *American Ninja Warrior* course. Now we're in an escape room arguing over a puzzle with seven minutes left.

"I think this a Freemason code," I say, looking at the sequence of right and obtuse angles opening in various directions, with some having dots inside. "I read a Dan Brown book about them."

We're trapped in a cabin (I can't remember for the life of me how we got here), and a crazed serial killer is expected back any minute.

"Nobody cares about your books and fascination with cults," Tyrese retorts. "Isn't there a calculus theorem, stating that each angle is equal to a certain number?"

"Wait, is there?"

"Ah, I don't know. I was hoping you would know. You are the only decently smart person here."

*I'll take that as a compliment. I guess?*

"Maybe those angles are in this room and there's a number or something on each corner," Blake conjectures, but after a quick search, we find that not to be the case.

I look up to see three minutes have rolled off the clock. Four to go.

"All right, Ollie, let's try your cult code," Tyrese finally relents.

I go to the dry-erase board laying on an oaken table and draw a tic-tac-toe board. I fill it in from top to bottom with letters, starting with "A" and ending with "H." I look at the coded message again and then back at the board. Blake peers over my shoulder and points out that I only have nine letters, and they all matched up to right angles, not obtuse.

Two minutes remaining.

"Hey, I th-think this m-might help," Slushie says, holding up a piece of laminated paper—the killer must take very good care of his property—bearing the same symbols on the wall, containing a letter within each one. He'd found the Freemason cipher.

"Where'd you get it?" I ask.

"It w-was rolled up in the shotgun b-barrel," he answers, pointing at the prop gun, leaning to the side.

"One minute, let's go," Dick demands, ripping the cipher out of Slushie's hands.

He quickly translates as we sweat it out, with one eye on the clock. Thirty seconds is all he needs, and after a quick conversion from letter to number (with A=1, B=2, and so on), we're free as the padlock falls to the ground.

***

Slushie's uncle owns a cabin in Pigeon Forge, which he surprisingly lent us for free during the busiest tourist season. And it's a real nice place if you can look past the heart-shaped jacuzzi and single king-sized bed. Slushie had forgot to mention it's a couples' cabin, not made for four teenage guys. But free is free, and we'll take it.

Blake has some cousins that live nearby that are having a Fourth of July party tonight. We're planning on going there in a couple of hours and are just passing time while watching *Rick and Morty*. We had moved the jacuzzi to the living room—real men relax in hot tubs shaped like hearts—and are taking turns in it. I win the rock-paper-scissors tourney and go first.

"Wow, Ollie," Tyrese praises as I take my shirt off and slide in. "When did you get so ripped?"

"I mean, I've been working out at Planet Fitness for about every day," I answer. "But that's only been since graduation. Mainly it's just been eating clean everday."

"Yeah, I couldn't do that," Blake says, patting his growing stomach.

"It really isn't that hard now that I'm not living at home. I'm trying to save every dollar I make and only have the bare necessities. Plus, I usually have a Swolboi frappuccino for a meal when I work. It's like a protein shake."

"The simple bare necessities," Tyrese sings, and is received with many questioning looks. "What, I can't like Disney because I'm black?"

We just shake our heads at this routine gag.

"And," I continue, "I have to look good for Jensen. Goodness knows she's out of my league."

Tyrese and Dick both nod at this, while Slushie asks, "How's it going w-with you two, anyway?"

"Cold," I answer. "Ever since State, she's not been the same. I mean she can barely look me in the eyes. We still hang out, but it's almost like—" (*she's terrified of me*) "she doesn't like me anymore."

"I'm s-sure you can w-win her back," Slushie consoles, and Blake and Tyrese nod in agreement.

"Let's just change the subject," I say, and they begin discussing their plans for college, with Slushie joining me at NKU, Blake to Louisville, and Tyrese enlisting in the navy.

I just sink into the tub, trying to disappear.

***

"Hey, T-Tyrese, how f-f-fast are you g-going?" Slushie asks nervously from the back seat.

We're on our way to Dick's cousins' party, with Tyrese driving us in his big yellow truck, aptly named Big Naner, on the interstate.

"Not fast enough, if you ask me," he replies, accelerating.

Blake looks over at the dashboard, then turns back at us, brown eyes raised with fear.

Oh great. If Dick's even slightly scared, we're screwed.

But then a flash of blue and red comes from behind us, followed up by a recognizable siren. I don't think I've ever been so happy to see the cops. Tyrese, however, just speeds up.

"Hey, uh, Tyrese, d-did you see the p-police?" Slushie inquires nervously.

He glances up at the rearview mirror. "Nope."

We had gone down a hill, and, with Big Naner going so fast, we have lost track of them.

Suddenly a militia of police roll off the next exit, and this time Tyrese acknowledges them and pulls over.

"Get down!" he hisses at me and Slushie. We numbly comply.

"And you," he says, turning his attention to Blake. "Follow my lead."

190

An officer walks up to the Naner and asks for his license and registration.

"Why didn't you stop for the officer by the Pine Grove exit?" he asks, sounding more tired than angry.

"I'm sorry? I didn't see anybody. I would've pulled over immediately if I did."

"Anyhow, you were driving really reckless—clocked you at 119—what's the hurry?"

"Well," he sniffs, "my mom has just gotten airlifted from a car crash. She's in critical condition, and they don't think she's going ..." a pause and another sniff, "going to make it. I just want to see her before she goes. Blake here was kind enough to accompany me in my time of sorrow."

I roll my eyes in the dark at Slushie.

"Well, if you drive like you were doing, you're going to join her. Here we'll escort you to the hospital. Which one is it?"

*Oh no, we're screwed.*

"The one off the next exit," Tyrese answers immediately.

"Oh, St. Joe's. They treated my dad there when he had cancer. Good people there."

The officer leads the way with his cruiser, and the Big Naner follows him.

Me and Slushie get up to see literal tears on Tyrese's face, glistening from the LED-lit dashboard—I'm surprised the cop said nothing about that.

"Impressive," I praise.

"This is not a first for me and Big Naner. I've gotten good at getting out of these situations."

Nobody opted to explore further, letting the matter rest, although I'm sure some of those dealings had to do with his crazy girlfriend.

We get to the hospital, and Tyrese and Dick pile out. They go inside as me and Slushie duck back down while the internal lights turn on. The police leave shortly after, and ten minutes pass before I get a text from Tyrese, asking if they were still there. Then they return to the truck.

"Good," Tyrese says, getting back behind the wheel. "We were starting to get weird looks in the waiting room."

"You kn-know, you should d-do drama," Slushie suggests as we pull out of the parking lot.

"Nah, I'm too good for them."

***

We finally arrive at Dick's cousins' place at a quarter till eleven. They have a decent property, but the greatest attractor is it's distant from neighbors. I'm sure this area is party central as much as my house is.

The party is well underway as we walk to the backyard, but we soon find out that we haven't missed the fireworks show.

"Hey, it's about time, Blake," a millennial with a bushy beard says as he approaches us. This must be one of his cousins, but I can't see any similarities.

Another man with the exact same looks sans beard joins him. Identical twins.

"I'm Jeremiah," the bearded one continues.

"And I'm Jonathan," the other one says. "Can we get you anything to drink?"

"Just a water," Tyrese answers. "I've already had one run-in with the fuzz. Don't need a DUI to top that off."

Slushie does the same, while Blake gets a Natty Lite.

"I'll take one too," I say, to the surprised look of my friends, at which I just shrug. "It's been a long night."

Seeing most people around me drinking beers made me fall into a bit of peer pressure, to be honest. But it has also been a very long night.

"You drink, Ollie?" Dick asks, surprised but smiling as if he's proud of me.

"Just whenever I can get my hands on something," I answer, meaning only rare occasion when I'm in a country with an eigh-

-teen-year-old drinking age.

"I guess you're not as innocent as we thought," Tyrese says, looking at me differently. I don't like it. For much of my life, I wanted to be someone other than "that nice guy." Have an edge. Hell, there were days I thought the only way I could gain some people's respect was by being the occasional jerk. Now, I just don't know.

"Yeah," I reply, taking a long swallow of the bitter substance and acting as if I enjoy it. I try to ignore the expression on Tyrese's face. "I guess not. And anyways, it's only one beer."

It's three beers by the time the fireworks start; five by the time we leave. With my low tolerance for alcohol, I'm fairly intoxicated now. My first time drunk. But as they help me into the Big Naner, I'm not too drunk to notice Slushie's disappointment at me. And I'm sober enough to realize that I used to be the one dragging him home from parties, where I looked at him that way, not the other way around. It was me that got him to stop drinking and go to church—although his girlfriend, Callie, did most of the heavy lifting there. Now I'm throwing up on him in the back seat. I've singlehandedly ruined the vacation—not the mention the Naner—we've all been looking for.

In my drunken state, I see that I'm a fuckup. I've screwed things up with my family, will most likely screw things up with Jensen, and now my friends probably hate me. I would do more good with a bullet in my head.

*Faith over Fear. For Fear only leads to death.*

# Saturday, July 20

**"This is why** I don't like the ocean," Jensen says as we walk hand-in-hand through a glass tunnel with sharks swimming around it.

Jensen had called me earlier, asking if I wanted to go to the Newport Aquarium. Despite Tyrese and Dick's warnings about there being too many fish in one area—I have a feeling that they weren't talking about ones that swim underwater—I of course accepted the invitation. How could anyone ever say no to her?

"It really makes you think if it really was seaweed that brushed up against your leg," I say, and we both shudder at the thought.

"How's work?" I ask after a minute. She had just gotten a job at the Ark Encounter, which is basically a theme park featuring a model of Noah's Ark built with the same dimensions as written in the Bible. It even has animals, although I doubt if there are two of each species.

"It's good," she answers. "They have me working at the gift shop right now, but I'm hoping to transfer over to the petting zoo in a year."

"That's great."

We exit the tunnel into the jellyfish room and stand in silence in front of a tank of Portuguese man o' war. The label states that it is extremely dangerous and apparently not even technically a jellyfish. Glowing in the blacklight, though, they actually look kinda pretty.

She turns to me. "We need to talk."

That's not a phrase any guy wants to hear. I turn away from the *Siphonophore* and face her. My eyes are already watering in expectation of what's to come, and I'm unable to meet hers.

"Ollie, I don't think this is going to work."

I almost nod like an idiot.

"We just don't have as many similarities as I thought. I think we should see other people."

It's really happening. My world is unraveling at the seams. Soon there will be nothing left.

I'm finally able to look her in her beautiful hazel eyes and see a lie.

"That's not the whole truth, is it?" I ask.

Now she's the one who drops her eyes. "No." She raises them up almost immediately. "Ollie. I just … don't like you."

It's better if I didn't ask. This is like a knife to the heart.

"You're a great guy and super nice. I tried so hard to like you but I just … can't. It's better for both of us if this ends."

That still wasn't all.

"There's more," I say.

She looks at her shoes, this time unable to return my gaze. "And you scared me. At State. Ollie, you terrified me. I just can't be with you, I'm sorry.

"I have a ride waiting for me." She meets my eyes for maybe the last time. "Bye, Ollie."

I turn to stare at the deadly creature. I feel empty. Hollow except for a fire growing slowly, deep inside me.

*Faith over Fear. For from Fear ensues heartbreak.*

# Sunday, July 21

**On a whim**, Tanner decided to close Swolbois for the day to have a barbeque at his house with his employees. There were a few complaints about not making any money today, but eventually, we all gave in. It doesn't really take too much convincing to get a day off and free food.

His house is located far out in the country, with the closest neighbor being four miles away. He has a nice place, which I guess is what happens when you own your own business, even if it hasn't become super popular yet.

I arrive fashionably late and park on the grass with the other cars. I walk around the back, following my nose as well as any basset hound.

"Hey, Ollie," Tanner greets from the grill. "I see you're as punctual as usual."

"Just so I can get your attention," I return.

I spot Emma watching a cornhole match with the pair of Chloë and Brie against another two attractive girls, who I assume work the morning shift. Excusing myself, I move toward them.

"Does this happen often?" I ask, sliding in next to her.

"This?" She gestures out into the yard. "No. This is a first. Maybe it's to keep us quiet."

We ponder that for a minute.

She glances over at me. "Are you okay? You seem off to-

-day."

Not too many people can read me through the façade I built up over years.

"Me and my girlfriend—Jensen, I think I mentioned her—broke up yesterday," I reply.

"Oh, I'm so sorry," Emma says. She actually looks genuinely apologetic, as if Jensen dumping me personally affected her. I've never seen that level of empathy in anybody.

A memory of Celeste hugging me during graduation flashes through my mind.

"Yeah, thanks." I stare off at nothing in particular.

"How are you doing?"

After the aquarium, I had driven home in some kind of trance, having less awareness of the road than a drunk person. I somehow made it home—I think that's the first time I ever called my apartment home, hmm—safely and walked past Slushie, without a word, to my room. There, sitting up on my bed, I had silently cried till I could no more.

"I've been better," I say. I take a look at all the friendly faces around me. "But I've also been worse."

"Hey!" Tanner hollers. "Burgers are ready."

Emma squeezes my hand and gives me a smile full of—*love?*—apology, before letting go to join the others.

Some misfortunes might just be blessings in disguise.

# Monday, August 12

**There's just a** week before college starts, so I'm trying to have one last hurrah before then. With Blake going to UK and Tyrese leaving for Virginia in a couple weeks for boot camp, this may be the last time I see them for a while.

It looks like most of them are coming, with the only exceptions being Mitch, who's still interning, and Wes, who just left the chat on *read*.

It will be different this time, though, as we're meeting at my apartment. Slushie's still on a grocery run when Celeste enters.

"Ollie, I'm so sorry about Jensen," Celeste says, startling me with a hug. It's warm and comforting, her chestnut hair smelling of shea butter and coconuts.

It … it feels like home.

"Thank you," I reply as we pull apart. "I think it would be better if we didn't talk about it. Keep things light today."

I say this more so Dick or somebody doesn't walk in and try to push the topic. I could talk to Celeste for hours.

"Well, if there's anything you need," she says, "I'm here."

Slushie barges in to interrupt our moment. "Time to start this party," Slushie announces, holding up grocery bags of soda and chips.

We sit around the couch, sipping Coke and snacking on hot fries as we catch up, waiting for the others to arrive. Both are obviously dodging any subject dealing with dating, including their own respective relationships.

"How do you two like living together?" Celeste asks.

"Well, it's nothing like home," I say bitterly, before realizing my company and quickly throwing on a smile. "But we could be in a worse place, and the freedom we have is nice."

"Yeah," Slushie chimes in. "You're d-definitely using that freedom to leave the t-toilet seat up."

"Oh, I'm sorry," I retort. "I didn't know you peed sitting down. I'll make sure to drop it next time, Your Highness."

"You guys are turning into an old married couple," Celeste notes with an amused smile.

Colton arrives a little later, with Tyrese and Blake following soon thereafter.

"Damn, Ollie," Tyrese says, admiring the apartment. "Nice digs. Why haven't you invited me over earlier?"

His question is answered as he sits down and throws his muddy shoes on the ottoman. I glare at him, and he takes them off, but not before giving me the bird.

"How are you doing?" Colton asks with concern, and the room grows quiet.

"Guys, I'm fine," I say, faking a smile. "Let's not bring up bad memories today. This may be our last time together for a while. Let's enjoy it."

"Just try not to vomit this time when you get drunk over her," Dick says, distractedly while unpacking Cards Against Humanity. He looks up as the room falls silent. "What? I vomited the first time I got drunk. It's a rite of passage."

"You got drunk?" Celeste turns on me.

"I ..." I open and close my mouth as I search for an answer, my face turning redder every second.

"I peer pressured him into having a shot of vodka," Tyrese lies. "And one thing led to the next."

Celeste looks between us, hunting for the truth.

"Let's j-just play the g-game," Slushie breaks the silence.

Dick deals out the cards while *Taxi Driver* plays in the background. Robert De Niro's character's mental state is rapidly deteriorating as he is currently threatening himself in the mirror while drawing a gun on his reflection, preparing for a murderous rampage he believes to be his purpose. *Here is a man who would not take it anymore. A man who stood up against the scum, the cunts, the dogs, the filth, the shit. Here is a man who stood up.*

This has to be my favorite movie.

"Have you b-been on c-campus yet?" Slushie asks Blake.

"Yeah," he answers. "I had orientation a couple days ago."

"Are the rum-mors true?"

"Oh yeah." Dick smiles devilishly. "That's where all the hottest girls go to party and screw. My type of place."

"What about you, Colton?" I ask.

"Yeah, I had orientation the other day," he replies from his spot by the TV, sitting in a chair he had pulled up from the dinner table.

He's going to Thomas Moore, which is just down the street from NKU.

"You met somebody, didn't you?" Celeste asks, staring at him closely.

He deeply blushes. "Uh, yeah. I've never met somebody like him."

"Well, go ask him out." Celeste always fancied herself a matchmaker.

"I don't even know his name."

"You can find that out later," she pushes. "If you wait, you might lose him forever."

My face drops a bit at this. If I had asked out Celeste earlier, I would never have had to deal with the heartache Jensen dealt me or have to compete with the likes of Jake. Now, I don't think I'll ever get another chance.

"Just ask him this," Tyrese suggests. "'Are you related to

Jean-Claude Van Damme? Because Jean-Claude Van Damme you're hot!'"

"No, don't listen to him," Dick counters. "Have him feel your shirt and then ask 'know what it's made of? Boyfriend material.' Works every time."

"Okay, scratch the pickup lines," Celeste says. "All Jake did was ask me out for dinner and a movie. Simple and not cringe-worthy."

I reflexively wince at that name but decide to throw in my two cents from my limited experience with dating.

"Here, this is how you do it." I turn to Celeste. "Look into their eyes. Deep into their eyes. Where it's just you and them. Nothing else, no one else. Just them."

I begin to feel a spark between us, albeit a small one. And like in every serious situation, I decide to end it.

"And then you say, 'how you doooing?'"

The room had gone deathly quiet while I had become trapped in Celeste's eyes, and now chuckles fill the room.

I look back at Celeste and see what I think may be disappointment in her green eyes before she laughs with the others.

*Dammit*

**The moment I** walk through the glass doors of Swolbois, I know something is wrong. The coffee shop is completely empty of both customers and employees. And as I move to the back, I hear crying. I rush through the swinging doors to find Emma—bruised and bleeding, with clothes torn—surrounded by Chloë and Brie as they try to console her. They turn to me as I enter, and nobody says anything for a second.

I finally break the silence, my voice laced with concern. "What happened?"

All three look at each other, while Emma wipes her eyes.

"None of your business," Brie answers bluntly after a minute.

"No, he should know too," Emma says, lips trembling. "Tanner's also his boss. He … he—"

"The little prick raped her," Chloë spits out.

My legs suddenly feel weak, so I fall into a chair at the table next to the girls.

"When? Where?" I ramble weakly.

She doesn't answer, but a look at her ripped Swolbois shirt and swollen face answers the last. Here. The bastard raped her *here*.

"He left immediately … after." Emma closes her eyes fiercely, trying to block out memories so atrocious that even my vivid imagination couldn't fabricate. "Said if I called the police, he'd

… he'd kill me."

She gives me a look of Fear so potent, it could never be replicated by even the greatest actress. "I'm scared, Ollie."

Like fighting fire with fire, sometimes using Fear is the only way to beat Fear.

I grab her hand and squeeze. "Everything's going to be okay. I promise you."

And everything will be.

***

I rip the covers off Tanner as he sleeps. He groggily opens his eyes and quickly sits up when he sees what I have in my hand. He begs, he cries, he bribes, but I have no mercy for a monster like him. I drive the kitchen knife into his chest, relishing in his screams, and then again and again.

"No, no, no," I say to myself, lying on my bed. "Too messy."

*You're plotting murder as if you're deciding what to have for dinner. C'mon, Ollie.*

Slushie is at a revival, leaving the apartment to myself, so the only person talking to me is me.

"It's not murder; it's euthanizing a rabid animal," I reason with the voice in my head. "I'm putting him out of his misery."

*You'll never be able to come back from this.*

It kind of sounds like Alex, come to think of it.

"I've got a plan. I'll get away with it."

*I know you will, dumbass.* Yeah, it's definitely Alex. I would never have thought he'd be the angel sitting on my shoulder. *I'm saying you won't ever be the same afterward.*

"He doesn't deserve to get away with it." I grit my teeth, trying to keep my voice down. "He has to die if Emma will ever be at ease."

*It's a dark path you're going down. You'll throw out any chance at a normal life.*

"And what normal life is that?" I clench my fist, wishing Alex was here, so I could slug him in the mouth. "Standing be-

-hind a bent-over eighty-year-old woman with some disgusting disease on her wrinkly, white ass? No, that is no life. That's just the first ring of Dante's Inferno."

I wait for a response, but there is none. Alex has given up. No, my subconscious has given up. Alex is dead. I mean, he's at home, our parents' home. These murderous thoughts have messed me up. But I need to do what needs to be done.

For Emma.

I slide open the drawer on my nightstand to reveal a Taurus .357 snub-nose I had bought on a whim one day on the way home from work. I have been shooting guns since I could first hold them and felt the need to have one, now that I have my own place.

At close range, that could blow off half his face.

I grab it, already loaded, and walk out of the apartment, dressed in all black.

***

Tanner is the perfect victim. He lives out in the middle of nowhere in a place where a gunshot is just a little late-night target practice. And at ten o'clock, he'll most likely still be awake, meaning the alarm will have yet to be set. But this is still Kentucky, where thieves leave in body bags, riddled with buckshot. Tanner doesn't seem like a gun-toting redneck, though neither do I. I'll have to be careful.

I pull up a mile from Tanner's house, still far off the main drag, and park in a ditch to the side. I sit in the car, the realization of what I'm about to do rushes over. I'm going to kill a human being, damn him to hell for eternity. I've seen enough crime shows to know that the criminal rarely gets away these days. I'll get caught and go to jail, and my life—no matter how dull and purposeless it may be—will be over.

But then I see Emma's face. The tears that had yet to dry on her face. Her ripped-up clothes. And worst of all, the Fear on her face.

I open the Camry's door and walk to Tanner, sticking to the edge of the woods.

"*Falls the Shadow.*"

The voice comes from deep within the woods.

"*Falls the Shadow. Falls the Shadow. Falls the Shadow.*"

Each repetition of the foreboding phrase comes from a different direction. And again I'm frozen in place from the ghostly voice.

After a minute, Alex emerges from among the trees. "*This is the way the world ends,*" he whispers.

I find myself able to hurry along at a steady jog.

"*This is the way the world ends.*" This time it sounds like he's just behind me. I pick up my pace, now at a sprint.

"*This is the way the world ends.*"

I drive my legs and pump my arms, trying to race my own shadow.

"*Not with a bang but a whimper.*"

I skid to a stop as lights glitter through the trees. Turning around, fearing what would be there, I see nothing but trees and the shadows dancing among them.

*What is going on?* That'll have to wait; I have more dire issues to deal with than chasing after a phantom.

I continue on and a few minutes later, his house comes into view. With all those lights on, he must not only be there but be awake as well. My plan is working.

I sneak up to his place, keeping to the shadows. I crouch against the brick wall and peer into a lit window to the right of the front door. I see the rapist sitting on the couch, watching the *Big Bang Theory* of all things

I originally planned on knocking and then blowing his brains out when he opened, but Kentuckians answer the door at this hour with a shotgun. No, that won't do. My best friend tonight is surprise. He'd never expect me to come to his place with a Taurus. No one would.

I take another peek inside to check if there's a gun or any other weapon in his vicinity. It's clear, and I try the doorknob, finding myself praying to God that it's unlocked. It is, and I almost believe He wants me to kill Tanner. Be His Angel of Death.

Almost.

I barge through the door, and Tanner jumps up, looking around for a weapon or maybe a way out.

"This is for what you did to Emma!" I scream at the top of my lungs.

I almost end him right there when a thought comes to mind.

"Please don't shoot," he pleads, as if that will help him.

"Sit back down!" I demand, and when he doesn't reply, I pull back on the hammer. He drops faster than a nerd during PE dodgeball. "Now beg for your life."

He's a blubbering mess, tears running down his face, mixing with his snot. Absolutely pitiful and disgusting, and I enjoy it more than I would've ever thought. But every minute I'm here is another minute I could get caught.

I touch the barrel of the revolver to the right side of his head, "Tell Satan I said hello," and pull the trigger.

My ears reverberate as I stare at what I've just done. I'm covered in blood. His blood. I'm unable to move. To do anything. To run and get the hell out of here. To breath.

Fear has taken over. Death has won.

*For from Fear arises evil.*

# Fall '19

*Between the idea*
*And the reality*
*Between the motion*
*And the act*
*Falls the Shadow*

—T. S. Eliot
"The Hollow Men"

# Thursday, August 15
## Oliver

Alexander Matthew Behr<br>
March 30, 2003–<br>
July 26, 2018<br>
Loving son and brother

**I stand in** the cemetery in front of his grave. Just six feet above my brother, who I would have sworn with my hand on a Bible, was still alive.

*I know you will, dumbass.*

Alex—my unconscious—whatever, knew I would get away with killing Tanner because I had done it before.

But I just saw him at church not even a week ago. I've heard that a traumatic event can repress memories, but create an entire person for over a year? I don't know. For all I know, this tombstone could just be a figment of my imagination, and Alex could be alive and well. Maybe Emma never got raped, and I didn't kill Tanner. These don't seem like things that could happen in my boring and simple life. Is this my nightmare? Or somebody else's? Maybe I'm in hell now. Or trapped in my own head by some James Bond villain.

I fall to my knees, grabbing my head and letting out an involuntary scream.

I don't know what's real now.

As I writhe around, a ruffling in my pocket draws my attention. It's a ripped piece of paper.

*Between the idea*
*And the reality*
*Between the motion*
*And the act*
*Falls the Shadow*

The word "Shadow" is circled frantically, cutting into the paper. I remember seeing this in English class but not knowing when and why did it.

"What did I do to you?" I ask my dead brother before everything becomes clear.

***

*"Are you drinking?"*

*I drop the bottle of Captain Morgan to my side. Alex stands in the doorway to my room, leering at me.*

*"It's just soda," I lie badly, trying to keep my voice normal. I only had a couple of shots so it wasn't too difficult. I just found out Celeste was talking to another guy and I needed it.*

*"That's the worst lie I've ever heard."*

*"I only had a little bit. Please don't tell Mom and Dad," I beg.*

*"What, tell them their perfect child is drinking in their basement." He laughs. "They'll kill you."*

*"Please, I'll do anything."*

*"Nothing you do will stop me from telling them," he says stubbornly and turns to leave.*

*I throw him into the closet door, banging his head against it, yelling incoherent obscenities.*

*"You prick!" I grab a heavy, iron lamp off my nightstand and slam it onto his head. "Just promise you won't say anything, and this will all be over."*

*No response. He's bleeding profusely from the contusion on his temple.*

*Bleeding way too much.*

*"Alex?" A million thoughts go through my head, none of them good.*

*I place two fingers on his neck, just like I had been taught in health class.*

*Nothing.*

*I hold the palm of my hand over his mouth.*

*Nothing.*

*I lay my head on his chest.*

*Nothing. Nothing. Nothing*

*I killed him, I realize in shock, not fully comprehending what I had just done.* I'm a murderer.

Oh lord, what have I done?

*This is not the time for thinking. I have to cover this up before everybody else gets home.*

*Mom and Dad are at Dylan's fall baseball game.*

*I don't have a lot of time.*

*I sling him over my shoulder, grunting from the effort—there's a reason they call heavy things "dead weight"—*

(Why am I joking?*)*

*—but, thankfully, he was pretty light when he was alive.*

When he was alive.

*I position his body so the blood from his death-wound*

(death-wound)

*will just drip onto me and not the floor.*

*I haul him up the stairs, keeping my mind focused on the task at hand. Or else it will collapse into insanity. Two flights later, I find myself standing in front of the attic, although it's not really an attic, a room, rather than a loft. Opening the door, I bring him and prop him against the wall in the attic while I catch my breath. I open and peer out the window above his sunken body. A four-story fall onto the hard, concrete driveway will do a lot of damage. Erase evidence.*

*I pick up Alex again*

*(for the last time)*

*and push him headfirst out of the window, creating a sickening noise.*

*I had worked at Honey Baked Ham for several days during the Christmas season. Throwing out the garbage sounded a lot like that.*

But when I looked to see the damage I did, I saw nothing. No, I did see his mangled body, but my mind is still keeping that sight locked up tight.

*I don't have much time. They could be home in as soon as twenty minutes. I need to clean up.* Why am I treating this like I'm cleaning up spilled milk, not my brother's blood?

*I run downstairs and hop in the shower, not giving myself the luxury of hot water. I scrub myself raw, trying to clean the blood that, in a way, will never come off. I get out five minutes later and go to clean up the blood from the carpet*

(where I fuckin' killed him)

*and the lamp*

(what I fuckin' killed him with)

*as best I could.*

*I'm not able to get all the blood off the lamp, but it's black and doesn't really show, especially if I face the largest splotch to the wall. The carpet, on the other hand, will be a problem. But there was a trick Mom had taught me that she herself had learned from Granjerry. Place ice over the bloodstains. It seems like fiction, but it really does the trick, and I've seen it in action. I run back upstairs, still naked, and fill a bowl with ice from the refrigerator. Back in my room, I dump ice over the large bloodstain quickly—why do head wounds bleed so much?*

(I'm talking about my brother here!)

*—and cover the stain up with some clothes, hoping that would hide it before the ice did the trick.*

*Then I quickly get dressed and hurry outside before remembering the attic and dash back in. I fill up another bowl with dish soap and water and grab a rag. In the attic, I get on my hands and knees and scrub at the drops of blood till they all come up.*

*Now I exit the house and stand at the scene, which I still cannot recall. I reach into my pocket and pull out my phone, dialing the three numbers no one ever wants to push.*

'911, what's your emergency?" *the operator asks.*

*I suddenly break down into real tears as I feel the walls of my sanity begin to crumble.*

I killed my brother.

I killed my fuckin' brother!

*"My brother just jumped out of the window!" I yell into the iPhone, legitimately freaked out. "He's … dead! Oh lord, he's dead!"*

**Friday, August 16, 2:00 p.m.**
**Casey**

**Colin and I** pull into the driveway of the victim's house. Unlike a regular crime scene, there's no police tape or a mob of cops. Instead, a lone officer greets us from the front door.

"Detectives," Officer Weber acknowledges us as we approach him. He's a bulky guy, spending more time at the gym then at work. "I'm afraid y'all wasted your time. The guy blew his own brains out."

The victim's brother, who resides in western Virginia, had called Verona's sheriff's office, filing a missing-persons case. The victim, a Tanner Wall, hadn't been returning any of his calls, apparently an unusual phenomenon. Weber had been kind enough to pay him a courtesy call. There was no answer to his knocking and after a few minutes, he turned to leave. But police instincts told him to take a glimpse inside through the window adjacent to the door.

And now here we are.

"I just want to take a look," I reply. "Call it boredom. Not much else to do around here."

That may be part of the answer but just a small one. His body had already undergone rigor mortis, meaning he could have been dead for anywhere from twenty-four hours to eighty-four. We'll have to wait for the coroner to find the exact time of death, but considering Wall's brother said he hadn't heard from him since Wednesday, he may have been dead for three days. And since Wall was the owner of the local business, Swolbois—having found this out minutes ago on the drive—he'd be missed. Something doesn't add up.

We walk inside with the door already ajar, and I flinch, taking a step back at the sight. This may just be a suicide—or at least appears to be—but there's not many violent deaths in Verona. I see Colin reacting the same way and feel a bit better. At least I don't feel like I'm going to puke.

The first thing I notice is the blood. It's everywhere, seeming to dot every object in the room. We put our booties on over our shoes and carefully approach the decaying body of the late Tanner Wall, suicide weapon—a Taurus .375 snub-nose if I'm not mistaken—lying next to him. I almost do lose my lunch, though, when I see that flies have taken solitude in Wall's death-wound, their black mass filling the gaping crater.

"Are you sure it's him?" I holler out at Weber. With half his face blown off, it is hard to tell.

"Yes, his brother said he had a, uh, very distinctive mermaid tattoo on his chest," the officer yells back.

I push down the collar of the vic's shirt to reveal it. *Tasteful.*

Now, looking around the floor of the corpse, I sense something's not right. I walk to the left of the body as the eyes seem to track me. I make a gun with my fingers and point it as close as I dare to his right temple.

"You see anything off, Colin?" I ask my partner.

"Well, you're aiming a finger gun at a decaying body," he answers dryly.

"Look at the floor behind me."

His eyebrows furrow as he tries to see what I see. "I'm not finding nothing," he finally gives.

"There's not much blood behind me when compared to the area to the right and left of me," I explain. "It seems to stop around where I'm standing. Something, or someone, must have been in that spot."

Colin peers at me incredulously.

"We'll have to wait for the blood splatter analyst to get a definitive answer," I continue, barely noticing his expression. "But I believe Wall didn't kill himself. Someone murdered him."

***

Wall hadn't had his nightly phone call with his brother on Wednesday. So, it's safe to presume that's when he died, which the coroner did confirm on his preliminary tests. This means he was missing for a whole workday. So why did nobody report it? Maybe it was his day off. Or he just no-called/no-showed. He owns the place, so why not. But something's not right. Why would someone want to kill him?

Colin and I walk through the glass doors of Swolbois, hoping somebody there can shed some light on the situation. He doesn't have any other relatives in the area, so there's not really anybody else to question.

"Hi," I say to the heavyset, attractive brunette manning the counter. "Can I have a minute?"

She takes a look around the empty parlor. "I guess I can spare a minute. But Tanner didn't do anything."

"What?" I glance over at Colin, who just shrugs.

"Oh damn, you're not police?"

"We're detectives." I show her my badge, Colin doing the same. "What did Tanner do?"

"First, why are you here?" She crosses her muscular arms.

I sigh. "Why don't you two come out," nodding to a pair of heads in the smoky windows of the swinging back doors.

Two other pretty girls push through, giving us a confused look, although the blonde one's was more of fear. Something happened before Wall was murdered. But what?

"Come over here," I continue, motioning to the other side of the counter, where there are several stools. "You might want to be seated for this."

Once they're all seated, I break the news. "Tanner Wall is dead. Killed himself." I'll keep the skewed blood splatter to myself for now.

"Oh lord," Brunette gasps.

The other two just stand there in silent contemplation. None of them sit down.

"I'm sorry for your loss," I say, "but I need to ask y'all some questions."

"I thought you said he killed himself," Ginger says snarkily. "So why are you here? I feel like being a bearer of bad news is under your pay grade."

"Humor me," I reply. "Was he here Wednesday?"

Brunette looks over at Blonde. "He can't hurt you anymore, Emma."

I raise my eyebrows at her.

"You don't need to tell him shit," Ginger snarls.

The blonde, apparently named Emma, looks down at her feet before raising her tear-filled eyes to me.

"He raped me Wednesday," she says quietly.

I breathe sharply through my teeth and wrap an arm around her shoulder, steering her to a table out in the parlor. Ginger tries to stop her; Brunette holds her back, shaking her head. I have a daughter who couldn't be much younger than Emma and cannot imagine that happening to her.

But would I kill the rapist?

We talk for a little before I give her the number of a guy I went to undergrad with who's a psychiatrist in the next town over. I stand up and thank the girls for their time, giving Emma what I hope is a reassuring squeeze of her shoulder.

"Oh, and one last thing," I say, directing my inquiry toward Brunette. "Why did you think I was here for Tanner when none of you reported the rape?"

Emma had told me about Wall threatening her.

"We thought Oliver might've said something about it. He

was pretty stirred up about it," she answers.

"Is Oliver a coworker?"

She nods. "He's off for the weekend. Begins college Monday."

"And what's his last name?"

"Behr, why?"

"No reason. Thank you for your time and cooperation."

*Not Ollie. It can't be Ollie.*

**Friday, August 16, 4:30 p.m.**
**Oliver**

**"Thanks for letting** me know, Emma. I'm sorry" I say, hanging up the phone.

*Thanks for letting me know?* Tanner mocks.

Tanner joined Alex in my head just an hour ago. I don't know what the hell is going on.

*You trying to get yourself caught?*

I ignore him, knowing Slushie is just on the other side of the wall. And that he's a voice inside my head.

*I'll give you some props, setting up my murder like a suicide. Raping Emma might've helped your case—you can thank me later. The guilt caused me to kill myself.*

*If you keep killing everybody to resemble suicide, though, you're going to get caught,* Alex adds. *You'll be linked to the victims. It's only a matter of time.*

"I'm not going to kill anybody else," I hiss through my teeth.

*Is that what you said after you killed me? It's what you're good at. It's your purpose.*

My purpose? God wouldn't put me on this Earth to kill. No, no. Only Satan plants those ideas.

*Are you saying the devil is more powerful than God? I thought you were supposed to be a Bible thumper.*

I'm unable to find solid reasoning, so I remain quiet.

*There are thousands of murderers out there. Why would God not smite them down if he didn't want them to do what they do? He wants them to cleanse the world of the immoral. Wash the scum off the street. Soldiers kill more people than you ever will. Do you think they are murderers, damned to hell?*

*And, hey, I accept my death, knowing it's part of God's will.*

*She screamed when I entered her,* Tanner muses. *I like it when they scream; it just gets me harder.*

My nails bite into my closed fists as I see his memories—no—when I imagine what he must've seen. He's not there; I'm just going crazy. Just going crazy, ha. Do insane people have awareness of their madness?

*You know,* Alex discloses. *I think I saw something on Discovery or somewhere that if you kill somebody, their soul becomes part of you.*

"You don't watch the Discovery Channel," I say absently.

*I'm more knowledgeable than you think.*

I chuckle under my breath—not entirely sure what about—trying to keep quiet but unable to quit.

"*Friends* is not that funny," Slushie hollers from his room.

"Watch more than one episode and you'll see," I retort, slapping the wall.

*See, you are born to kill people like Tanner,* Alex continues. *I was just the catalyst that got this reaction going. A true honor, really. You're going to do great things, Ollie, I know it.*

"I'm not evil," I whisper unconvincingly to myself.

*No, you're just insane,* Tanner reassures.

I close my eyes. Maybe I'll wake up, and this will all just be some screwed-up fever dream. The voices say this will not be the case. They're right.

# Monday, August 19
## Oliver

**I can't remember** the last time I was completely on my own. Not like alone alone, of course, but without friends or family. People I'm acquainted with. In college, I won't know virtually anybody. I guess there's Slushie, but we don't have any of the same classes together and aren't even on campus at the same time most days. I'm starting anew. A fresh start. Or as much of a fresh start I can get with two bodies buried because of me thirty minutes away.

*You'll never be alone with us,* Alex speaks up.

*We've got your back,* Tanner joins.

I ignore them. The only way they'll disappear is if I ignore them. I'm in control, not the other way around.

When I pull into the parking lot I had parked in for orientation, I'll have to face the first challenge of the day sooner than expected, as it's completely full. I drive to the next. Full as well. There's a couple of parking garages on campus too.Full and full. What the hell. It was so empty just a couple weeks ago. I get back onto the main road then take the third exit on the roundabout to get back on campus. BB&T Arena is on my right, and I pull into its parking lot. I have to find somewhere closer to park in the future.

I glance at my dashboard and see I have ten minutes till my class starts. I grab my bag and hustle to where I guesstimated the science building was, around a glorified pond dubbed Loch Norse, past a statue of a dragon—what I presumed was the Loch Norse Monster—finally making it to the dull, gray building with a surplus of windows. I check my schedule for the twentieth time in the last twenty-four hours and walk to the third floor. I pause outside room 308, refer again to my schedule. Damn it! It's 208. I run back downstairs, glancing at my watch as I do. Shit, a minute late. How am I supposed to make a good first impression on my professor if I'm a minute late?

*Kill them*, Alex offers.

I take a deep breath and walk in, awkwardly nodding my head at the professor—a middle-aged guy rocking a ponytail—while I don't make eye contact with a single peer as I take a seat in the second row. Everybody knows that the front row for the stereotypical kiss-asses, while the back row is where the slack-offs sleep through the lecture, so I decide to go with a happy medium.

Now safely seated, I pull out my Surface laptop and open up a previously saved Word file from an already-made file: "Chemistry 120." I glance around and attempt to maintain a complicated composure of both indifference and excitement to win the approval of my classmates and the professor. An extremely attractive girl smiles at me from the far side of the front row. I shyly return it before ducking behind my computer.

"I apologize for starting late," the hippie professor starts. "I had technical difficulties."

Maybe my first impression isn't completely terrible.

"My name is Dr. Sampson, but you can call me Joe," he continues. "We'll keep today chill and just go over the syllabus and try to get you guys out of here a little early."

Maybe college professors aren't the pompous, stuck-up people I thought they were.

"Let's start off with an icebreaker," Joe says. "I know you guys hate this as I did, but it not only helps me get to know you guys, but it also helps you guys get to know your peers, who you guys could very well be taking many classes with."

*How many times is he going to say "you guys"?*

"We'll start with the young lady over on the end," he says, gesturing over at the girl who had smiled at me.

"Hi, I'm Kat," she looks around the room, eyes like that of a forest in the middle of the summer straying on me—or was that just my imagination? "I'm a chemistry major on the pre-pharm track. Um, and I like to write. More specifically, I like to write novels."

*A hot chick that's a writer*, Alex says. *Marry her.*

I ignore him, staring at the back of her platinum hair.

*"Ollie, can you give me any tips on becoming a New York Times bestselling author?" she asks as we sit together in a hot tub. "I know you're a screenwriter, but after winning an Oscar for 2020, you must have a few tricks up your sleeve."*

*I move closer to her lean, tan body, wrapping my muscular arm around her. "Come over sometime, and I'll show you."*

*Gunshots fill the rec center, followed by screams. I separate myself from Kat and hop out of the tub. The gunman comes around the corner, firing into the nearby pool. I look at the red pool, filled with floating bodies, and then at Kat. She stares back at me, shaking with fear. I run at the man as he turns to shoot at me. The* dack-dack-dack *of the machine gun fills my ear as the bullets whistle by me. I feel an excruciating pain in my left shoulder as I'm hit. But I don't stop and form tackle him. I grab the gun and unload it into his face till it's just an abstract painting.*

*I limp over to Kat, keeping pressure on my wound, now bleeding profusely. She meets me halfway and helps me to the ground.*

*"Why did you do that?" she asks with tears in her eyes.*

*"Because living without you would be more painful than death," I* rasp.

*"I love you, Ollie."*

*"I—"*

"And you, sir?" Joe asks, looking directly at me.

I jerk toward him, startled out of my daydream. "I'm a biology major on the pre-med track. And I, uh, like to write. More specifically, I like to write scripts. And yeah."

Kat looks back at me, surprised but smiling widely.

College gives us a fresh start. And Kat *will* be a part of it.

**"What have you** done, Ollie?" I ask no one in particular.

I sit in my cramped office at the rundown police department. In front of me is the file on Alexander Behr, Ollie's brother. We don't usually keep files for suicides, but the brutal nature of it called for us to do it. And also there's not much to do around here.

Alex had killed himself by jumping out of the attic window. He was just fifteen. There was only one other person home—Ollie. The body itself was pretty beat up, but jumping from three stories would do that. No signs of a struggle were reported. It was a simple case of suicide, and I had quickly marked it up as so.

But now that's two apparent suicides connected with Ollie, and, oh, I really hope these are just coincidences. With them being almost a year apart, there's not enough evidence to pursue this investigation. No judge with any sense would give me a warrant, and privately interviewing Ollie is grounds for a possible unpaid suspension.

Remaining sedentary, however, could result in another murder disguised as a suicide. Serial killers are terrifying by how they blend in so perfectly with the rest of society. It's ridiculous to think Ollie could be one of them, but I have to keep my mind free of feelings and bias. I'll have to tread carefully on this one. Lives may depend on it.

**"One Butterscotch frozen**—the frappucino—Swolboi with extra protein," I say as I give the drink to a guy with a string tank top, squiggly veins popping in his shoulders. "Have a good day."

That was Emma's and my second customer in the past ten minutes. Swolbois is really starting to pop.

"Business is booming," I express my thoughts to her, really just wanting to start a conversation. She's been understandably quiet lately. I want the old Emma back.

"Yeah," she says softly. Her face is still pretty swollen with the sickly yellow of a healing bruise and her nose at a crooked angle that would never be quite the same. The area under her eyes is pitch black. I don't think she's gotten much sleep—if any—since the … incident. "I'm sure Tanner would have bought us all a steak dinner with how many customers we brought in today. Who knew his death would've put us on the map?"

Tanner had gotten his own segment on the seven o'clock news—goes to show what little happens here. They *mourned* the bastard. They talked about how much of a loss it was to the community. How he would've been a huge success one day. Emma wanted to keep the rape secret, so now Tanner dies a saint. It all pisses me off, but at least Emma's safe, along with many other young women. I slew a monster. I'm the hero, not him

"That bastard deserved what he got," I say.

"Deserved what he got? His suicide?"

*Shit.* "You know what I mean."

"What he did to me," she says slowly, "is unforgivable, and I know he'll rot in hell for it. But he was there for me long before Swolbois. I was a foster child my entire life. I never knew my parents. His parents were fostering, and I was with them for the last three years before I turned eighteen. I didn't get along with any of the girls—they were all just super prissy and all into shopping and boys. Tanner was the only one I could get along with. And before you say anything, I didn't ever have a crush on him; he was like my older brother. By the time I had turned eighteen, he had bought this place and started Swolbois with the money he had saved up for college—he dropped out in his first semester. He gave me a high-paying job when he really couldn't afford it at the time." She starts to tear up, and I wrap an arm around her. "I really don't know where I'd be without him  . But I guess I do know how much I meant to him."

*See,* Tanner says, *you just killed her ride-or-die. You really think she's happier now that I'm gone? You'll never be able to replace me. Never.*

*She would never be—or feel—safe with Tanner out there,* Alex refutes. *Taking his life possibly saved hers. A few weeks of grief is better than a lifetime of Fear.*

"I'm sorry, Emma." I hug her. "I didn't know."

She sniffles and wipes her eyes with the back of her hand.

A customer walks through the front door and approaches the counter.

"I got her," I say, nodding at the short girl, wearing only a sports bra and yoga pants, her blonde hair pulled into a loose bun. "Go take a break."

She nods and pushes through the swinging doors.

"Hi, how can I help you?" I ask before noticing that her eyes are watery.

*This is not my day.*

"This is the first time I've been here since he … since he passed," she says, looking around as if seeing it for the first time.

I pick at some imaginary speck on my shirt.

"I'm sorry. I should introduce myself." She puts a strained smile on her face and sticks her hand across the counter. "I'm McKaela. I don't know if Tanner mentioned me at all."

"Just briefly."

*That bitch is my ex.*

"Well, a lawyer came by yesterday with Tanner's will. He gave me this." She gestures around the parlor. "Plus a considerable sum of money."

I open my mouth to ask why but then see that her stomach is bulging slightly—I really need to work on my awareness; lack of it will get me caught. She's pregnant. Pregnant with Tanner's baby, whose father I had just killed.

*And now my son will grow up without ever knowing his father,* Tanner says. *Who's the real monster here?*

What have I done?

*You saved a kid from being abused and then abandoned,* Alex says. *You prevented other young girls from being in the same situation.*

*And not to mention he was with Chloë when he knocked McKaela up. Growing up without a father is better than it being Tanner.*

I apologize with a deeper meaning than she realizes. I'm unable to meet her eyes.

"I'm going to keep it," she says without me asking, almost thinking out loud as if I wasn't there. "I don't think I would have it in me to kill my own child. I just don't understand why he would leave me alone with it."

She wipes the corner of her eye with the back of her hand, and I hand her a napkin. I open my mouth then close it. How can I reassure the woman carrying the child of a man I murdered?

*Just confess,* Tanner offers. *Or kill her and my unborn child. That seems to be the way you like to deal with your problems.*

"If there's anything I can do …" I finally say.

"No, thank you. I've probably burdened you too much already."

*More than you'll ever know.*

"It's just been a long several days." She straightens herself. "Now where's everybody else? I came here to meet my, uh, employees, I guess, before I got a bit sidetracked there."

I lead her to the back room, thinking I'll never be able to escape the darkness of my short past. Escape the Fear.

# Thursday, August 22
## Oliver

**As part of** Chemistry 120, I have to take a three-hour lab. Partaking in anything school related that long will usually turn me off, but I'm actually looking forward to it. I'll get to make explosions and melt stuff, basically do some Walter White stuff. It sounds amazing.

I find my way to the correct laboratory, and sitting on the near end is Kat.

*Sit next to her.* Thankfully only I am taking residence inside my head right now. I think.

I walk past her to the other side of the room, attempting a soft smile accentuated by a slight head nod, but instead grin madly and move my head sharply. She smiles politely, her eyes lighting up with recognition. I sit down next to a skinny black guy who introduces himself as Marcus.

"Welcome to Chemistry 120 Lab. My name is Dr. French, and I expect to not be called by anything else." The professor rises behind her desk, and I realize why I never noticed her when I walked in. She's tiny; I'd say five-foot-two at the most and weighing no more than a hundred pounds. Even being so short, she stands tall, her chin pointed up and flat chest out. It almost looks like she's got a stick up her ass.

"Today we will discuss safety measures to a great extent, as that is the most important part of each day."

*Yeah, there's definitely something lodged up there.*

"But before that, I will quickly assign you into groups, based on your GPA—I realize most of you are freshmen, so I took the initiative to collect it from your former high schools. Everyone will do their part of the lab or fail.

"Oliver Behr, Marcus Julius, Diego Martínez, and Katherine Watters are Group 1, sitting right where Miss Watters is. Congratulations on being the smartest in the class." She looks at us coldly, her perfectly straight black bob giving me some serious Edna from *The Incredibles* vibes. "You four better not disappoint me."

"She looks like she hasn't been laid in like … ever," Kat notes as I sit next to her.

"Yeah, a total bitch," I agree, and she laughs loudly and pleasantly at that, although quickly covering her mouth with her hand, glancing over at Mrs.—Dr. French. She was fortunately berating a few scared-looking guys at the bottom of the GPA scale.

"You said you like to write, right?" she asks me. "Have you finished any novels?"

"Actually, I write screenplays," I reply. "And I finished a thriller but couldn't find anybody interested in it. I'm working on a dystopian right now. What about you?"

"Oh yeah, I remember now. That's so cool. I've written a couple of literary fictions that remain unpublished."

I open my mouth to continue our conversation but am interrupted by French. "You are responsible for your own pair of goggles, but I will provide some for today's lab. And when I say goggles, I mean goggles, not the more comfortable safety glasses. They need to adhere to your face all around your eyes, and if they don't leave a red imprint, then they're not tight enough.

"Next, you will have to wear gloves at all times. We won't be handling any overly caustic chemicals," *Darn.* "—but many can cause persistent irritation."

For the next half-hour, she goes over all the safety measures for each piece of equipment and chemical we will be handling throughout the semester. Finally, she directs our attention to the materials laying out on our tables.

"For today's experiment, you will be performing a titration to determine the concentration of sodium hydroxide, a base, by neutralizing the acidic potassium hydrogen phthalate dissolved in water. This lab requires acute precision to get an accurate measurement, as you will need to slowly drip the sodium hydroxide from the burette into the flask containing the KHP solution until it turns pink—caused by an indicator called phenolphthalein. To pass this week, you must have a percent RSD of 2, which means your measurements can only differ by a one-hundredth of a milliliter. The rest of the procedures are found on Canvas, but I expect you to arrive next week with a detailed protocol for that day's experiment. If you have any questions, I'll be at my desk."

I pull up the instructions on my phone and start reading it.

"So, where are you guys from?" Kat asks us.

"I live just thirty minutes south of here," I answer. "You?"

"I'm from all the way up in southern Michigan."

"That seems like a long drive for a commuter college."

"We have to move around a lot for my dad's work, but I spent the majority of my teenage years here. I used to go to Lincoln P. Douglas, and a lot of old friends came here. You've heard of it?"

I realize I had made a face when she mentioned Douglas. "Yeah, I have a friend that graduated from there."

"Oh, that's cool! What's their name?"

"Colton Dunner."

There's no reason to bring up Jensen.

"Oh, that name sounds familiar," she says in a way that suggests it does not. "But anyway, what about you two?" directing her question at Diego and Marcus.

"Mexico." Diego is the first to respond. "Lived there all my life."

"Why'd you choose here?"

"They have a really great international student program."

"Are you an international student too?" I ask Marcus.

"No, I'm from Cincinnati."

"Oh. Cool." I hurry to change the subject. "Okay, does anybody know if we're going to do any Walter White shit?"

"Walter White shit," Kat repeats, giggling. "No, I glanced over the syllabus, and looks like it's not going to get much more exciting than today."

"Awesome," I reply and open the bottle with the NaOH label. "Damn it." I had already gotten some of the base on me.

**"Now faith is** confidence in what we hope for and assurance about what we do not see,'" Pastor Paul Lewis reads from Hebrews in his usual button-down. "'By faith Abel brought God a better offering than Cain did. By faith Enoch was taken from this life, so that he did not experience death. By faith Noah, when warned about things not yet seen, in holy fear built an ark to save his family. By faith Abraham, when called to go to a place he would later receive as his inheritance, obeyed and went, even though he did not know where he was going.'"

Even though I haven't spoken or seen my family since I found out I killed Alex, I still go to Zion Baptist. God is my only chance of redemption.

*You already redeemed yourself when you killed Tanner,* Alex says after being absent for some time.

*Heyyy,* Tanner responds, sounding actually hurt.

*And you will continue serving the Good Lord by being His sword,* Alex continues. *His Angel of Death.*

*I'm not killing anymore,* I add to my swirling thoughts.

*I'm sure every serial killer has thought that at some point.*

I try not to think about that and return my attention back to Lewis.

"—these legends of the Bible dealt with more hardships than most of us will ever experience. Abel was murdered by his own brother, for goodness sake. I've had some spats with my siblings, but that goes beyond imagination."

*You can imagine, can't you, Ollie?* Alex antagonizes.

"But they kept their faith in God that He would deliver them from their sufferings. And God didn't always come through for them like with Abel. Without faith, though, we become the jealous Cain. Without faith, we become the temptress Hagar.

"If you put your faith in God—if you place faith over fear—you will prosper. None of these people got what they wanted, but they were all rewarded for their faith. We all want something in life, praying to God constantly that He will give it to us. Whether it be a job or a spouse, or the Bengals to win a Super Bowl. Even though we may not get what we're asking for, if we remain faithful in His plan for us, He will commend us for it."

I glance over at Colton like I had done many other times the message had struck me any sort of way, before remembering he had joined a church closer to UC. I suddenly feel lonely.

*You still have us*, Tanner says.

*Yeah, we'll always be here*, Alex joins.

That's what Faith has gotten me, two victims I had killed now stuck in my head. Lewis is wrong; he doesn't know the power of Fear and the frailties of Faith. Fear is what's going to keep me going. Keep me from killing again. Fear of the police, Fear of the ghosts inside my head, Fear of getting close to others. Fear of myself. Faith is dead. Fear is all there is. All there ever will be.

**"I c-can't b-believe** this is all of us," Slushie says.

"Have any of y'all heard anything from anybody?" Celeste asks.

We're back at GloGolf for the first time in what feels like years, which probably isn't far off. But this time we invited the entire group, except, well, no one other than us showed up.

"I talked to Tyrese a few days after we last met up. But nothing since," I answer.

"What did you talk about?" Celeste inquires.

"Uh," I stutter, formulating a lie. "You know, just guy stuff."

They both give me questioning looks for good reason. The "guy stuff" you talk about with Tyrese is sex. I just shake my head, not bothering to come up with a better answer. Some things just need to remain a secret.

*You got that right*, Tanner agrees.

"All right." I drop my neon blue ball on the glowing green and attempt to change the subject. "How's college been going for you guys?"

"I never t-thought I w-would say this, but I m-miss high school," Slushie replies. "Everyw-where I look, t-there are strangers. I m-miss b-being able to see you g-guys every day."

"I can't say I miss high school," Celeste says, "but I do miss the familiar faces. I love you guys …”

I putt the ball up the slight incline, where it lines up right next to the hole.

“… and you're my best friends, yet I barely see y'all anymore.”

Great, now I got blue balls.

“I love you too,” I say, but somehow am unable to meet her eyes. Why is it that whenever I'm around her, my feelings always rush back at me? She has a boyfriend, and I like Kat. Right?

*A girlfriend would just get in the way of the Lord's plans for you,* Alex says. *You control your feelings, not the other way around.*

*I think you should go for it,* Tanner disagrees. *I mean, look at that ass.*

I find myself blushing and hide it by walking to my ball.

“How's it going with you and that girl?” Celeste asks Slushie. “What's her name again?”

“It's Callie,” he answers. “And w-we broke up last w-week.”

“I'm sooo sorry.” Now it's her turn to blush. “I didn't know.”

“It's okay.” He shrugs as he lines up to putt. “I broke up w-with her, actually. God removed the scales from m-my eyes, and I realized she's not as good a person as I t-thought she w-was.”

She hugs him, a side hug, but I still feel a red-hot nail of jealousy strike through me. *I killed two people who are now stuck in my head, and fear I will continue down this road, because the seed of evil inside me has blossomed into a shepherd's tree—damn my bio lab professor for his botanical zeal—its strong roots grown deep into my heart. Can I get a hug for that?*

“What about you?” I ask quickly as I tap the ball in, not meeting her eyes. “You still with Jake?”

“Yeah. I don't get to see him as much as I'd like, with him going to Michigan State.” She examines her fingernails. “Although I don't know how long I can do this long-distance thing. I love him, but …” She swings her club and hits the red ball. It rolls gently up the slope, falling softly into the hole. A hole-in-one, but there's no celebration.

I'd been looking forward to this, as I'm sure they were too, but it seems like we all can't let go of our past. Slushie acts like he's over Callie, but I heard him crying on the other side of the ever-so-thin wall just a few days ago. Celeste is trying to hold together a failing relationship. And me, well … it's Celeste. The forbidden fruit that I yet again want to sink my teeth into. Although, this time I might have a chance. But I might just be setting myself up to be heartbroken. I'll have to play my cards right in the coming weeks and months.

"Ollie?" I realize I had zoned out and Celeste had been calling my name. "Are you talking to anybody?"

*Yes, actually. She's super hot, and I think—*

"Nope." I smile wanly at her. "I'm dry as the Sahara."

## Monday, September 30
## Oliver

**The rec center** at Northern is super nice, which I guess is what I should expect for paying three thousand plus dollars a year—and that's with a nice scholarship—to go here. On my right when I enter are two basketball courts with a volleyball net lining the center of one of them. On the left are the locker rooms where I enter. There are two types of lockers, one which costs you a certain amount I never bothered to find out and can be used throughout the duration of the semester, and one that's free. I went with the free one, even with its disadvantages of there being a lock with a temporary code that doesn't even work—maybe it's not so nice. It's not like we really need it, with NKU being one of the safest colleges in the country.

I get changed into my workout clothes—a faded Adidas tank with shorts a bit too short—mix my pre-workout and exit as quickly as I had entered. I walk up the stairs, peering down through the window at teens swimming around in the indoor pool. I eye the empty hot tub—

*I love you, Ollie.*

—for a second before moving on. The gym itself really isn't that big given the size of everything else in the building, but it's not the quantity that caught my eye, but the quality. There are only free weights, not like the smith machines at Planet Fitness. The barbells go over sixty pounds. Just things like that. Also, there's a power room, where you can deadlift and clean-and-jerk to your contentment. I almost feel like a professional bodybuilder lifting here. It's an iron paradise. A sanctuary of sweat. I need a sponsorship for Project Rock.

Mondays are chest days to start the week off right, so I go grab myself a free bench. I throw on a forty-five on each side and lie down, preparing for my two-minute mental setup.

"Hey, Ollie!"

I sit up quickly, banging my head on the bar. It's Kat, and I stand up to meet her as she smiles with pleasant surprise that only widened when I bumped my head. She's wearing a sports bra with yoga pants, her tan, lean body exposed to the world. I go to respond but am attacked with a sudden hug. It's just a quick one, over before I can even relax.

"Uh, hey," I say, my cheeks on fire and my hand going to scratch my opposite arm in the typical awkward fashion. "You getting swole?"

"Oh yeah, haha." She seems distracted, but I choose not to pursue it. At least not yet. "Just a little bit, I guess."

We stand there for a bit, awkwardly looking around the gym.

"Well, I'll let you get back to getting *swole*," she finally says, turning to go, and that's when I see a dark, oblong bruise, just above the waistband.

*None of your business*, I try to tell myself, but I can't resist. And I swear if somebody did that to her ...

"Hey, Kat." She turns around. "That's a nasty bruise you have there."

"I was just playing softball with some people and took one on my back," she says, smiling softly. Was that a slight twitch of her nose? A sudden glance to the left? She's lying. Woe to the son of a bitch who did that.

*Maybe she is telling the truth*, Tanner suggests. *Not every girl you crush on has an evil boyfriend.*

*Coming from the guy who raped Emma*, Alex disagrees. *That's not a bruise from a softball. That's a belt, Ollie. You can't let pieces of shit like that get away. He'll continue abusing her till he kills her. You have to protect her, Ollie.*

"Oh, okay," I reply, faking a smile. "I hope it gets better."

"Thanks." *There! A tremble on her lips.*

Once she leaves the gym, I pull up Instagram and type her name into the search bar. I don't have to scroll far before I see her beautiful face in the profile picture. No guy, good sign. I click on it. Nothing incriminating in her bio—just NKU '23 with a black-and-yellow emoji—but my investigation stops there. It's a private account. I'm sure she'll accept my follow request, but I can't send it just after I talked to her. That might come off a bit creepy. I'll send it this evening.

Even if she does have a boyfriend, it could be from somebody else. I can't be rash. I have to play this out smartly. But the bastard who did that will get what he deserves. I swear to God he will.

**"Some parts were** translated from a fifteenth-century Syrian manuscript when this work was introduced to Europe around 1700."

"*Arabian Nights*," Emma answers the Final Jeopardy. We're on break in the back, while Chloë and Brie cover up front.

"What is *Aladdin*?" the three contestants scribble on their podiums. "What is *One Thousand and One Nights* or *Arabian Nights* is the correct answer," Alex Trebek says. "Ruby you bet $6,288, bringing your total to $2."

"How'd you know that?" I ask, taking a slurp from my Fruity Pebbles frozen Swolboi

"I don't know." She shrugs. "It's a good book."

"I didn't think you could even read." I stare at her blankly before breaking into a smile. She just glares at me.

"Anyways, how'd your date go?" I inquire.

"It went really well, and he seemed like a really great guy, but …" She swirls the straw around in her own frappuccino. "I don't think I'm ready for a relationship yet."

I nod but don't say anything. I mean, what can I say. *I know how you feel?* None of us know how she feels.

"Enough with that." She comes out of her cloud. "What about you? Is there a special girl in your life? Or guy?" She smiles without showing her teeth. "I'm still not convinced you're straight."

"Actually, there's two of them. Two *girls*," I admit.

"Thirsty much?"

"No, I don't know. I think I like one, then I'll see the other and my feelings will completely flip."

"I see. Yeah, that's tough."

"It gets better. They both have boyfriends."

Kat had accepted my follow request just a few minutes after I had sent it. It didn't take long to determine she is seeing someone; you don't take multiple pictures with the same guy if you're not dating him.

*Unless you're just really close friends*, Tanner disagrees.

I tune him out. What does he know? He's a rapist and. But I do need to wait and see. Rashness will get me arrested. Although I think a part of me thinks that would be for the best. Everybody close to me would be a lot safer then.

*No*, Alex argues. *They'll be safer if you're free to protect them.*

"Oh, that sucks." She grabs my hand laying on the table beside my drink, but then quickly retracts it. "I'm sorry."

"Yeah, I just wish I could control my feelings," I say, opening up for the rare occasion.

"Me too," she says quietly.

McKaela barges in before either of us could say something, leading me to jump in my seat. There's now a noticeable bulge under her Swolbois T-shirt.

"Weren't you guys just on break?" she asks.

We just play with our hands. Apart, not together.

"Ah, you guys know I don't care." She leans against the wall, tired. She has been at it nonstop. Even close to a month after Tanner's death, she's being pulled into meetings with suits to discuss his assets. On top of that, she's trying to run a shop that's been getting more and more attention by millennials every day. "I just wanted to let you know that I'm gone the rest of the evening; I have a potential parent who wants to meet with me."

McKaela had decided she couldn't raise that child at her age by herself but didn't want to abort it, believing it equal to murder. She still wants to be in close contact but just can't handle the responsibilities associated with having a kid while running this business. Not to mention it's a bastard.

She leaves, and I excuse myself to the bathroom.

*She's giving up my child*, Tanner says. *What a bitch.*

"It's my fault," I tell my reflection. "I've caused all this. Without me, she'd still be working at Planet Fitness and be able to raise the child with its father."

*As I've said a million times*, Alex assures me, *it's better for that kid to have a loving family that cares for him, rather than a dad that beats him.*

I know that as long as I work here, I'm going to feel the guilt of my sins, whether it's right or not. I leave the restroom and walk past Emma—staring off into space and absently sipping her Swolboi, as she's been prone to do ever since she was raped—to McKaela's office. Grabbing a pen and a pad of paper, I jot down a quick note. Two weeks from today, I will be leaving Swolbois permanently.

**"Barth just announced** he's running for president for another term," I read from my iPhone. "I think he's finally going to put China in its place."

"Good, Wall will just let Xiang walk all over us, relying on them more and more," Celeste agrees. "We may even become socialist if Barth doesn't win."

"No politics at the dinner table," Missy says, annoyed. Her family's extremely liberal, so it's a miracle we got together. "Anyway, Barth would probably just start World War III."

"And would end it before it even started." I casually knock down her rebuttal and then turn to my daughter. "I can't even imagine what it's like at Thomas Moore."

"It's not as bad as I thought. Most people stay away from politics. But you can still tell that most people—students and professors—are liberal."

I take a bite out of my burger. "Have you made any friends there?"

"No, not really." She sips her water. "I really only hang out with Ollie and Slushie."

How can I tell her he's a possible serial killer without telling her he's a possible serial killer?

"Has Oliver been acting any *differently* at all?" I try to ask this nonchalantly, but I was never a good actor.

"I mean, he's been a little quiet, but he's never super talk-ative anyways." She looks at me oddly, suspiciously before a small smile touches her lips. "Why? Do you think I like him? Dad, just because things aren't going great with Jake doesn't mean I'm going to jump to the closest guy to me. I mean, Ollie's a great guy, but I don't like him that way. It'd be weird like dating a …" she trails off.

"Brother?" Missy asks.

She nods, a slight blush rising to her cheeks.

*She likes him. Why does she have to like him?*

"It was just a simple question," I defend myself, raising my hands.

I need to find concrete evidence that he killed his boss and brother. I've hit a wall, but there has to be a weak spot. I just have to find it.

"This is great corn pudding." I change the subject, waving around the veggie delicacy on my fork. "Did Jamie finally give you her recipe?"

"What are you talking about?" Missy asks, hiding her smile behind her cabernet. "It's always this good."

"Yeah. She definitely stole that from the Hoppis," Celeste agrees.

Until I find something against him, she'll be in constant danger. And I can't just stop her from seeing Oliver.

I have to find something.

# Monday, October 28
## Oliver

**"Bohr's Model is** used to illustrate the quantum energy levels of electrons as they orbit around the nucleus," Joe lectures, drawing four circles, each inside the other. "When the electrons absorb energy, they will rise to the next level, and then they will relax, releasing light and generating a line spectrum."

This sounds a lot more boring than the quanite stuff Wes raves about.

He moves to a blank area of the board. "In 1926, Erwin Schrödinger created his own model to show this on a more detailed level. The s-orbital here—" He draws a circle. "—is found starting at the first level, containing at max two electrons. The p-orbital—" A figure eight. "—is found starting at the second level with a maximum of six electrons. And finally the d-orbital—" P-orbital with a donut-like shape in the middle. "—is found starting at the third level and contains a maximum of ten electrons. There's also an f-orbital, but we won't worry about that now."

I frantically type all this down on my Surface, switching back and forth from the pen and keyboard. I have to keep my mind fully occupied, or else it will drift away. Drift away and be taken hold of by my victims.

"Schrödinger also created an electron orbital diagram as part of his model to illustrate the atomic orbitals with the spins of the specific electrons." He begins to draw this before glancing at his watch. "It looks like I'm out of time. Next class, I will go over some later rules that add to this model. For now, make sure to review today's lecture. This isn't like high school; you guys won't pass by cramming the night before. Enjoy the rest of your day, you guys."

I shut my laptop and place it delicately in my backpack.

"Hey, Ollie."

I jerk my head up to find Kat standing in front of my desk.

"Hey." I stand up, simultaneously pulling my bag over my shoulder. "Did you get any of that?"

"Bits and pieces," she answers in a way that implies that she *does* fully *get* it and probably already *got* the next lecture. "Are you doing anything Thursday night?"

"That's Halloween, right? I have work till eight, but I'm free after."

"Oh, that's great! My boyfriend's having a party at his house. It doesn't start till ten, and you're more than welcome to come."

A picture of the bruise on her back flashes through my mind. A bruise most likely inflicted by her boyfriend. Alcohol and weed uncover many secrets.

"I wouldn't want to be anywhere else." I flash her a smile that never quite reaches my eyes.

**Law is impersonal.** It is objective, not subjective. Based on fact rather than feelings. It shuns a grieving mother with a cold heart while wrapping a matching pair of semen samples with a warm hug. Law is effective at establishing order and ripping killers off the street. But what about stopping them after their first victim? If the police had believed Konerak Sinthasomphone—wandering around naked in the street, drugged out of his mind and with hydrochloric acid injected into his brain—Jeffrey Dahmer would have been arrested two months earlier, and he and four others would still be alive.

Sometimes you have to put the law in your own hands to achieve justice. To save lives.

Now I stand in front of the Behrs' garage, planning to cause a crime to stop one. If Oliver did kill his brother, it would have been messy. Evidence may still be around.

I know Oliver has a younger brother at the age to be trick-or-treating, and with having only one son still living at home, the house should be empty during this time. But to be certain, I Uber to a home down the street—the driveways are so long here that I probably wasn't noticed—and hiked the rest of the way, stopping two hundred feet away in the neighboring woods. When I see a large, gray SUV pull out of their equally long driveway, I wait fifteen minutes to make sure they didn't forget any-

-thing and return, before approaching.

The garage faces away from the only visible neighbors, so I flip the pad cover without any fear of being seen. I pull out a small notebook with a series of four-digit numbers written down, from birthdays to Doug's and Megan's  marriage year. Almost all of these potential codes I was able to find relatively easily online. I start with the date of their nuptials, and it's a winner as the garage opens a little too noisily for comfort.

I move past the overflowing bins of various sporting equipment to the door leading inside. I ready myself to quickly press in the same code for the alarm and then press down on the handle, wondering what I would do if the door was locked. It's not, and there's no blaring of a security system that welcomes me. I check the security pad next to the door and see it blinks green as expected. Who sets their alarm when they're just going to be out for a couple hours?

Meaning to go up to the attic, where Alex supposedly killed himself, I find myself in Megan and Doug's room. I drift slowly across the carpet to a series of framed photos on the wooden drawers placed facing the king bed. I pick up the closest one; it's her and Doug standing together on a beach—Jamaica, if I remember correctly.

*Damn, she was beautiful. Was and still is.*

I realize my slight infidelity and quickly back out of the door, setting the picture down where I hopefully remember it was.

I now move up to the attic, opening doors at random—the report on Alex's apparent suicide had mentioned the attic was accessible through an actual door rather than having to climb a ladder—and pause outside of what I imagine was Alex's room. Photos of him with friends still remain above the made bed, along with his other possessions. I solemnly close the door. You'd have to be messed up to premeditatively kill your brother. If Oliver did kill him, it was most likely a crime of passion, but still. I really, *really* hope he's innocent.

I open the door across the hall, and bingo. It's dark, and after fruitlessly searching for a light switch or cord, I use the flashlight on my iPhone. There actually appears to be no lighting installed, but the light from the phone reveals that the few items present are covered in a fine layer of dust; probably haven't been touched since the Behrs moved in. I shut the door behind me and turn off the flashlight; now the only light comes from the large window. Next to it is a bar chair. I move a box of books smelling of mildew from below the window and pull out a spray bottle of luminol that I had swiped from the lab. I spray the now-free area, and drops of a substance glow blue. Blood. If Alex had indeed committed suicide, there wouldn't have been any blood inside. A judge, however, might say that might not even be his blood without bothering to test it; it's an old house. I need more evidence.

I turn in the direction I had entered and spray some more of the luminol, revealing several more drops. I continue this process, following the sparse trail of blood until I find myself in Oliver's old room. It's mostly cleared out, just a naked bed, a shelf containing a few knick-knacks, and a bedside table with a lamp. I spray the ground in front of me, revealing a large mass of the glowing remnants of blood.

Oliver murdered Alex. Killed him right here. This is what I had expected, but I'm taken aback, nonetheless.

I take a few pictures at different angles before turning to leave. The lamp catches my eye, and I pick it up with a gloved hand, spraying it completely. It glows brightly. I now have the how and where with enough evidence for cause to bring him in for questioning. But what bothers me is why?

# Thursday, October 31, 10:30 p.m.
## Oliver

**I don't really** know what I was expecting, but it's not this. No LEDs flash outside the windows. No beer cans litter the front yard. It doesn't even look like a party besides the low drum of rap and an underlying scent of marijuana in the air as I get out of my car. I walk across to the suburban home and knock on the stained-glass door. It swings open to reveal a young guy with shaggy, sweaty hair, holding a Corona.

"Shup, man," he says drunkenly. He turns aside, throwing me a strong whiff of weed. "Come gerab yershelf a beer."

He stumbles a little as I follow him inside. *How drunk can he be? The party only started thirty minutes ago.*

There's a surprisingly small number of people here—couldn't be more than ten. I grab a White Claw from the cooler—goes down a bit easier than beer—and take a sip, managing not to cringe at the taste.

"Ollie!" Kat appears around the corner, a guy right behind her, and gives me a side hug. "You came!"

I smile back at her and eye her shadow. He's skinny with jet-black hair that is slicked back. His dark clothes and glittering stud in his left ear add to the emo impression. A literal shadow.

*The Shadow.*

"How's it going?" He acknowledges me with a voice that is more vibrant than his appearance suggests. "Kat has told me a lot about you. Said you like to write too."

He says this without any signs of jealousy. No arm slung tightly around Kat. No watchful reproach. The prick doesn't even think of me as competition.

"Yeah, but I don't think I'm as good as her." I give her another smile that suggests something more than a simple gesture.

Still, he doesn't react. "Well, it's good to finally meet you."

"You too, Logan."

He looks at me curiously, as I realize he never told me his name, but then shrugs it off, probably assuming Kat had mentioned it. Kat, on the other hand, opens her mouth to pursue this.

"Hurricanes!" the drunk hippie yells from the kitchen, taking a long sip from a red Solo cup and saving me for the moment.

"Conner, haven't you had enough to drink tonight?" Kat yells.

"Thasha good one, Kat." He spills his drink onto the carpet. "Oops."

I follow the couple to the island where the cups are separated into five different groups.

"The ones over here—" A blond-haired guy, who looks even younger than me, comes from behind Conner and gestures at drinks at the far left. "—are Category 1. The ones here—" He points to the bunch on the right. "—are Category 5. You can figure out the rest.

"I also poured them, not Stonehead here. So, you can be sure they have the correct ratios of alcohol." He notices me for the first time. "I don't think we met. I'm Anthony, Logan's brother."

"Oliver. I go to school with Kat."

"Another Norse, huh." He grabs a Category 5, but Logan doesn't even react. "I never really considered going to college. I could be making as much money as an electrician as I could with a four-year degree except with the debt. With my grades, I wouldn't be able to get into any decent school, anyway."

"How old are you?" I can't be out-drunk by some kid.

"Sixteen." He points the drink in my direction. "Cheers, mate."

Kat and Logan both take a Category 5. I know I should just stick with the 2 or 3—I learned after a night with Tyrese that being wasted allows Tanner and Alex to get a bit of a step hold in my mind—but peer pressure trumps all, and I join them.

***

One drink in, my head already feels foggy. My own thoughts being taken over by my victims.

*Don't get too drunk*, Alex advises. *You need a clear head to kill him without getting caught.*

You can't just rely on us to guide you, Tanner adds.

Logan challenges me to beer pong, and with Kat watching me as well as the influence of the hurricane, I agree.

A card table is set up in the corner with the red Solo cups already placed.

I smile at Kat through a slight haze before taking my turn. Back and forth we go, beer running down both our faces. He's much better from plenty of practice, I'm sure. And soon he lands the ping-pong ball in my final cup. I chug the warm booze that seems to go down a bit easier than the last few.

"Hell of plaaayer," he congrats. I had only made four of the ten.

***

Two drinks in, me and Logan argue on the couch.

"Aaare you kiiidding? The Rwock would mesh hiim up." Logan laughs.

"He's the fuuckin' Wolverine," I defend Hugh. "He would do some Kungfuuu or shiit. The Rerock was just a fake wreshla."

"He's huuuuge thooo. And you don't mess with a Samoooaan."

"Size don't matter."

"You ushe that one a lot, don't'a."

"Oooh, fuuck offf." I storm off to the kitchen. "D'ya want a drrrink?"

"Heeell yeah, brooo."

***

Three drinks in, the voices begin to speak for me.

Me and Logan are back on the couch with Kat between us. He takes a puff from a brown cigarette.

"Want shum kussh?" He reaches over Kat with the doobie.

"Yes," Tanner answers for me, accepting the joint.

I take a long drag of the weed, falling into a coughing fit then pass the joint to Kat.

"How'd you get a gurl like 'er?" I inquire, staring at her, but she doesn't seem to notice.

"Oh, hell. It wush at shum partee like dis." He grabs the weed from Kat. "We both got stoned, and I screwed 'er. We've been 'gether e're since."

I see red through the haze. I almost stand ready to kill him now before Alex stops me.

Soon, Alex whispers in my head. Soon.

***

Three drinks and half a joint in, they take over.

My eyes linger uncontrollably over Kat's sizeable breasts. I need to kill Logan while I still have semi-control of myself, but drunken horniness persists.

"Mind if I borrow 'er for a shecond?" I ask Logan.

He waves his hand. "But if I catch ya with yer dick out, Imma kill you."

"Wattabout you?" I twirl her light hair between my fingers. "Ya wanna ... talk in da next room?"

She doesn't say anything, her small body unable to handle the amount of liquor we've drunk tonight. But when I stand up and pull her to me, she gets up. I guide us to a bedroom, which looks like it has already been used, as there's a soggy condom lying in the corner next to a hypodermic needle.

Tanner then pushes me deep into my own mind. He doesn't waste any time and rips off her blouse. His experienced hands nimbly unclip her bra, letting it slide to the floor. Then he stands there for a second as we both ogle at her perfect breasts, oscillating to a hypnotic rhythm, as she drunkenly sways with them. Now he flicks an erect nipple, eliciting a moan. Too loud of a moan.

Logan barges into the room. Apparently, the alcohol and the weed didn't affect his hearing.

"I told ya I'd kill ya if you tried to screw 'er," he slurs. "But first—" He pulls his penis out, flopping it lazily around. "Imma screw ya."

He marches toward me, pushing the still-dazed Kat out of the way. She hits the wooden floor hard, but he doesn't notice. Or doesn't care. She's just his plaything, but for some reason, she sticks with him. I'll help her with that.

It's Alex's turn to take over. He grabs Logan by the shoulders and twists him around, but not before his enormous, semierect penis (*is that why she sticks with him?*) rubs against me. I try to scamper away, but Alex is in control now, and he wraps my arm around Logan's throat and squeezes. We're both about equal size—at least in regard to height and weight—but Logan is drunk, while Alex is sober. I'm not sure how that's possible, and my head is too foggy to attempt to understand it.

Logan's knees buckle, and he slides down me, his penis now at a more modest size. His breathing ceases after five minutes. Alex maintains pressure for another five before releasing him. He brings me over to the bed gathering up the sheets and forming a noose. He ties the top end to the light fixture above us, yanking a couple times. In the corner next to the condom and needle is a desk chair with a velvet seat. He places it haphazardly under the fixture and slings Logan over his shoulder, teetering the literal dead weight. After many annoying attempts, he finally is able to loop the noose around Logan's neck. He steps back and admires his handiwork, enjoying it a bit too much. He puts a frown on my face when he realizes a rather large problem. Pulling Logan's pants up was a bit harder than it should have been and would have been rather funny under different circumstances, but finally, he's able to get the jeans zipped and buckled.

As Logan sways back and forth, I realize I don't care. I don't feel any satisfaction or any regret. Just nothing. That scares me more than anything else.

*Now you know what we have to do*, Alex says, forcing me to look at Kat. She looks pitiful lying there, eyes glazed, her breasts flopped over to the side.

*No, she's done nothing wrong. I—we—did this to protect her. What's the point if she dies?*

*She's seen too much.*

*Look at her. She's' wasted. She won't remember the last three hours.*

*We could always just rape her*, Tanner speaks up. I can hear the thirst in his voice. It disgusts me now that killing Logan had sobered me up.

*No. Rape is too messy*, Alex disagrees. *Too much DNA on her. And inside of her.*

*Imma kill you if ya touch 'er*, Logan adds. It took less than ten minutes to occupy my mind; they're coming faster.

*Okay, Ollie, if you want to keep her alive, we'll keep her alive*, Alex reassures me. *You're the boss.*

I stare forlornly at Kat—eyes closed in merciful sleep—and, now with full control of my body, I approach her.

"I'm sorry," I say quietly as I crouch down to run my hands through her soft, pale hair.

How much killing can I do before I lose myself?

*We'll take care of it, Ollie*, Alex says. *Now go to sleep.*

I lie down next to Kat and close my eyes. As I drift asleep, and my victims debate among themselves in my head, I know

I've already lost it.

# Friday, November 1, 9:00 a.m.
## Casey

**"Why did you** call so late?" I ask the young, pretty girl whose boyfriend is swinging in the next room. "You'd have to have noticed him."

Kat wraps her arms around herself from where she sits on the chair, dealing with something no girl her age should have to deal with.

*Damn, she's Celeste's age.*

"I … we were asleep," She's not able to meet my eyes with her tear-filled ones. Obviously hungover and with the place stinking of weed, I doubt that. Febreze only covers up so much.

We had gotten the call about an hour ago; there were just a few people here, the whole place scrubbed clean. The suicide obviously made me suspect Oliver, but I would've expected him to remain here. That would be the smart thing to do at least, which is what Oliver seems to be—covering up two separate murders is no small feat. Unless he's on to me, which would put Celeste in danger. I'll need to have someone to constantly watch her.

"Yeah sure," I continue. "Who was here?"

"Just us." She gestures at the three others gathered in the living room.

*Even with her boyfriend swinging from a ceiling fan, she remains loyal.*

"What about Oliver Behr?"

She glances up before returning her gaze to her lap. "No, I mean, he's in my chemistry class, but he didn't come. Not even after I invited him."

I take a slight risk, going against something we're taught not to do. "Okay, here's the deal. I know he was here, and I know you were all drunk, probably high as well. Oliver is my nephew. He had asked me to be his DD. He never called, but my boss did. And now I'm here. Just help me out. He has answered any of my calls."

"Show me."

"Excuse me?"

"The calls."

Pulling out my phone, I show her my call history with the local McDonald's that I spammed before I came here. I created a contact under the name "Ollie" with that number. Nobody memorizes numbers these days.

Kat scrutinized the iPhone for a minute, then sat back and picked at some loose skin on her right thumb as she considered it. "I don't remember much," she says finally. "Honestly. I woke up half-naked in that room, with Logan …"

"Go on," I push.

"I think he had taken advantage of me when I was out and killed himself from a mixture of guilt and alcohol."

"What's the last thing you remember?"

"Uh—" She grimaces and massages her temple. I fill a cup with water and take some Excedrin from the cabinet she points out.

"This was a lifesaver back in my college days," I say, handing her two tablets with the water.

"The last thing I remember was that they were arguing—"

"Arguing? About what?" I ask a bit too hastily.

"Just about who would win in a fight between Dwayne Johnson and Hugh Jackman," she says, a smile touching her lips for the first time this morning. "They were really drunk. We all were. I really don't remember anything after that."

I look for any signs of lying, but there are none.

"Okay, I believe you." I stand, motioning for her to do the same. "You can go now.

"And," I add as she turns to leave, "I'm really sorry. I have a daughter your age and couldn't fathom this happening to her."

She pauses but doesn't turn away before continuing on her way.

I walk over to Colin, who has just concluded his conversation with the forensics expert.

"Oliver was here," I tell him.

"You have to quit with this shit," Colin responds. "Just because you hate the kid doesn't mean he's some serial killer."

"I don't hate him—"

"No, you hate his mother. For dumping your ass in college for his father."

"That doesn't matter. This is the third suicide he's connected to in the past year and a half."

"You think an eighteen-year-old kid is responsible for all this? That he's smart enough to commit all of this without being caught?"

"Yet," I say dourly.

"Just listen to yourself; you're thinking crazy."

"I found blood in his house—"

"Casey, please tell me you had a warrant." He sees the truth in my face before I can answer and swears under his breath. "You know how much trouble you could get in for that?"

"Blood *inside*—"

"Shut up. Come on, I don't want to be complicit in your break-in." He looks at me sharply and with care. "Casey, you have to get yourself together. Take some time off. Go home back to your wife and daughter. Don't come back until you get your head clear. I know I'm not your boss, but I think it's best for everybody if you stay away from the department in the meantime."

I slowly nod, more for his benefit rather than actually agreeing. Oliver did this, and I will stop him from doing it again. And if that son of a bitch goes for Celeste, so help me God—

# Friday, November 1, 2:00 p.m.
## Oliver

*Between the idea*
*And the reality*
*Between the motion*
*And the act*
*Falls the Shadow*

**"Dang it, Eliot,** *why do you have to be so cryptic?" I ponder aloud at my desk.*

*I had already painstakingly gone through the first four parts of his lengthy poem, carefully annotating as I went. Five more stanzas and I'm done.*

*Underlining "Falls the Shadow," I write in the margins next to it "repetition" as it recurs twice more.*

*"So, between a dream and the truth, between a proposal and the response, lies the Shadow. But what is the Shadow?" I rap my pencil against the dark wood of my desk. I probably will have done more than everybody else, but it's better to be overprepared than underprepared.*

*"Ollie!" Mom calls from upstairs. "We're leaving for Alex's funeral in ten minutes."*

*I don't reply as the haunting, torturous memories return to me at a dizzying speed. And for a minute, the only sound is the scritch scritch of my pencil.*

*"The Shadow," I say almost in a trance, staring at the A. J. Green*

*bobblehead in front of me, except I was seeing inside myself. "I know what it is. It is rage and sorrow. It is death and evil. It is Fear. It is the Fear within."*

***

Sunlight leaks from the blinds, momentarily blinding me as I crack my eyes open. I slowly sit up in my bed (*how did I get here?*) and groan as my head beats in time to my heart.

*Thirsty, so thirsty.*

With an agonizing lunge out from beneath the covers, I walk languidly to the kitchen, wary of the blood rushing to my brain. I squint against the light coming in from the opened blinds in the living room and quickly close them as my skull screams. Now with the apartment at a moderate lighting, I fill up a cup with water from the tap. I take a sip, sighing around the cool liquid as it soothes my sore throat. After another cup, my head begins to clear, and I'm able to think. I was at Kat's house, no, her boyfriend's house, Logan. And he's dead. Alex killed him. No, Alex is just a piece of my unconscious. I killed him. I control my body. Right?

The apartment door swings open, squeaking just enough to send a needle of pain through my brain.

"Ollie." It's Slushie with his backpack slung over one shoulder. "W-what the heck, man?"

"Shh," I say, winching at his loud voice.

"W-why are you n-naked?" he asks but does lower his tone.

I look down, and sure enough, I'm as nude as an OnlyFans girl.

"Oh, sorry," is all I say, my head still a bit foggy.

"Are you hungover?" he follows up, fully aware of what it's like to be in this state.

I nod.

"You didn't even go to class, did you?"

I shake my head.

"Where were you last night?"

"With Tyrese and Blake," Alex answers for me. News of Logan's "suicide" may have spread itself around campus already. It's best he doesn't know I went to the same party where he apparently killed himself.

"W-with them, really?" He seems disappointed as I guess he should be. "So, D-Dick doesn't like b-being called that anymore?"

*Shit, Alex.*

"Yeah, I guess he's maturing now, finally." I try a small laugh; it doesn't go well.

"G-go get some clothes on," Slushie insists, done talking about it.

He seems to be in a better mood when I return.

"Apparently someone from school k-killed themself last n-night," he says from his spot on the couch, *South Park* on the TV. "It's b-been kept hush-hush, but the w-word on the street is it's your friend Kat's boyfriend."

I look at him quizzically.

"I heard you t-talking about her to yourself," he explains. "You k-know you c-can tell me anything."

*Yeah, I don't think he'd be saying that, knowing what you'd done*, Tanner disagrees.

I see that he suspects I was there, but I just nod in response.

Slushie copies the gesture, ending the discussion.

"Oh," he adds, not bothering to look up from the screen, "Celeste broke up with Jake."

Hope. Finally, hope. She is the only thing that can cure me. This is like some *deus ex machina* shit. She becomes available at my lowest to bring me back to the light right before I hit the point of no return. God's the greatest author, but I've got to write this down. This will make a great movie. An Oscar-winning movie. My victims will have no hold inside my mind. She will *free* me. Faith will finally overpower Fear.

For the first time since I killed Tanner, I don't see a future for myself that ends in utter pain and destruction, but one filled with love and happiness alongside Celeste.

# Friday, November 1, 6:00 p.m.
## Oliver


**"You like her,** *don't you," Tyrese prods as we sit in the bed of Big Naner.*

*"Who?" I ask, knowing full well there's only one girl he could be talking about.*

*"Celeste," he confirms. "It's obvious you like her. I know, she knows—"*

*"Did she say so?" I interrupt and quickly query, staring eagerly at him.*

*"No, but how could she not? You're not hiding your feelings for her very good."*

*I take a sip of Natty Lite. Tastes like crap, but I drink it anyway. It helps with ... with everything.*

*"Why don't you ask her out?" Tyrese leans back, using his left arm as a kickstand. "What's there to lose?"*

*"What's there to lose?" I repeat, my voice rising. "Everything. Our friendship will never be the same if she says no, and it will eventually fall apart like all the other ones already. When I try to imagine a future without her, all I see is darkness ... and Fear."*

*"But what if she says yes?" Tyrese takes a hit from his Juul, breathing out a white vapor with an underlying scent of cucumbers. "Then you'll have everything. The initial pain you'll feel from a rejection will never come close to the lasting agony you'll have from never asking her."*

*"All right, Sherlock," I say, eyes following a murder of crows. "What*

*do your deducing skills say about Celeste's feelings to me? Will she even say yes?"*

*"I don't know. Girls are a lot harder to read than guys." He smiles, looking at something other than the rural scenery. "I've been with Mia for nearly three years and still don't really know what's going on inside her head."*

*"But even if I was able to gain the confidence to ask her out, there's still Jake." I continue to reach for excuses.*

*"He's in Michigan now; long distances don't work. It'll be only a matter of time before they break up."*

*I finish off the beer and crush it onto the steel of the bed.*

*"If you really do care for her. If you love her. Do everything you need to get her, and don't let anybody stand in your way."*

***

And I go to do just that.

Not trying to overthink it, I just put on a sweatshirt and shorts but do steal some gel from Slushie—absent, so he must've left to go to work—to control my shaggy hair a bit. A picture of me, Celeste, and Slushie from graduation draws my eye. Celeste had bought us both a matching frame as a graduation gift. Now, I caress her pixelated face with my thumb, almost feeling her soft skin through it.

*Yesterdaaay he tried to fuuck ma gurl,* Logan says. *Now he's rubbing the shame thuumb he flicked Kat's nipple wiith on a picture of another gurl's face."*

I ignore him, knowing everything he said is true, and walk out of the door.

***

A nightmare awaits me as I pull up to her house.

*One you desherve,* Logan reverberates in my skull.

"The bastard," I hiss through my teeth. Slushie's Civic is parked in her driveway.

*Now, let's not jump to conclusions,* Alex tries to rein me in. *He could just be hanging out with her. Possibly reassuring her over her breakup.*

"He's screwing her, isn't he?" I barely hold in my rage. "Screwing her right as I'm sitting here."

*I'm sure he is*, Tanner agrees. *I would too if I was still alive.*

"Shut up, shut up, shut up!" I scream, hands gripping the steering wheel.

*Karma's a bitch*, Logan retorts.

*Investigate before you act*, Alex suggests.

I drive into a nearby cul-de-sac and park the Camry. Head up, back straight, I walk with confidence to Celeste's house as if I am supposed to be there. I move around back with an equal countenance, circling around till I find them through a window. They're sitting on a couch, legs just far enough to not be touching, talking about something. I lean up against the window, knowing that with the sky fully dark, I'll be invisible looking out, and strain to hear something. Nothing. Damn, I wish I could read lips. And suddenly, before my mind can comprehend what is going on, they kiss.

I'm gone before they're part.

*Wait till he leaves, and kill him when he gets home*, Alex instructs. *I'm thinking drug him with pills and then slice his wrists in the tub.*

*No*, I deny absently, returning to my car in a much more dejected composure than how I came. *She kissed him. She likes him, maybe even loves him. I ca- … I can't do anything about that.*

Now in my Camry, I break down over the wheel, heart shattered for what I think might be the last time.

# Friday, November 1, 7:15 p.m.
## Oliver

**Characters in movies** always made the barrels of guns look small when they stick it into their mouth to blow the back of their heads out. But the cold end of my .357—a new one, bought from a different retailer—instead triggers my gag reflex, so I remove it.

*Quit it, Ollie!* Alex demands. *You don't want to do this, and you know it.*

"Give me one good reason I should live," I say in a daze while I sit on the edge of my bed, every atom in my body trembling in a maddening cocktail of depression, ire, and most of all Fear.

*You have a purpose—*

"To kill innocent people with the screwed-up idea that I'm protecting them?"

*Nobody's innocent …*

"All I've done is cause pain. I haven't helped anybody. I murdered the father of an unborn child. I killed a guy I just met, solely on a hunch that he's beating a girl that I liked for all of three months. I even bashed your head in, dammit. My own brother, just because he caught me drinking over a girl.."

Nothing.

"So now you're quiet." Fresh tears stream down my face. "You finally believe I'm getting what I deserve, huh?" I find myself laughing insanely. "A poetic end. I kill people and create a tableau of suicide. Now it's my turn to be found with half my head blown off."

*Have patience and Faith, and God will show you the way,* Alex says.

"This isn't God's plan. I'm not ridding the world of evil; I am evil. Killing myself would be the holiest thing I've done in the last eighteen months. I'm not even sure God's real at this point. I mean, why would he take everything away from me? From someone who's already screwed up in the head enough?

"But here's what I'll do." I remove one bullet from the cylinder and spin it. "If this really is God's plan and not yours, I'll live." I point the revolver at my head, waiting, almost hoping, that Slushie would walk in and stop me. But nothing, not even my victims speak.

A .357 Taurus snub-nose cylinder contains five chambers. With one empty, there are four bullets. Four chances to die, one to live. A twenty percent chance I walk out of here. Eighty percent I don't. I'm not sure which I want.

I reach over to grab the graduation picture, temporarily laying the gun next to me. I remove the frame and pull out the actual photo. With great care, I tear Slushie from the other side of Celeste. I want her to be the last thing I see if I die, not that traitor.

I brush her pixelated face. "I love you, Celeste." I return the cocked Taurus to my head and wrap my finger around the trigger. The muscles in my neck tense in anticipation, while the ones in my arm threaten to cramp up.

"Ahh!" I scream and throw down the gun to the ground—not thinking that it could go off, but it doesn't.

Breaking down from the coiled nerves, I lie down in a fetal position, rocking back and forth as if I was four.

"Why can't I die?" I sob into my arm. "Why the fuck can't I die?"

*Because you want to live, Ollie,* Alex explains.

And deep down, I know that's the truth, but I'm not sure if that's a good thing or just a weakness.

What am I going to do? What path will I tread? How … how can I go on?

The voice that answers me is not who I was expecting.

*"If you really do care for her. If you love her. Do everything you need to get her, and don't let anybody stand in your way."*

I stand up now that my legs feel a little steadier and return the bullet I had removed from the snub-nose to its waiting chamber. I'm going to need it for what's coming.

# Friday, November 1, 10:00 p.m.
## Casey

**It's a weird** thought to be completely convinced of the necessity of killing another human, no less an eighteen-year-old kid. To gain the nerves to do so is a whole other devil, and it requires the use of spirits. But killing him, I don't know. I just don't know if I have what it takes to kill him, even seeing what he's done and what he could do. I'm not sure if anyone knows what it takes to kill premeditatively. What kind of neurological process unlocks the motivation to murder another human being. All I know is that I'll need a lot more Jim Beam.

In the back of the Kroger parking just across the street from Oliver's apartment. I'm three shots into the bourbon, and it's nowhere near enough. I take another shot and pump the air conditioning. It's starting to get warm in here.

*What if he's not even in there?*

That is strangely welcoming and hopeful. But I need to do this. If Celeste is ever going to be truly safe, I need to kill him. The law's not going to do anything, and by the time he trips up, giving them the evidence in probable cause to arrest, Celeste will be gone.

But if he's not there, what will I do? Do I wait inside in the dark for him to return like an MI-6 director bringing James Bond out of retirement for the umpteenth time? No, he lives with Gideon. Maybe I'll wait in the parking lot. Or do I check his old house? Would that mean he suspects me? He couldn't suspect me, right? I haven't seen the kid since Celeste's graduation party.

*Don't overthink it, Casey. Take one thing at a time. One thing at a time.*

I take another shot to uncoil my nerves. I can't even taste the whiskey anymore. I pour another shot with a shaky hand but don't drink it. Too much more liquor and I won't have the awareness to cover it up. I look over at the complex and decide to swallow the burning liquid. Setting down the bottle in the passenger seat, I remove a picture of Celeste from my wallet. It's one from graduation, dressed in her black gown. I brush my thumb across her pixelated face. "I love you, Celeste," I express, and then add, "I'm doing this for you." Although, I'm not sure if that's the truth.

Returning to my wallet, I now pick up my Colt 1911, instead of my police-issued Glock. I'm no forensics expert, but I think they can determine what type of gun—maybe the exact gun—that fired the bullet. I bought the pistol from a pawn shop, so there's no record that it's registered to me. This will not be framed as suicide; I'm too drunk for that.

I pop open the cylinder to make sure each chamber is filled. I'm going to need each bullet for what's coming.

# Friday, November 1, 10:00 p.m.
## Oliver

**Like an MI-6** agent bringing James Bond out of retirement for the umpteenth time, I wait, sitting in the dark, for Slushie. The only difference is that in my hand sits a loaded gun. One that shakes considerably. Slushie's not like the others; he's not a dick. Come to think about it, he's never said a single harsh thing to me, except for a slightly hurtful joke every now and then.

*Everything's a joke to you,* Alex says. *Nothing is serious to you. You want—need to be liked, so a part of your brain disguises the fact that others actually hate you.*

"Slushie doesn't hate me," I tell him firmly. I'm not going to let him corrupt me. Or at least not any further.

*Maybe not hate, but disgust. Did you see the way he looked at you this morning? He was ashamed of you for drinking but didn't give you the helping hand you gave him a long time ago. He's only friends with you because he feels bad for you.*

"No." My voice and beliefs begin to waver.

*Don't forget he's screwing your girl,* Tanner adds.

"No, not screwing, they wouldn't do that," I disagree absently. "He doesn't know I like her, anyway."

*So let me get this straight,* Alex says. *Tyrese knows how you feel about her, but your best friend, who you also live with, doesn't?*

My hand tightens around the trigger. Thankfully, the hammer is not cocked.

*And also, he hears you talking to us. It's only a matter of time before he hears something incriminating and tells the cops. He's suspicious of you already.*

I remain silent.

*You have to kill him to remain free.*

*They'll screw ya tiny ass,* Logan agrees.

I nod, resolute but wishing I had some alcohol to steady my hand.

The doorknob turns, causing me to straighten up.

"Ollie, w-we need to …" He trails off, eyes wide as he stares at my revolver. "T-t-t-t-alk," he finishes.

"Talk about what? How you're with Celeste now? Yeah, I know," I add in response to his even more startled expression. "I was stalking you and saw you making out with her."

"O-o-o—"

"Sit down," I cut him off, keeping my voice even, not to be heard by the neighbors, while gesturing with the Taurus at the far end of the couch.

We stare at each other for a moment. Me, not sure of what to say; him, too scared to say anything.

"I like her, you know," I finally say. "Love her, actually."

"Ollie, I d-didn't—"

"Shut up!" I say quickly, jabbing the snub-nose in his direction. "I don't want to hear your lies. That's all you've done, isn't it? Lie, lie, lie. You never really liked me, did you? Don't you answer," I snap when he starts to open his mouth. "If Eve had just killed the snake before it convinced her to take a bite of the godly fruit, we'd still be in Eden.

"You know I killed them, don't you? Answer!"

"Wh-wh-wh-who?" Slushie asks, trying to appear shocked, desperate to prove his false innocence.

"Don't. Play. With. Me," I cock my pistol, eyes wide with insanity. "I know you know. Which means you will have to die."

"P-please, t-t-this is c-crazy," he pleads, actual tears flowing down his cheeks.

"Did you screw her?" I have to know.

"No," he answers honestly. "We d-don't b-believe in pre-marital sex."

*He screwed her*, Tanner disagrees. *You can see it all over his face.*

*Yeaah, he shcrewed her*, Logan concurs.

But through the burning fire of rage and the crowded haze of my mind, I see truth. He didn't know I'm a murderer. He didn't realize I love Celeste. And he certainly didn't have sex with her.

But he knows now. And for that, he must die.

Slushie sees the anger on my face be replaced with sorrow and presses himself against the end of the couch. He knows that I can't—won't—be reasoned with. I'm no longer Oliver. I am Fear.

But again, I find myself unable to pull the trigger.

"Help me," I plead with Alex though my teeth. "Take over as you did at the party."

"Wh—"

"Shh!" I interrupt, distracted.

*I can't do that, Ollie, and deep down you know that too*, he replies. *You fondled Kat. You killed Logan. We are just a part of your unconscious. I've told you all this before, but you purposely forget it. Even those times when I'd visit you at night. You know why? You created us, because you need somebody to put the blame on, so you'll believe you're actually a good person instead of a fuckin' lunatic. I'm only telling you all this because when you wake up tomorrow, you'll forget we ever had this conversation. So, see ya later, big bro.*

"Ahh! Fuck!" I scream as I stand up and flip the ottoman into the wall, not bothering anymore to keep quiet.

"Do you know what's happening in here?" I ask Slushie, jabbing the barrel of my gun into my temple. "I hear the voices of the people I killed. Alex, Tanner, Logan. They bicker inside of my head *all the time*. And let me tell you something, Slushie, I really do love you—truly I do—but I can't have you sputtering inside of my' head like a goddamn idiot."

His eyes turn to saucers as he witnesses the full extent of my insanity.

"So, here's what we're going to do." I twirl the Taurus in the air like some true diabolical movie villain. "I'm going to cut your tongue out." He lets out an involuntary yelp at this. "Ah, don't worry, you'll still live. I'm not sure how my unconscious works, but I don't think removing your tongue will keep you quiet. But I'm also going to chop your hands off, so you don't go writing my name down."

In response he just stared at me with a look, not of rage, sadness, or even Fear, but of remorse. He pities me. The bastard pities me, and that *pisses* me off.

"Cat got your tongue?" I ask as I remove the shimmering blade and approach him. "Oh right, I do." I laugh sickly at my own terrible joke but find myself unable to stop.

"I'm sorry," I say, wiping my eyes with the back of my head as my laughter finally ceases. "I'm afraid I've become utterly and perfectly insane."

His countenance remains the same. I push back his head hard against the couch armrest, enraged he isn't begging through his tears.

"Remember, if you scream, I'll kill you."

He nods and opens his mouth without resistance, angering me even more. I grasp the slippery muscle and rip it out of his mouth, hoping for at least a whimper, but get nothing. Even after I easily slice off his tongue with the burning knife, he remains mute—which will be the norm for now on. Tears fill his eyes as I start on his hands, yet still he remains silent, not giving me the satisfaction I desire. I pause for a second, watching the blood drip onto his lap. My stomach doesn't even churn the slightest. Maybe I really should've been a doctor.

He's passed out by the time I reach the bone, which is prob-

-ably for the best since I have to break it with the butt of my .357.

Once I have finished the grisly work, I call 911 on Slushie's phone, swiping right to use the emergency pad. And just as I drop it into his bloody lap, a large mass slams against the apartment door. I hurry quickly, not trying to see who's on the other side. For all I know it could be Death himself, finally collecting his due.

*Or the Shadow.*

I unlatch the window leading out to the fire escape, remembering just then that I never locked the door. The person on the other side realizes it at the same time and enters the gory scene just as I leave it. But before I do, I catch a glimpse of the intruder.

It's Mr. Lynch. Celeste's dad. And worse of all, he saw me too.

# Friday, November 1, 10:20 p.m.
## Casey

**Oliver did kill** *all of them*, I realize almost with glee, feeling immediately ashamed of my drunken joy.

I hobble over to the window in slow motion, drawing my revolver as I do. I peer down the fire escape, resolving that I'm too crocked to make an attempt at climbing down there.

*Uggghh.*

I turn quickly around to find the source of the monstrous noise. I recoil at the sight of the

*(meatbag)*

disfigured person and hurl up the Jim Beam down the escape.

*Uggghh.*

Oh lord, it's Gideon. I should've known something like this would happen. Oliver is jealous.

*(just like his dad)*

He would suspect Slushie of dating my daughter.

This is on me.

I walk over to him, stepping on something hard and slippery. I lift up my foot and nearly faint, once I see what's there.

"Gideon, I'm going to get help," I fruitlessly reassure him, placing a hand on his shoulder, wet with a mixture of sweat and blood.

*His hands. Where are his goddamn hands?*

Another wave of bourbon bile decorates the other side of the couch.

"Hello, anyone there?"

The voice comes from a phone, covered in gristle, lying in his equally gory lap. I reach for it but hesitate before picking it up. How will I explain what I was doing at the apartment of a kid I've been obsessed with the past few months? Especially since they'll smell the whiskey on my breath from a mile away. I could have my badge permanently taken away.

"Radiant Apartment Complex. Room 18. Ambulance needed," is all I say, distorting my voice slightly with my hand, hoping that's enough.

I hurry back to the Kroger parking lot. *He's getting away.* My head is swimming from the liquor, but that doesn't stop me from taking a long pull from the bottle.

Where now? Return home to Celeste to protect her? No, Oliver is obviously in love with her, in some sick, twisted way. He wouldn't hurt her, but he might try to see her, knowing his life as an innocent kid is soon to come to a close. But not covered in gore. He'll need to get cleaned, dress in his normal clothes so as not to send any warning signs that something is wrong. But where?

His home, obviously.

I start the car and careen onto the main road.

# Friday, November 1, 10:50 p.m.
## Oliver

**Home is where** our story begins.

But where does it end?

That question looms before me as I pull up in front of the house of people I haven't seen since midsummer after a lunch filled with anger. My time as a free man is close to an end now that Officer Lynch has seen me.

*So why am I here?*

I should be with Celeste, so I can confess my love for her while she still sees me as what I was. Yet my internal compass takes me here. *Where my story begins.* And is this where it ends? I'll admit it's a nice ending. A movie with a similar one would be praised for it. Is this God's plan coming to fruition? The master storyteller must have a taste of the irony.

It sure beats *The Stranger*'s.

I climb the steps before the front door, weighed down by sins no longer supported by the persons they were done to. I raise my hand to knock yet am unable to bring it forward.

*I have sinned against heaven and against you. I am no longer worthy to be called your son.*

I turn to leave, but the door is thrown open.

"Ollie," Dad says, with tears in his eyes.

*For this son of mine was dead and is alive again, he was lost and is found.*

"I'm sorry," I cry out as he wraps me in a choking hug.

Soon we're joined by Mom and Dylan. I look for Alex before remembering what I did to him. I don't deserve this and break away from them.

"What happened to you?" Mom asks with concern rather than with fear when she sees my blood-soaked clothes. Actually, concern is a bit of an understatement; she looks like she is bordering on a panic attack. "Are you hurt?"

"Slushie's hurt. Mr. Lynch. Tortured. No hands. No tongue. Escaped," I blurt out in quick succession, crying out tears that weren't all fake and hyperventilating.

"You were attacked at your apartment by Celeste's dad?" Mom starts. "Oh, shit. That perverted prick."

She seems like she's about to spiral out of control. Dad looks more controlled, while Dylan's face holds nothing but Fear.

"Megan, take Dylan to our room," he says, surprisingly calm for the circumstances.

When she tries to argue, he just tilts his head to Dylan. She understands and leaves.

"Did you call the police?" he asks once they're gone.

"He *is* the police," I answer, shaking in what I hoped to be the proper rhythm for this situation.

He pulls me inside and directs me to the kitchen table, while he moves away to the living room, pulling out his phone as he does. I strain to hear what he says and get nothing before he returns moments later.

"They already got there," he says. "Gideon must have called them before he passed out. They said it's too early to know if he'll survive; he's lost a lot of blood. They also said they were coming here to interview you."

I noticeably react.

"Don't worry, I told them they would have to wait till tomorrow morning." He sits across from me, face grave. "Tell me exactly what happened."

I make a show of slowing my breath. "Mr. Lynch broke into our apartment and pointed a gun—" I shudder at the false memory. "—at us before we could react. He said we had raped Celeste." I speak slowly, attempting to create the greatest story of my life. "I would never do that. You know that, right?"

"I believe you," he answers, and his countenance supports it.

"Then he started torturing Slushie, cutting his tongue out first." My eyes are glazed as I relive those moments with no glee. "There was so much blood. And I was *right there*."

"It's okay," he reassures me and moves around the table to place his hand on my shoulder in an awkward manner. He's never been the consoling type. "How did you escape?"

"When he—went for Slushie's hands, he had to use both of *his*. Oh lord, I can still hear his screams. He was distracted, so I ran for it; we were never tied up. He was drunk, I think, and I was down the fire escape before he could …" I trail off before a jarring thought pops into my head. "He could be here any minute. Is the alarm set?"

He realizes my very real fear and goes to do just that. Then he hurries downstairs without any word of why.

*Slushie's going to be okay, right?* I ask the voices inside my head.

No answer.

Oh yeah, I forgot they're retired for the night.

A loud bang by the garage door is followed by the tone of something heavy hitting the ground. I then hear the door swing open and the alarm system being fiddled. Shortly, a beep sounds, indicating it has been shut off. My pace quickens further as Casey appears around the corner. He is tall and skinny with blond hair cut short and obviously drunk.

"You really need to change your code to something a bit more peculiar." He opens a couple of cabinets, murmuring under his breat—something about bourbon—before settling on a mostly full bottle of Skyy from the fridge. "Everybody uses their marriage date for everything."

"Mr. Lynch, please don't hurt me," I say loudly. "I didn't rape Celeste. I would never do anything to hurt her."

Lynch pours himself a finger of the vodka into a glass he had scavenged but then decides to take a long swig from the bottle.

"Not yet maybe." His cheeks are red from the alcohol. Eyes bloodshot and filled with insanity. They seem familiar. "But it's only a matter of time."

His gun is stuck in the front of his pants, uncocked. I could make a run for it as I did before. He's certainly drunk enough to elude. But how confident am I in my chances of escape? I think it will be best to wait and keep him talking. Anyway, I don't think I could move, even if I wanted to.

"What do you think I did?" I ask, trying maybe too hard to keep my face innocent.

"Don't play that shit with me," he says, setting down the liquor and ripping out his revolver like some drunken Clint Eastwood. "I know you—"

The boom of the shotgun shoots rivers of Fear down my veins as I stare at the remains of Lynch's head.

"Jesus! God—fuck! What did you do?" I scream at Dad, who stands on the edge of the family room, holding a double gauge.

"I saved your life," he answers slowly but firmly, and one look at his eyes tells me he didn't just kill Lynch to protect me.

Mom sprints into the room, screaming from the top of her lungs when she sees the grisly scene. Dylan follows close behind, recoiling and then immediately bending over, his tears mixing with vomit.

I stand up, my legs shaking violently, now covered in the blood of two men. Lynch's death is my fault. Dad might've fired the bullet, but I aimed the gun. That's five people I've killed, three in the last twenty-four hours. When will it end?

"Wait ten minutes before calling the police," I tell no one in particular, my voice beginning to even out. "I'm going to take a shower and get changed."

It's a weird thought to realize you have more experience with death than your parents. To be the level-headed one in the face of it.

Mom is on the ground with Dylan, rocking back and forth as they cry. I'm not sure who's cradling who. Dad remains where he was, the shotgun still aimed at the spot where Lynch's head used to be. Blood dots parts of his shirt and face; he doesn't seem to notice. However, he does nod at my instruction, but in such an absent manner that I don't think he actually understands what I said.

I trudge slowly downstairs, wishing more than ever for the comfort of my victims.

Tonight will be The End.

# Friday, November 1, 11:45 p.m
## Oliver

**Dressed in gray** slacks and a white button-down, I walk up the steps to the Lynches' residence. I fiddle with my tie and straighten my oversized sports coat as I check my reflection in the glass door.

*I look like I'm going to a funeral.* I realize my ridiculous outfit, before recognizing that, like Death, the funeral follows me.

I knock on the door while lightly brushing my gelled blond hair. *Damn, I have a huge forehead.*

"Ollie?" Celeste stands in the open doorframe, her brown hair hanging freely below her shoulders. She's dressed in faded blue pajamas. I forgot how late it is, yet there's no sign of sleep in her bright-green eyes, the color of the purest emeralds. "What are you doing here?"

She notices the way my face drops and the fancy state of my clothes. "Come on in."

"Celeste, I'm really sorry for coming so late. I just had to see you," I tell her while I follow her to her room.

This is the first time I've been in her room—a surprise, with so many years as friends—and I don't really know what I expected, but it wasn't this. Lights are strung up along the walls in neat rows and columns. It's like stepping into another universe with Celeste at the center. My head even starts spinning a bit as I get trapped in her orbit. And among those stars are pictures. I move to the nearest one and see me, her, and Slushie standing in front of the Capitol Building in Frankfort on a field trip we had taken in seventh grade. I continue onward, finding pictures from the last six years of the three of us, many that I had completely forgotten about. Like one where we had both kissed her cheeks simultaneously in what I believe was freshman year. The last is our graduation picture.

"Ollie, are you okay?" She lightly touches my shoulder, and I realize I had been crying.

I wipe the tears with the sleeve of my woolen coat. "I know about Slushie."

"Ollie." She removes her hand quickly. *She knew I liked her.* "I don't know what to say. It was a mistake. He—"

"I'm not here to win you over." I cut her off, turning around to face her. "I just wanted to know if you ever liked me. If I even had a chance if I had asked you out earlier."

"I love you, Ollie, but like a brother. You mean more to me than most, but I never had those kinds of feelings for you."

I sigh and sit down at the edge of her bed. I know now that this is truly the end. An awful way to finish a story, but I guess that's just life; it's a bitch. She joins me after a moment, leaving plenty of space between us. We sit there in silence for what seems like an eternity before I finally speak. "I love you, Celeste." Her eyes widen at my confession, but she keeps her soft, pink lips sealed. "And not like a sister. I know you don't feel the same, but I just had to tell you. I think I've had a crush on you since the first day we met, but I just didn't understand those feelings then.

"Celeste, it's always been you. You're the first thought in my head when I wake up and the last before I fall asleep. You're my sole source of true happiness and Faith. I would do anything for you. You're my dream, Celeste, you are my *dream.*"

"Ollie, you're starting to scare me." And indeed she appears to be.

"I'm not going to kill myself if that's what you're thinking.

I'm transferring to South Carolina University, and I don't know when I'm going to see you next."

A simple lie, for she has no need for the truth.

I push a loose strand of hair behind her ear, and to my credit, she doesn't flinch or pull away. Then the door slams open, revealing two police officers and a plainclothesman, all with their guns drawn.

I throw myself in front of Celeste.

"Freeze!" the plainclothesman demands. "Step away from her now."

"What?" I ask. *They found Lynch. I thought I had more time.*

"Don't play dumb. We know you killed Tanner Wall, Logan Ewing, and even your own brother." There was no pride in his expression at finding the killer. Only shame. "Tanner had never registered a Taurus .357 snub-nose."

*How could I be so stupid?*

"Alex killed himself." I look back at Celeste and she's expectantly shocked, but there's also a bit of doubt as well. "I was there."

"Exactly, you were the only one there." He gestures at an officer next to him, who pulls out a pair of handcuffs behind his back and approaches me. "Oliver Behr, you are under arrest. You have the right to remain silent ..."

I turn around to say goodbye and see legit tears in her eyes. She really does care about me. But if she finds out what I've done or even suspects it, she'll no longer. I'd be dead to her and everybody else. Better to die innocent than live guilty.

"I love you," I mouth to her before reaching into my coat and rotate to face the cops as the world slows down. The fat one yells at me to remove my hand, while the officer sent to arrest me drops the handcuffs, replacing it with his handgun. I quickly remove my hand to the tune of three Glocks firing—

*the world really does end with a bang*

—at me. The woolen suit Dad had bought for his wedding

is shredded as the bullets ram into me. I fall—

*Falls the Shadow*

—to the ground—barely feeling anything as I land. Even the bullets only sting as if I was just bitten by a sweat bee, not lead fired at twelve hundred feet per second.

"Ollie!" Celeste appears by my side.

"Look into my eyes," I say with my dying breath, still holding on to the bloodstained picture that killed me. "Deep into my eyes. Where it's just you and me. Nothing else. No one else. Just us."

And then she kisses me with her brilliant eyes wide open as the Shadow laughs from behind.

# Authors Note

So . . . that was brutal.

As someone enjoys the mind and has an almost sick fascinations with serial killers, I wanted to figure out the "why" of their horrendous decisions. This was the goal of *Shadow of Fear;* it even had the working title of *Becoming Evil* at one point.

First, I had to create a serial killer. The base of Oliver's character was not hard to figure out: depression, anxiety, and a search for their purpose. The majority of young people—including myself—have dealt with these feelings to some extent.

And then I needed an ingredient that separates him from the so-called "normal" people. One: the Shadow (I'll let you guys try to figure that one out) and also misogyny. But nothing too forward. Maybe an objectifying statement here and there presented as a joke. This combined with how he falls for four girls in about a year but with the inability to maintain a relationship, gives him the sexual complex of necessity and incompetence that most serial killers posess. Ollie's sexual complex also consists of a feeling that he needs to protect the women in his life, never considering that they might not need him. All he needed was a catalyst in the form of Emma's rape.

Finally, his lack of purpose, sexual complex, and the recall of his repressed memories create the deadly aggregate of insanity. The severity of his actions splits his unconcious into pieces, subjugated by—explicitly—his victims voices, but really it's their personality.

Through his madness, he is convinced killing any possible threats to the women in his life is God's plan for him. This is of course not true, but I wanted to get inside a serial killers head and find reason, fearing the alternative of just pure evil.

Now, I'll leave the rest of the book up to y'all to unpack. I just wanted to give some justification for my writing, so you guys don't hate me as much.

# Acknowledgments

These past four years have been extremely tough as I graduated high school and began college. I lost many, many friends. I had good days and really bad days, and occasionally I would have a great day. I've strayed far from God's path for me during this time and can only pray I'm back in the vicinity. But through all these trials, I at least can say I published a damn book.

I had kept this novel and the unpublished one before it a secret, not sure how it would be received by those closest to me. And now here it is. You probably didn't love it—I don't blame you—but hopefully you didn't hate it. It took two years of writing and another year of pain in the ass self-publishing, so if you did maybe it wouldn't hurt to lie. On that note, constructive criticism is great as I will be writing and publishing books--hopefully by a traditional publisher next time--for probably the rest of my life.

Keeping this book a secret, meant not many people really directly helped with the process. So, I would like thank to Joe Pierson for his help in editing *Shadow of Fear*, not holding back AT ALL. And also, many thanks to Xavier Comas for his spectacular cover design that I know will garner much attention. Finally, I would like to thank Stephen Van Zant—author of *Far from Good: The Trial of Sam Cray*—for guidance in the world of self-publishing, as well as taking the time to edit this novel.

Starting college just a month before the world shut down to a super virus is not ideal for making friends. It was a struggle and I didn't make any my freshman year, but the next year I started going to the BCM on campus, where I made many friends (especially thank you Paul Miller, Ashley Frazier, Josh Skipper, Matt Wallen, Cornelius Smal, Josh Skipper, Justin Lucas, Kaden LaFleur, and Max Cantrell). But the best thing that happened to me since I graduated high school—and that includes publishing this book—was quitting my job at the Kroger deli and joining the Better Blend team, who became like family in no time at all. Especially, thank you Isaac Hamlin, Macy Stiles, and Casey Cox for giving me a chance. Now I'm going to list everybody I worked with (at the time of writing this): Manny Aguirre, Zack Ajwa, Natalie Allen, Grace Birch, Logan Blaut, Tessa Gastright, Ben Elsten, Zach Ernst, Nathan Halfhill, Courtney Hansel, Haley King, Cory Knaley, Caleb Lanyi, Zach Lowe, Chad Michels, Jess O'Connor, Ian Sears, Paige Snyder, Mollie Tagher, Riley Tompos, Eva Vallandingham, and Marcus Watson. Thank y'all for being the best.

I also have to give thanks to several people from Kroger who I would never have made it through two years without (since I don't know all y'all's lastnames, Imma just list first names): Philly, Mike, Lynn, Connie (both), Rhonda, Robin, Jake, Shawna, and Dillon.

Now there are a few friends from high school who have still been there for me: Logan Weber, McKaela Harris-Dinser, Cody Morehead, and Layne Simpson.

And finally, last but certainly not least, my family. I really don't know where I'd be without you guys. Coming home to you, Mom and Dad, after long days and just talking about what happened were sometimes the highlight of my days. So, thank you for pausing the TV to talk to me for ten minutes. Thank you for putting food on the table, showing up to high school games no matter the weather to watch me sit the bench, paying for my schooling, guiding me in my faith, and just giving me an amazing (will be twenty-one) years. I'm just so fortunate to have you guys as parents for an amazing twenty-one years. I'm just so fortunate to have you guys as parents.

And Luke and Adam, thank you for being the best brothers anyone could have. Seeing you guys, I know I did a good job at being your big brother.

I would never be able to write and publish this book without you all, so thank you so much for being there, even when you never knew I needed it.

# About the Author

**Ben Naas** is the author of this book, believe it or not. He lives in Verona, Kentucky and currently attends Northern Kentucky University.. You can catch him slinging blends at his "job," Better Blend. He welcomes you to his website (bennaas.com) and his social media    (@bnaas30).